MW01611280

JUSTICE FOR SAMARA (POLICE AND FIRE: OPERATION ALPHA)

BLUEGRASS BRAVERY BOOK 16

DEANNDRA HALL

Dear Readers,

Welcome to the Police and Fire: Operation Alpha Fan-Fiction world!

If you are new to this amazing world, in a nutshell the author wrote a story using one or more of my characters in it. Sometimes that character has a major role in the story, and other times they are only mentioned briefly. This is perfectly legal and allowable because they are going through Aces Press to publish the story.

This book is entirely the work of the author who wrote it. While I might have assisted with brainstorming and other ideas about which of my characters to use, I didn't have any part in the process or writing or editing the story.

I'm proud and excited that so many authors have loved my characters enough that they wanted to write them into their own story. Thank you for supporting them, and me!

READ ON!
    Xoxo
    Susan Stoker

INTRODUCTION

In most of these books, I didn't name names. I simply gave you enough information to be able to look up the crime if you cared to.

But not this one.

It was two miles from my home. Just thinking about it makes me furious, and it was so convoluted and twisted that *Dateline NBC* did an hour on it entitled "Consumed"– Season 24, Episode 37, first aired on April 8, 2016. It was also featured in an *Investigation Discovery*'s Season 5, Episode 8 broadcast, "Fatal Vows: Reduced to Ash," originally aired on July 1, 2017. It's a story of middle-aged crisis, betrayal, and murder.

Keith and Julie Griffith had been married for thirty-six years. He was a traveling lawn mower salesman. I've never found a reference to Julie's vocation. They had two adult sons and loved riding motorcycles, playing golf, and spending time with their grandchildren. In 2013, Keith had weight-loss surgery, and the change in him was considered remarkable by friends and family.

On January 17, 2014, first responders were called to a fire at 307 Tudor Boulevard in the small community of Reidland just south of Paducah, Kentucky. There were discussions of recent burglaries in the area. But as the responders combed through the rubble, they found what they initially didn't even recognize as a body. Upon further inspection, they not only recognized it as a human body, but they found the bodies of two dogs nearby. The medical examiner confirmed that it was a female victim who died by three gunshot wounds, .45 caliber; the dogs had been shot as well. Keith Griffith was two hours away in Indiana for business. The fire seemed to have been set, rather than a malfunction of the new HVAC system, which was their first suspicion.

Then-Detective Matt Carter of the McCracken County Sheriff's Department took over the investigation (he later became Sheriff Matt Carter and has recently retired). There were no hair fibers, footprints, or anything else useful—the arson had destroyed all the evidence. However, the department didn't tell anyone that it was a homicide.

At first, it was treated as a robbery gone wrong, except that nothing seemed to be missing. There was another problem with that as well. One of the dogs was a Great Dane named Cleo, and the dog never let anyone unknown to her near the property. That tidbit led Det. Carter to suspect it was someone the Griffiths knew.

On January 28, when Keith Griffith returned, he was questioned by Det. Carter. Keith claimed that his relationship with his wife was fine. He stated that he left the hotel about 11:00 p.m. for a drink and again at about 4:00 a.m. to get a donut and a soft drink. He also revealed that he owned a .45 ACP handgun that was kept in his work truck and had never been loaded. He was asked about the clothes he was wearing, which he says were the clothes he was wearing the previous day. He also had a receipt from the hotel, confirming that he stayed there.

However, during the questioning, a text message came in from a woman asking if Keith made it home okay; Keith said the woman was more "like a guy friend." He was released to take care of his wife's arrangements.

Oddly, when he was told the death was a homicide, his only comment was, "Okay." Keith went straight to the home of some friends and said he'd been questioned as though he'd committed the murder.

The text message had come from a woman named Deanna James, later known as Deanna Cloe. It had come in at 6:49 p.m. the night of the murder, simply asking if he'd arrived at home safely. That led Det. Carter to make arrangements to speak with Deanna. She said she and Keith had met at a vendor fair, and he'd asked her to dinner. After several dates, he wanted more of a relationship, but she didn't, as she was going through a very traumatic romantic breakup.

A period of time passed, and then she got a flirty text. He began aggressively courting her, showering her with flowers, jewelry, etc., but she wanted to keep it just friends. At the time Det. Carter met with her at the police station in Indiana, she said she'd never been intimate with Keith. She also said he seemed to be very bound to a woman he called his ex-wife. He was talking long-term with Deanna, wanting to look for property in Mooresville to buy so they could be together. When Det. Carter told Deanna that Keith was still married and they were investigating the murder of his wife, she was shocked because she never suspected he was still married.

Initially, Julie's family was angry that the investigation was focusing on Keith. They were distressed that he'd been involved with another woman, but they accepted it as a mistake and were convinced that he didn't kill Julie. Their friends felt the same way.

In the meantime, Det. Carter was convinced that Keith had murdered Julie. Then he uncovered a bombshell at the hotel. Keith said he'd been at the hotel and only gone out twice, coming back between. But security video from the hotel showed that he left there at 11:00 p.m. and was gone for six hours and thirty-four minutes. Det. Carter and a partner got in the car and tried the drive. Could he have made it to Reidland and back in that amount of time?

Yes. With twenty minutes to spare.

When Keith went to trial February 2015, Prosecutor Raymond McGee laid out a formidable case. Hotel security video footage was key. He had been asked by Det. Carter if he had changed clothes and he said he hadn't; the video showed that he came back to the hotel in other clothes. His family stood by him.

The prosecutor brought proof that he'd taken out several life insurance policies totaling $250,000.00, one of which had taken effect eight days prior to Julie's murder. The defense was handled by the best criminal attorney in town. He claimed they didn't have any DNA, no forensics, and no confession, saying they got it wildly wrong. He also claimed that Deanna's story was nonsense, and that Keith only wanted a port in every storm. And he added that Keith wouldn't have driven his regular vehicle, an SUV everyone would recognize, to commit the crime.

When he was asked on the stand, Keith claimed he had a sex addiction and that the night Julie was murdered, he was out looking for women, but had been too embarrassed to admit it. He said he went to a massage parlor, a bar, and a couple of strip clubs, but found no takers. He then said he went down to the river to watch the boats before going back to the hotel.

The jury was hung, and a mistrial was declared. A retrial was then scheduled. Their youngest son, who had come out as gay, been ostracized by his parents, and had only recently begun to rebuild a relationship with his mother, listened to all the evidence presented and knew his father was lying. He sent his father a "Dear Dad, you are dead to me" letter. His sister-in-law also believed Keith had murdered Julie. Their oldest son, however, still believed his dad was innocent.

A few months before retrial, Det. Carter got a call from the jail that an inmate there had information related to the case. Keith had gone to the inmate and said he wanted Det. Carter killed. The inmate said Keith had given him a map of what he believed was Carter's residence and suggested the caliber of weapon that should be used. When the informant asked Keith what should happen if Carter's family was present, Keith responded, "Tragedy." Those revelations pushed the older son to agreement with his wife and brother, and he wrote his dad a letter, telling him to man up and confess.

Keith Griffith finally did confess. Friends who were in the courtroom were shocked and heartbroken. As he stood there, he said, "There's no excuse for what I did, and I can't take it back. And she was my best friend. And I don't know what happened to me. But I did it, and there's nothing I can do about it." When asked why, Griffith said, "All I can tell you is that I, uh, had a lot of bad thoughts, wrong thoughts, mistakes. I really can't tell you. I mean, I don't know. I mean, just a bad decision." He insisted that it was not a delayed midlife crisis. "I have a hard time believing that I did what I did." When asked why he didn't consider divorce, he replied, "Never crossed my mind." He says the remorse began the minute he left the house. "Trying to get out of the subdivision, crying before I ever get out, regretting what I'd done. I probably drove a hundred miles an hour all the way back, hoping to get caught." He says he's prepared to die in prison, and he has nothing to live for except the hope of forgiveness from his sons.

In his retrial, Keith finally pleaded guilty to murder, first-degree arson, tampering with physical evidence, and two counts of animal cruelty. Additionally, he even pleaded guilty to trying to hire a hitman to kill the lead investigator. Based on his plea, Keith was sentenced to 30 years in prison in 2016. At present, he remains incarcerated at the Roederer Correctional Complex in Oldham County, Kentucky, and will be eligible for parole in 2034.

My husband attended the same church with Keith and Julie as he was growing up and says that Keith was always an entitled, arrogant person who believed himself to be a "preacher" and above reproach. Regardless, it's a waste of two lives, and a loving family has been scarred and broken apart by one person's vicious and loathsome character.

It occurred to me just days before publishing this book that there were two more men who murdered their wives in that same subdivision, and those two murders took place in the same house. One simply shot his wife and went to prison. Several years later, the other shot and killed his wife and left her body lying on their bed, only to go to the bedroom three days later and kill himself, his body falling across his wife's. They were found several days later by family.

It appears if you're a man who wants to kill his wife, Canterbury Subdivision in Reidland, Kentucky, is definitely your kind of neighborhood.

CHAPTER 1

THE PHONE RANG AGAIN. And then again. She'd called at least eight times in thirty minutes, and he just couldn't take it anymore. He'd decided he should probably call her and was looking for a place to put his trowel when the phone rang once more, so he just dropped the trowel on top of the bucket of drywall compound and grabbed the phone. "Yes, Mom, what do you want?"

"Mikey! Is that any way to talk to your mother?"

"I didn't mean to sound cross, Mom."

"Oh, it's okay. I've got dinner ready, honey. Are you coming home pretty soon?"

"Mom, I'm trying to get some work done. I ..." In his mind, he could see her face and how disappointed she'd be if he didn't show up. "Okay, look, let me finish these last few passes and I'll be home."

"Okie-dokie, son. I'll see you in just a little bit. Bye-bye."

"Bye, Mom." *God, she just won't stop*, he thought as he leaned into the wall, intending to pound his head on the surface. And he forgot there was fresh wallboard compound on it. "Shit," he muttered as he wiped at it with his hand, just spreading it even more.

"Hey! Lookin' good!" a voice called from somewhere behind him, and he spun to find the source.

"Oh, hey. Um …"

"What the hell happened to you?" Sheriff Melton asked, laughing. Carter Melton wasn't just the sheriff; he was Michael's boss and friend.

"I just got off the phone with my mom …"

"Say no more. I know what you're gonna say. You know Wilda Fern drives me crazy. I swear, that woman can see what I'm doing from miles away and calls me at the absolute worst times. Yesterday, the washing machine was bumping and walking across the laundry room floor, water was leaking out from under the kitchen sink, and I was up to my elbows in poop, trying to change Angel's diaper, when she called. And when I tried to tell her how busy I was, she just forged ahead."

"Yeah. Same here."

The sheriff spun around, looking at everything. "I've gotta say, Edwards, this is looking nice. What else have you gotten done?"

"You can walk through and look if you want. The bedrooms are done, and the front bathroom. I've got the master bath to do, and the dining room needs some repairs. I'll be glad when I can paint everything. But I think this is coming together pretty well." He'd knocked out the wall between the kitchen and living room, installed some decorative columns to take some of the weight, and turned it into an open floor plan. It made the whole house feel roomier.

Sure, it was just a sixties kit house, but it had two nice-sized bedrooms with large closets and a surprisingly large laundry room and pantry. As soon as the wallboard was done, the doors were hung, and everything was painted, he could put down the flooring and he'd be in business.

"Hey, one of the guys told me that you do this kind of work on the side. Think I could hire you to do some stuff around my place? I'm not the handiest guy around."

"Sure. I don't know why not. What have you got in mind?"

"Not a lot. Maybe some shelving in my home office, a new toilet, just some things like that."

"Then I'm your guy. Be glad to. And don't worry. I'm not going to charge you anything. I'll do it for …"

"Oh, no, you absolutely will not," Carter said, his voice stern. "I'll pay you like I'd pay anybody else. And while I'm here, there's something I need to talk to you about." Then Carter snorted. "I'll make it quick so you don't get in more trouble with Marjorie." Carter knew Michael's mother. He knew what she was like. "Lewis is leaving."

"What?" That was the first Michael had heard of it.

"Yeah. Met somebody and he's moving. To Little Rock."

"Little Rock? Of all places … Must be serious."

"Oh, it is. They're getting married."

"How did I not know about this?" Michael asked, finally putting voice to that question.

"Nobody did. Apparently they've been doing the long-distance thing on his days off, and they just decided to go for it."

Michael couldn't believe his ears. The chief deputy was leaving? "What's her name?"

"*His* name is Miguel Santiago."

"Well, damn. I had no idea ..."

"I'd suspected for a while, but I didn't know for sure. And now we all do. So I wanted to talk to you."

"Yes, sir. I think Justin would be a fine candidate."

Carter stood there for a minute, seemingly deep in thought, before he finally said, "I wasn't thinking about Watson. I was thinking about you."

"M-m-me, sir? I mean, Watson's been there five years longer than me, and I'm not the sharpest knife in the drawer, and—"

"You were sharp enough to save my life. If it hadn't been for you, I'd be dead now. So yes—I think you're a great candidate."

"But Justin—"

"This isn't Justin's call. Besides, you've got one thing Justin doesn't."

"What, sir?"

"You've got a way with people, Michael. They like you. They trust you. I've watched you in action, and you're the real deal. So consider this the informal version of me offering you the spot as chief deputy, but say nothing until I make the formal announcement."

Michael couldn't think straight. Carter wanted him to be the chief deputy? He wasn't even sure what he should say. "You ... Are you *sure*, sir?"

"I'm as sure as I've ever been about anything. I think you'd be the perfect person for the job."

He was dreaming. He had to be. "Uh, okay."

Carter let out a little chuckle. "Is that a yes?"

"Yes. I mean, yes! It's a yes! Yes, sir. I'll take it. I mean, thank you for your confidence in me and I'd be honored to serve as chief deputy under you. You're a great sheriff, hard-working, fair, sharp—"

"You can quit kissing my ass, Edwards. You've got the job," Carter said with a smirk.

"I'm not, sir. I ..." Michael tried to quell the excitement and also the sadness he felt. "You've been like ... like a father to me, sir. You truly have."

"Well, first off, I'm not that much older than you," Carter said with obvious sarcasm. Then Michael saw the muscles in the sheriff's face soften. "But thank you for saying that. I know you miss your dad. The whole damn county does. Wilson Edwards was a man among men. And I can tell you that he was very, very proud of you, Michael. Very proud."

Getting mushy in front of the sheriff wasn't something he wanted to do, but his heart was still raw. Everybody in Trigg County said his dad had been the best county judge executive they'd ever had. He'd been returning from a conference when the little plane he was riding in crashed on federal land, Land Between the Lakes. He, the county attorney, and the mayor had been killed, along with the pilot. The whole town had mourned, but Michael and Marjorie had been totally and completely lost. His mother adored his dad, and being the only child, he and Wilson had spent a lot of time together. "Thank you for saying that, sir. It means a lot to me."

"You're very welcome. So I'll just plan on making it official next week." Then Carter laughed. "Now, you'd better get home and eat whatever your mom has made or you'll never hear the end of it."

"Boy, that's sure true. Thanks, sir. I really appreciate it."

"You're welcome. See you tomorrow." Carter gave Michael a backhanded wave as he meandered out the front door, and Michael stood there in shock.

Chief Deputy Michael Edwards. He'd never thought he'd hear those words all strung together. A promotion. A pay raise. A house. Now if he could just find a woman to make it a home with.

Fat chance of that.

THERE WAS A SLOW DRIZZLE SLICKING UP THE ROADWAYS, and Michael stopped only once on his way to the department to call in an accident. Mr. Henry had been going a little fast around the bend and slid into a tree. The last thing he heard Mr. Henry say as he headed to his car made Michael sad. "I guess my daughter will stop me from driving now." He'd known Mr. Henry all his life, and the old man was patient and kind. Michael decided he'd offer the fellow a ride from time to time. It was the right thing to do.

Everyone's cruisers were out front when he pulled up, so he grabbed a cup of coffee and settled in behind his desk. Voices wafted up the hallway from the far end, and he knew it was Carter and Gray Lewis. What little he could hear sounded friendly, so he assumed it was discussion of what would be happening once Gray was gone. Carter had always respected Gray's opinion, and Gray had always been nice to Michael, so he had no reason to think the soon-to-be-former chief deputy would try to torpedo him.

As the ink from his pen was drying on the report he'd just finished, Gray came out and Carter appeared in the hallway's entrance. "Edwards, could you come back here for a minute, please?"

"Yes, sir." After slipping the report into a folder, he wandered down the hallway and into Carter's office, then pointed at the door. Carter nodded, so Michael closed it. "What's up, sir?"

"This is where everybody thinks I'm offering you the position. Of course, Watson doesn't know yet, so he has no idea what's going on."

"You don't think Gray told him?"

"No. I know Gray didn't tell him. Gray wouldn't tell him. There's a lot you don't know."

"Got it, sir. None of my business."

"I have a feeling it will become your business in the very near future. Now, I want you to go back to your desk, don't say a word, and I'll call Watson back here."

"How do you think he's going to take it, sir?"

"I have no idea, but we're about to find out. Did Marjorie jerk a knot in your tail last night when you got home?"

"Tried, sir, but I told her you came by."

"Shit. You didn't tell her about the promotion, did you?" Carter hissed.

"No. No, sir. You told me not to say a word, and I didn't."

"Good. Because I know these women around here. If you had told her, she would've called five of her friends and everybody in town would know by now."

Michael chuckled. "Yes, sir. I'd say that's an accurate assessment."

"Okay. Back to your desk. And if he says anything to you when he comes out, tell him to take it up with me. From this moment forward, if anybody gives you any lip, remind them of who you are in this department. Don't take it from them. You're no longer just one of them. You're their boss."

"Yes, sir." Michael stood and headed for the door, but he turned with his hand on the knob. "Thank you, sir."

"You're welcome. Thank you. Leave it open." Michael nodded and in seconds, he was back at his desk.

"Watson, could you come into my office for a minute, please?" Carter called from the end of the hallway.

"Yes, sir." When Justin walked by Michael's desk, he was grinning like the Cheshire cat. *He knows about Gray*, Michael surmised. They'd probably been talking about it, even though they weren't good friends. Michael heard Justin ask, "What's up, sir?"

But he didn't close the door.

Carter kicked off the conversation, and their voices were just loud enough that Michael could hear everything. He had a feeling that was by Carter's design. "I just wanted to let you know that Lewis will be leaving in a few weeks. He's taking a position in Little Rock."

"Yes, sir. He told me."

"Did he tell you … Never mind. That's his business. The reason I called you back here was to tell you about some changes in personnel around here."

"Yes, sir?"

"With Lewis gone, that leaves a position open in the department, and I already know who I want to fill it."

"Yes, sir. And thank you, sir."

"You're welcome. I don't mind keeping everybody informed."

"No, I mean—"

"I've chosen Edwards to be the new chief deputy."

"Wh-wh-what, sir?"

"He'll be assuming Lewis' old position as soon as Lewis is gone. I trust there won't be any issues."

"But sir … Edwards? Seriously? I've got five years on him in the department, and I've been—"

"Let me tell you what you've been, Watson." *I can't wait to hear this*, Michael thought. "Every time I've asked you to take some overtime, you've told me you had something else to do or already had plans. Every. Time. I can't think of a single time when you've accommodated the department in that way. Always a fishing trip with buddies, or your cousin's wedding, or something like that. Edwards, on the other hand, has done everything, and I mean *everything*, I've ever asked him to do."

"But sir, if I'd known it meant that much to you—"

"You don't have to know how much it means to me. If I ask you to do it, I obviously want you to do it. And you haven't. Do you know what happened last week?"

"Uh, no, sir."

"Let me tell you. Angel was sick all weekend. Really sick. Sick enough that my medically-trained wife thought she needed to go to the doctor. When she got the baby there, the doctor sent her to the hospital for some tests. To the *hospital*. My baby. And I couldn't go because we had a funeral procession to escort and there was no one else to do it. I'd already given Edwards another assignment for the day, and Lewis was on the other side of the county working a break-in at a residence. So my wife took our baby to the hospital for tests alone. I had asked you if you could come in because I knew we were going to be short-handed, and you told me you couldn't. Going camping with your family. You want to know why you're not getting the promotion? Shit like that is pretty much it."

"So you're saying that there's really no advancement for me here?"

"If you're saying that you're going to leave because I promoted Edwards, that's up to you. I'm not going to beg you to stay. You're a good officer, but this is a small department, and we have to expect to make some sacrifices to be sure that coverage is provided. I really don't want you to go, but I've got to hire someone to take Edwards' position, and I can hire two as easily as I can hire one. Totally up to you. What'll it be?"

"Can I have a while to think about it, sir?"

"Oh, sure, but if you leave today without giving me an answer, I'll consider that your answer and act accordingly. Now, go get busy. Dispatch just called a few minutes ago to say there's a stranded motorist out on I-24. Mile marker forty-seven."

"Yes, sir." Michael could hear Justin's footfalls as he stormed back up the hallway. He passed Michael's desk and glared at him. "You've got to be kidding me."

Michael remembered what Carter had said. "No. It's no joke. Don't you have somewhere you're supposed to be?"

Justin stood there for a few seconds, his left hand twitching, before he mumbled, "Yeah. I do," and headed out the door.

Michael watched him go until a *thud* made him turn, and he found a stack of folders in the middle of his desk.

Carter stood at the end of the desk, his arms folded across his chest. "Those are potential hires. I want you to go through them and pull the ones you think sound promising. Come up with five. We'll talk to them and if none of them work out, you can choose five more."

"But, sir, do you really think I ... I mean, do I really have—"

"Yes. You have the ability to do that. I wouldn't have given you this position if I didn't think you could do the job. Don't rush. Really look the files over, and if you need to, you can take them with you and finish them up tonight."

"Yes, sir. I'll get it done."

"And as soon as Lewis moves out of his office, you can move on in. Hell, I'll even order you a plaque!" Carter said with a laugh as he disappeared down the hallway.

His own office. A plaque on the door. And he got to go through job prospects' applications. That was his first official duty, and he wouldn't let Carter down.

———

"So who's next?"

Michael marked a name off the list and looked at the schedule. "Samara Futrell. Eight years with the state police. Before that, four years with McCracken County Sheriff's Department. Graduated in the top quarter of her class at the academy and only lacks about ten credit hours getting her degree in criminal justice." There was a beep when the front door opened, and Michael stood. "I'm guessing that's her."

"Bring her on back." Carter had already picked up a

pencil and was waiting.

The woman's back was to him when Michael took a spot behind the front counter. "Hello. Chief Deputy Edwards. Can I help you?"

She spun, and every molecule of air evacuated Michael's lungs. He was one hundred percent sure he'd never seen a woman that beautiful before in his life. From her long, dark lashes, to her shoulder-length hair and big coffee-colored eyes, she was a vision standing before him. *Oh, god, please don't let it be ...*

"Yes. I'm Samara Futrell. Here for an interview."

Michael's inner toddler fell to the floor, writhing and shrieking. *Why? Why, why, why? A gorgeous woman and I can't even hope to date her. Shit.* "Yes, ma'am. Come on back and I'll introduce you to the sheriff." They'd no more than cleared the doorway when Carter stood and extended a hand. "Miss Futrell, this is Sheriff Carter Melton."

The woman smiled broadly and reached for Carter's hand. "Pleasure to meet you, sir."

"And you as well, Miss Futrell. Please, have a seat. Would you like some coffee? Or a soft drink?"

"Um, do you have any diet soda? I was running late so I didn't stop at the convenience store and I could sure use one."

"Yes, we sure do." It got quiet, and then Carter barked, "Edwards? Can you get Miss Futrell a soft drink, please?"

Shit! I look like an idiot! his brain screamed. "Oh, um, yeah, sure. Uh, I think we have Coke and 7up, and maybe Dr Pepper."

"Any of them diet?"

He wanted to say, *You don't need a diet drink. You're perfect just as you are.* "Yes. I think the Cokes are."

"That'll be fine."

"Comin' right up," he said and hustled out of the room. He was certain that she thought he was an idiot, and she wouldn't be far from wrong. Women flustered him so badly that he'd never find anyone to date in a million years. He grabbed the can, rinsed the top off in the sink, wiped it down carefully with paper towel, and opened it as he made the trip back to Carter's office. "Here ya go." Would she notice that he'd cleaned it for her? Probably not. It would be nice if she did.

"Okay, so let's get down to business. Edwards here was in charge of pulling applications, and yours was one of five that we pulled. You're our fourth interview. Can you tell me why you left the state police?"

"It was the new post commander." Michael had heard about him, and the man sounded like someone he wouldn't want to work for. "It took about a week for the other two female troopers and me to look around and realize the three of us were in the office while the guys were out on patrol and taking calls. After the years I'd worked there without any problems, why he suddenly did that is still something I don't understand. I'm sure he's a good man, sir, but I guess he doesn't believe in women policing, and he basically turned us into secretaries."

"I see. We don't have a big enough department for me to do that," Carter said, never looking up as he studied her application. "And you're only ten hours away from your degree. So do you intend to finish it and move on?"

"No, sir. Honestly, I can't afford it. I have four siblings, so college money from my parents was nonexistent, and I already owe enough. And with what law enforcement typically earns, I can't see that ever happening."

Carter leaned back in his chair and locked eyes with the woman. "If I could come up with a way to subsidize your tuition and books, would you even consider it?"

"Oh, yes, sir. I certainly would. What's your thinking on that?"

Oh, shit. He's going to replace me, Michael told himself. But he was worried for nothing. "I've been thinking about the fact that our patrol officers have to act as detectives too, and I'd really like to have one dedicated detective. And I know that, as state troopers, you have to be your own detectives, unless KDCI is involved."

"Yes, sir. We did. The Department of Criminal Investigation has extensive resources and equipment, but they don't do patrols of any kind, so we had to do pretty much all of it, at least in the way of evidence collection and dissemination."

"Right, right. Done any crime scene reconstruction?" Then Carter chuckled and shook his head. "Wait. That's a stupid question. Of course you have."

She smiled, and that smile was dazzling. Michael was entranced. "Yes, sir. I've done pretty much everything. McCracken County was a great place to get my feet wet because it's a good department but not an extremely large one. We could do our jobs but not get lost in the shuffle. I wasn't a detective there, but I did work closely with them. Once I went to the state police, I missed that small-town work, but the money was so good that I couldn't walk away."

"I hear ya there. Not tootin' my own horn, but we actually have a pretty decent pay scale compared to most, and decent benefits too."

"Yes, sir. I saw that."

Carter laughed. "Checked us out, did you?"

"Of course I did, sir. I didn't want to waste my time or yours if I wasn't a good fit here."

"And? Do you think you'd be a good fit?"

"Can't imagine why not. Being back in a department this size would be perfect for me. I enjoy the small-town stuff. Can I ask about housing though? Are there places here? Because I'd definitely have to move."

"Not many. Edwards? Can you think of some places?"

"Not right off, but I'm sure there are some. I'll look around while I'm out and about. We don't have apartment buildings or things like that, but there's usually a house or two for rent, and sometimes even a few for sale."

"Thanks. So how soon will you be making your decision?"

"Within the next two wecks. My former chief deputy will be leaving and I'd like to have someone in place before then, since Edwards won't be as active in patrolling as he has been."

"Got it."

"So, overall, Miss Futrell, does this look like a place you'd want to work?" Carter asked, and Michael held his breath.

"Yes, sir. It does. If I get another offer before then, I'll give you a call." She rose and stuck out her hand again. "Thanks so much for giving me a chance, sir. And you as well, sir," she said, turning with an outstretched hand after she'd shaken Carter's.

Michael took her hand and was instantly impressed with its warmth, softness, and strength. "You're quite welcome. I'll walk you out," Michael offered as he stepped out into the hallway and waited for the woman to move in front of him. That was a view he appreciated.

But when they got to the front, she motioned for him to follow her out, so Michael called out, "Stepping outside the door, sir. I'll be back in just a second."

"Take your time," Carter called back.

As soon as the door closed, she smiled at Michael. "So, tell me, what's it like working for Sheriff Melton?"

"He's tough but fair. He doesn't try to be our best friend, but he also isn't standoffish. When he and Mrs. Melton got married, we were all invited, us and a guest. That day, he was Carter and she was Sharla, and we all had a great time. When he came back from the honeymoon, it was business as usual. I guess I'd say that we all highly respect him and want to do a good job for him. And he instills confidence in us. Can't say enough good things about him."

"If you'd known then what you know now, would you still have taken the job?" she asked, a hip cocked and her arms folded across her chest.

"Yep. Sure would."

"Got another question. Is there another woman in this department?"

"No, ma'am. Matter of fact, you'd be the first."

"Is there another officer of color here?"

"No, ma'am. Not because of any racial bias. Just because no one of color has applied before. There isn't a lot of racial diversity here."

"So do you think the locals would have a problem with me as a woman of color and also a deputy sheriff?"

"No, ma'am. I mean, you'd run into a few hicks and maybe the stray white supremacist, but that's about it."

"Good to know. Thanks for being straight with me."

"I'd never be anything but," Michael assured her.

"Good. Hey, thanks for pulling my application and I hope I hear from you guys."

"You're very welcome. Have a great afternoon."

"You too, Chief Deputy Edwards." He watched as she climbed into her Jeep Cherokee and pulled out of her parking space before he headed back to the door.

The metal frame had no more than snapped shut before Carter barked, "Wanted to talk to you alone, didn't she?"

Was that a bad thing? Had he done something wrong? "Uh, yes, sir."

"Good. I trust you told her the truth."

"Yes, sir. I sure did."

"Okay. Good enough. Who's up next?"

Michael checked his list. There was one more, a man named Hank Mason, and he hoped the guy didn't show. If he had to look at Miss Futrell every day, it would not hurt his feelings.

Not one little bit.

IT WAS HARD TO DRIVE WITH SHAKING HANDS, SO SHE pulled over and stopped at an abandoned gas station, slammed the Jeep into park, and sat for a few seconds to collect her thoughts. The two men she'd met seemed nice, but she never really knew what to expect until she was on the job. Her old commander had been great, and so had the guys from Paducah at the McCracken County department, but the new KSP commander had really done a number on her self-esteem. She'd never thought of a vagina as a drawback, but for Commander Porter, it had been.

Truth was, it wouldn't matter if the two men at the Trigg County Sheriff's Department had been real dicks. She needed a job, and she'd struck out everywhere else. Seemed like no departments anywhere had any money except Trigg County, and that was only because they were losing one employee. Did she even dare to hope? Black female police officers were common in big cities. In places like Cadiz, not so much.

She dropped her forehead to the steering wheel and sighed. If this one didn't pan out, the only places left were Clarksville and Nashville, and she really didn't want to move to Tennessee. She'd lived in Ballard County, Kentucky, her whole life and was one of only nine black kids there when she graduated. McCracken County had been an oasis for her. And until Commander Porter, she'd loved the Kentucky State Police. There was nowhere else to try.

"Guess I'd better learn to sing 'I'll Leave My Heart in Tennessee,'" she muttered aloud as she pulled the Jeep back onto the two-lane highway. YouTube surely had the music and lyrics, and she'd always been a strong singer.

"WHEW." MICHAEL DROPPED INTO THE CHAIR IN FRONT OF Carter's desk. "Glad that's over."

"Wow. What a blowhard. And a bigot. So I guess that 'black boys better stay in line' goes over okay in some places, but not here and not with me." Carter looked positively furious.

"Yeah, not me either. I mean, what the hell? Could he not see the pictures of you and your family behind you?"

Carter's eyes were almost shooting laser beams. "Oh, yeah. He saw them. He was trying to make a point. He's probably in his car right now, mumbling to himself about those blacks and whites and how they can't remember to stay in their respective places. There's no doubt in my mind that as soon as he saw those pictures, he no longer wanted this job, and that's fine with me, because he's sure as hell not gonna get it. Not now, not ever."

Michael sighed again. "Okay, so of the ones we interviewed, which one?"

"Actually," Carter said as he dropped his forearms onto the desk's surface and stared off to the side, "what would you think about hiring two?"

"Two? Can we afford that?"

"It'll be tight but, yeah, we can. I mean, I'm pretty sure Watson's gonna skate on us, and if he doesn't, then we've replaced Gray *and* we've got an extra person as a detective."

"You thinking Futrell?"

Carter nodded. "I am. I think she'd be well-suited to the job, and I think she'd do a good job. She's sure not lacking in experience, and if she went on to get her degree and then went to the forensics program online, she'd be an even better detective. I'm pretty sure she's a great one already."

"Yeah, I'm betting so. Who was the other one?"

Carter looked through his notes. "The second one. Anand Chadha. Seemed like a nice guy, knowledgeable, and familiar with small-town policing. I could see him doing the DARE program at the schools."

Michael nodded slowly. "Yeah. I could too. Seems like the type who'd enjoy that. He'd bring more racial diversity to the department. Not a reason to hire him, but still a good thing. And he's got a wife and kids, so he's steady."

"My thinking exactly. Okay, so let's call him and offer him the job."

"And the second opening?"

Carter smiled. "Futrell."

It was hard to hold his excitement. "Right. I'll get Chadha on the phone."

The call went well. Anand Chadha seemed excited to get started. When his mother had been diagnosed with cancer, he'd left his position and home in Carbondale, Illinois, to move to Murray, Kentucky, and take care of her. His wife wasn't happy about it, and neither were his kids, but they'd done it. The only work he'd been able to find was some minor security guard positions, and then his mother died. With the house willed to him and his sister, he and his family at least had a place to live, but he wanted to get back into the swing of things, and Trigg County could provide him with that opportunity.

After they'd hung up with him, Carter nodded toward Michael. "Call Futrell."

Michael picked up the desk phone, punched in the number, hit speaker, and let it ring. After two rings, a female voice said, "Hello?"

"Miss Futrell?"

"Yes?"

"This is Chief Deputy Edwards from Trigg County. Have you had time to think about everything we talked about?"

"Yes, sir."

"Then Sheriff Melton and I would like to formally offer the position to you."

There was a moment of silence before she said, "Oh, god, thank you so much. Thanks for calling. When do I start?"

Carter held up a finger to Michael. "Miss Futrell, this is Sheriff Melton. We've got a proposition for you. We'd like to have you as a deputy but also acting as our department's only detective. Would that be something you'd be interested in?"

"Yes, sir! Very much, sir."

"I'm going through the budget. Your probationary period will be over ninety days after you start. Even though I know you've been through what KSP gives you, I'd like to send you to the academy's online school for detectives. Are you interested?"

"Yes, sir. Very, very interested."

"Okay. Come in tomorrow and let's get your sizes for your uniforms. We'll get them ordered and until they come in, you can stay here in the office and go over the way we do things with Edwards. And Miss Futrell?"

"Yes, sir?"

"I'm *not* making you the secretary. I just want to be able to put you to work before your uniforms show up, and that's the easiest way."

"Yes, sir. I understand, sir. I'll be there tomorrow."

"Great. Day shift starts showing up at about seven."

"I'll be there, sir. And thank you so much."

"You're very welcome. Thank you. See you then."

"Yes, sir. Thank you, Chief Deputy Edwards."

"Thank you as well. See you in the morning. Bye." He sat back in his chair and stared at Carter for a couple of seconds. He wanted to say something so badly, but he wasn't sure how or what.

Carter beat him to it. "There's something on your mind. Spill it."

"Uh, well, sir, I ... It's just that ..."

"Yes. I was watching you. I'm not crazy about the idea, but you're grownups. I would hope to god you could be professional here."

"But, sir ... How did you ..." And he stopped.

"It was written all over your face. I had to hire her. I was afraid if I didn't, you'd quit and follow her around until she got a job, then apply there yourself."

Michael's cheeks were burning and he could feel reality setting in. "You don't have to worry about it, sir. She wouldn't give me the time of day."

Carter reared back in his chair and folded his arms across his chest. "And why would you say that?"

"Because, I mean ..." How could he explain it without sounding like a complete loser? Unless, of course, he was a complete loser.

"What? Any woman would be lucky to have you. But know this: She'll have to be tough as nails or Marjorie will walk all over her."

Michael shook his head and rolled his eyes. "Boy, you got that right."

"Yeah. But she seems like a tough lady. Give her time to get to know you."

"Oh, yeah. Not a problem." *Yeah*, Michael thought. *I ain't got nuthin' but time.*

Because when it came to women, that was definitely true.

CHAPTER 2

MAKING nice with your new coworkers seemed important to her, so Samara stopped on her way to the station and bought a box of fancy cupcakes. No donuts for her coworkers. She was a lot of things, but she wasn't a walking cliché.

There were only two cars there when she arrived, and she grabbed the box of cupcakes before heading in. "Hey there!" a voice called out, and Carter appeared at the head of the hallway. "Good morning!"

"Good morning, sir. Brought a little surprise for everybody."

Carter groaned. "Oh, god, not … cupcakes! Oh, wow! Everybody brings us donuts."

"I'm not everybody," she said and grinned.

"I see that! Come on back and fill out some paperwork. When Edwards gets here, he'll help get you measured for uniforms and we can go from there."

"Sounds good. Mind if I grab a cuppa …" she asked and pointed at the coffee maker.

"No. Go right ahead. Matter of fact, I'll take it all into the conference room and you can work on it in there."

The radio squawked to life. "TCSD base, this is TCSD unit one forty-eight, do you copy?"

Carter ran up the hallway and grabbed the mic. "Roger that, unit one forty-eight."

"Be advised, got a fifty-six thirty-two in the six hundred block of Bloom Avenue. Individual is standing in the middle of the street, waving it around."

"Roger that. Do you know who it is?"

"I think it's Blake Everett. Show me code six."

"Roger that, unit one forty-eight."

"Drunk this early in the morning?" Samara asked.

"What else are they going to do? They're drunk or doing meth. I'll take the former over the latter, but the gun is not good."

In just a couple of minutes he heard Michael's voice. "TCSD base, unit one forty-eight, one in custody and I'm fifteen to the jail. Repeat, fifteen to the jail. Copy?"

Carter sighed. "Roger that, unit one forty-eight."

"Was that Chief Deputy Edwards?" Samara asked.

"Yeah. That's on his route to work. Seems like every morning on his way to work he runs into some idiot and has to stop."

"How far away is the jail?"

Carter pointed down the street. "Just across the way there, at the back of the courthouse."

She grinned. "At least it's on his way."

"Yep. He'll be here in a minute. Get the paperwork filled out and we'll take it from there."

"Yes, sir." Samara retrieved her coffee from the counter and took off down the hallway.

"Hey!" Carter called after her. "Aren't you going to take a cupcake with you?"

"No, sir. I bought a baker's dozen."

"Oh, food tester to make sure nobody's going to poison us, huh?" he asked, laughing.

"Yes, sir! If that's what you want to believe, go right ahead." Samara was laughing too.

She could hear Carter out front. "Oh, god, they're cream-filled," he was mumbling with a full mouth, and she smiled. She really liked her new boss. He was a fun guy.

There was still paperwork to be finished when she heard the door open again. "Edwards, that you?"

"Yes, sir. It's me."

"You get that idiot straightened out?"

"Yes, sir. Fucking gun didn't even have bullets in it."

"The fucking gun didn't even have bullets in it?" Samara shouted back to ward off Carter's dress-down of Edwards.

"Futrell, is that you?" she heard Edwards ask.

"Yeah, unless you've got a couple of other female cops around here who I haven't met yet."

"Nope. You're the only one. Sorry for the language." The guy showed up in the doorway of the conference room, and for the first time, she took a really good look at him. He looked to be mid to late twenties with dark, wavy hair cropped into a high and tight. His smile was pleasant, and when he smiled, his eyes had very shallow lines that wrinkled the outer corners. And those eyes. They were a deep hazel, almost like toffee. She didn't know why, but when she looked into them, she felt a calmness. He just had an air of … What was it? Innocence? No. Not that. Wholesomeness. That was the best way to describe it. Of course, she could be wrong, but she was pretty sure if Edwards told you something and it wasn't true, it was because he actually thought it was, not because he was lying.

"Don't apologize. I drop my share of F-bombs. Y'all won't bother me."

"Edwards? You got a tape measure out there?" his boss called out.

"No, but we carry them in the shops for measuring circumference of things."

"Grab one and measure her for a uniform so you can order them."

"Uh, yes, sir."

Samara was fighting laughter. The look on his face told her that Edwards was grossly uncomfortable with the idea of measuring her. The thought crossed her mind to fuck with him a bit, but she shut it down. She had to get along with this guy, and he seemed really nice. Fucking with him wouldn't be nice at all.

When he came back, he had a tape measure in one hand and a piece of paper in the other. As soon as he laid the paper on the desk, she could see it was an order form from the uniform supplier. "Okay, we need a chest measurement, waist measurement, hips, sleeve, back length from top of spine to waistline, and inseam measurement."

Samara stood and took her jacket off. "Okay. Hand me the tape." She curled it around herself across her breasts. "Looks like … thirty-nine inches." Edwards marked it on the sheet. "Waist … twenty-nine inches. Hips …" She drew it around her hips. "Is it where it's supposed to be?"

"Yeah, I think so."

"Can you read it?"

She watched as he looked at it. "Yep. Thirty-five inches. Okay, give me the tape." She handed it to him and held one end while he drew the other up to her shoulder. "Thirty-one." She could feel him holding the tape at the top of her spine, then running it down her back. "Twenty-eight. And last but not least, inseam." Handing her the loose end, he waited while she pressed it on her thigh just below her crotch, and then he dragged it down the inside of her leg. "Thirty-one. I think that's it. Do you want short sleeves?"

"Yes, please, for summer. I wear longs in winter."

"Me too. That should do it. Oh, they have two choices, tailored or relaxed fit."

She had no idea what that meant. "Which are you wearing?"

"I wear the tailored shirts. They just look more professional. But I wear the relaxed version of the pants in case I have to run. Makes it a little easier."

She smiled at him and watched his cheeks pink just a little. "Sounds good to me. Hook me up with your special combo there."

"Will do."

A minute later, she could hear the fax machine going, and she assumed he was sending the form to the uniform company. As soon as she finished filling out her paperwork, she stepped over to Carter's door. "I've got the paperwork filled out. Anything else you want me to do?"

"Yeah." He took the stack of papers she held out to him, looked everything over, and handed it back to her. "I want Edwards to take you to the courthouse to give them to the clerk over there so they can put you on the county payroll. Then he can take you to the jail, city hall, bank, post office, places like that, so you can get familiar with the area. While you're out, go ahead and have lunch. As soon as that paperwork is filed, it'll register your duty weapon, and you'll be available for duty. And when you get there, they'll want this." He handed her a black presentation box, and she knew what it was. "You'll need to put the number on the paperwork when you get there. Welcome aboard, Deputy Futrell."

"Thank you, sir."

"Edwards! Assignment! Futrell will tell you."

"Yes, sir," Michael's voice called back from somewhere up front.

The hallway spit her out at the front desk again, and there was a deputy standing there, one she hadn't met. He turned and eyed her up and down, then stuck out a hand. "Deputy Justin Watson."

She took his hand and shook it, making sure to give him a solid grip. "Deputy Samara Futrell. Pleasure to meet you."

"And you too." Then he turned and went back to what he'd been doing. *Uh-huh. There's something going on there*, Samara told herself. She didn't know what, but there was a good chance she could get it out of Michael at lunch.

About that time, another deputy walked in. "Damn that Mrs. Bloodworth. She called me about her cat again. I swear ... Oh, hello. I'm Gray Lewis. You must be Deputy Futrell." When she took the hand he extended, she felt something pass between them, and she knew what it was. It was a knowing that she recognized.

"I am, but you can call me Samara. Just not on the radio," she quipped and he grinned.

"Not in a million years! Oh, wow. Cupcakes. Edwards, you do this?"

"Nope. It was her," Michael said with a grin as he pointed over his shoulder, never looking up.

"I keep eating like this, I'll never fit into my wedding dress," Gray said as he took a cupcake from the box. She heard Michael chuckle, but she also caught the look that passed over Justin's face—pure fury. *What the hell is that about?* she wondered.

"Oh, I'm sure you'll look great. Uh, Deputy Edwards, Sheriff Melton told me to take this paperwork over to the courthouse and said he'd like to have you show me around. Do you have time to—"

"I'll make time. Let me finish this report and we'll go. Won't take but a second." She watched as he went over the form again, then pointed at something and turned to show her. "See this box? Yeah, I didn't for a long time. Sheriff Melton didn't either. I got in trouble for not checking this on a document, so make sure you do."

"Good god, that's tiny," Samara said, leaning over and squinting at it.

"Yeah. No shit. Got a judge who picked on me for a while and he tried to get me fired over it."

That was a shock. "He still on the bench?"

"Yeah, unfortunately, but Carter cleaned his plow and he's backed off now."

"Why would he be like that?"

"Long story. I'll tell you while we're touring. Hey, Carter, want anything while we're gone?"

"Nah. Got a lunch meeting with the mayor," his boss called back.

"Oh, well, yay you. You have fun with that," Justin said, laughing.

"Oh, yeah. Always a real hoot," Carter barked. So there was a story there too? Seemed with every moment that went by, she was presented with yet another set of questions to pose to Michael.

He slipped the form into a bin and turned to look at her. "Okay, so you've got your badge. We've got a couple of extra tool belts in the closet back—"

"I have my own. Is that okay? I like it because I'm familiar with it."

"Oh, absolutely. Bring it in, we'll get it filled up, and then we can go."

After Samara retrieved her belt from her Jeep and they'd loaded it with equipment, Michael opened the door. "Got your paperwork?"

"Yep." She held up a manila envelope. "Ready to go."

"Good deal. We'll go to the courthouse first and then move around town." They reached the parking lot and Michael headed straight to a Ford Explorer with the TCSD crest on the outside.

"Nice ride."

He grinned. "Yeah. They asked what I wanted, and this was my choice. It was this or a Charger, and I really don't like those. This seems like a better choice. Roomier and more cargo space."

"Yeah, most of the departments are going to these now for that reason." To her surprise, he unlocked the door and held it for her, so she slipped in. As soon as he was behind the wheel, she turned to him. "You didn't have to do that. I'm just a fellow officer."

"You may be a fellow officer, but you're also a lady,

and my mother raised me to be a gentleman. If it offends you, I won't do it again. Just a courtesy."

Samara wasn't quite sure how she felt about that, but it was a nice gesture. "Oh, it's fine. Just not used to it."

"We're not KSP here. We still have a small-town code we follow, whether it's hokey or not. But if we're actually working, that won't happen. You'll be just another officer."

"Got it. So we're going to the clerk's office with these?"

He nodded. "At least three offices to stop at in there."

Forty-five minutes later, her paperwork was all filed, including her insurance forms, she'd seen the jail and met the jailer on duty, walked into city hall to look around, found the post office, and ridden past all the schools in the county. "Looks like antiques are popular around here," she commented as they drove down the main street on their way back.

"Yeah. We have a ham festival too. Used to have a couple of companies here that made country hams, but not anymore. They're all gone. But we still have the festival. It's fun. They have a rod run and a carnival."

"Does sound like fun. And a nightmare for law enforcement."

He nodded. "Yeah, a little, but the Cadiz Police Department is mostly responsible for that. We still help them though. It's just the right thing to do."

Michael kept driving and it looked like they were leaving town. "Where are we going?"

"To lunch. Unless you don't want to."

"Oh, no, I definitely want to."

He smiled. "Okay, so that's where I'm going." He

pulled up in front of a building that had what looked like a grain silo attached to it. The sign out front had two different names on it.

"Which one are we going to?"

"Coach House. The other one is Harley's Barbecue. It's great too." She hoped he wasn't upset that she didn't wait for him to open her door, but she got out anyway. He was waiting for her at the front of the SUV when she rounded it and they walked in together.

"Hi, Michael! How ya doin'?" the young woman working as hostess asked.

"Good. You doing okay?"

"Oh, yeah. Mamaw's in the nursing home now, so that's kinda bad, but she's okay. Just two?" she asked and eyed Samara.

"Yeah. Oh, Lindsey, this is Deputy Futrell. She's new at the department."

"Hi! Nice to meet you! They're finally gettin' a lady cop. 'Bout time! Everybody thinks we're in the Dark Ages around here, but we're really not."

"I see that," Samara responded, trying hard not to sound patronizing. Compared to a lot of places around there, it was indeed pretty backward, but everyone had been friendly and welcoming, at least to her face.

The food smelled delicious, but she really wanted to order and then get down to asking questions. They'd chatted in the SUV while he drove, but she was waiting for the right time to start with the things she really wanted to know. As soon as they ordered, he turned to her solemnly. "I'm guessing there's a lot you'd like to ask me."

"Damn. A mind reader. I'm in trouble," she said with a laugh.

"No mind reader. It's just that if I were you, I'd be asking some questions too."

"Okay, well, first off, what's with Gray? The door in the hallway says chief deputy, but I thought you were?"

"I am. He's leaving. Getting married and moving to Little Rock."

"Husband?"

Michael reared back and stared at her. "Yeah! How did you know?"

"My brother's gay. My gaydar works extremely well."

A smirk replaced his smile. "Ah. Hope you don't get that vibe from me."

"Nope. So, wife and kids. How many? Of both," Samara asked with a grin.

"Zero and zero."

That couldn't be right. "You're not married? Divorced?"

"Nope."

That seemed strange, especially if he wasn't gay. "Never?"

"No." Michael slumped back in his chair and sighed. "Might as well get this out of the way. I'm the butt of jokes from the other deputies. I live with my mother."

"How old are you?"

He rolled his eyes. "How did I know that was going to be the next question? I'm almost twenty-seven."

Good lord, the guy lived with his mother? She wasn't going to make a joke, but she had to admit to herself that it struck her as odd. "Do you have any intentions of moving out?"

"I have a house."

"Why aren't you living there?"

"Two reasons. Not so long ago, my dad and a couple of other county officials were killed in a plane crash in Land Between the Lakes."

She remembered it well. "That was your dad?"

"Yeah. He was the county judge executive. The mayor and the county attorney were on the plane too. I was super close to my dad, and he and my mom were high school sweethearts. It's been really hard, and I felt like she needed me there, at least for a little while."

She nodded. "Yeah. I can see that."

"And the reason I'm not living in my house is because it's a fixer-upper. But I'm almost through with it and when I am, that's where I'll be living. And between my savings and the insurance money my dad left me, it's completely paid for. I'm paying for the renovations as I go, so when I move in, I'll be on the hook for taxes and utilities. Nothing else. Which I think is a pretty good thing."

"No, it's a really good thing." Samara was impressed. The guy had thought it all out, and being kind to his mother had also allowed him a financial advantage that most people wouldn't have. "Can I see it sometime?"

"Sure. Whenever you want. If I'm not on duty, I'm usually there working on it, except to sleep." He stopped and closed his eyes, then opened them again. "Everybody except Carter has made fun of me, but they won't for long when they're making mortgage payments and I'm living in a house that I own free and clear."

"I'll say. That's never gonna happen for me."

He smiled and shook his head. "Don't say that. If you'll stick with Carter, you'll have a career for life. He's a great guy to work for."

There was another question she'd been dying to ask. "Are those his kids in the picture on his credenza?"

"Yes and no. The older girl, Chelsea, is his wife's daughter. The boy, Lionel, is his wife's nephew. They're raising him. His sister, Tamara, was the one who killed Trooper Palmer."

"Oh my god. Yeah. He was my training officer. A trooper and a veteran."

"Yeah. That's how they met. Carter's bullet was the one that killed the girl, but Sharla understood that he was just protecting himself. It was a tragic time, but they made it through to the other side and they're very happy. Oh, and the baby was dropped in the drop box outside the station during that tornado we had a while back. Turns out she was the granddaughter of his cousin on his dad's side, and the mother said she'd only put it up for adoption if a relative would take it. So she signed off on Carter and Sharla adopting her. He's also adopted Chelsea and Lionel, even though they're adults now. As far as he's concerned, they're his kids too."

Oh my god, what a nice guy, Samara heard her inner voice whisper. He'd taken on a teenage boy of another race, a baby, and a teenage girl, even though he didn't have to. "Wow. My respect for him just shot through the roof."

"Everybody in the county respects him. And we share a common bond."

"Yeah?"

"Yeah. Both of us have mothers that drive us absolutely crazy. Don't worry. You'll meet Marjorie and Wilda Fern soon enough," Michael said with a laugh and took a bite of the bread the server had left on the table. "What about you? Husband? Kids?"

"No. Never had time. Too busy trying to stay in the game that the big boys wanted to exclude me from."

"I hear ya."

"Hey, what's up with Watson?"

Michael chuckled. "He's royally pissed. He thought he should have the chief deputy position, but Carter gave it to me, and he's really frosted about it. I'm expecting to have some trouble from him when he just can't rein it in anymore."

"Most likely."

"Yeah, and we've got another new deputy coming on board in a couple of days. We were afraid Watson would walk, and that would leave us shorthanded. Plus I hear he's going to give you a lot of detective duties."

"Yep."

"Good. We need somebody to do that."

"He said he'd help me get my education and certifications."

"If Carter Melton tells you he'll do something, it'll happen. He's a man of his word if ever there was one. So, your family—are they here?"

"No, and I'm staying in a little motel over on Highway 41 for right now, but I've got to find somewhere to live."

"Yeah, I've been watching and so far, nothing, but I'll keep watching. Would you mind living out in the county?"

"No. That would be fine."

"Then hang on just a minute." He pulled his phone out, punched on the screen a few times, and put it up to his ear. "Hey, don't you know Mr. Ramsey? Out at the cattle farm? Yeah. Yeah. Okay, well, I have somebody who needs a place to live, and I just remembered that he has a cabin on that property. Can you call him and ask about it? Thanks. Love you too. Bye." He pressed the screen and slipped the phone back into his pocket. "My mom. The Ramseys go to the same church she does. She'll call Mr. Ramsey and ask him."

"Oh! Thanks. Nice place?"

"May be a little rustic, but it'll be in good shape. He's good about taking care of his property." The server stepped up to the table and placed their plates in front of them. "Thanks, Tasha."

"Y'all are welcome. Enjoy."

The girl sashayed away from the table and Samara watched as Michael took in her sweeping backside. "Nice girl," he mumbled.

"Nice-looking girl," she said, thinking nothing of it.

His brow wrinkled downward. "Are you a lesbian?"

Samara started to laugh. "God, no! I was just watching *you* watching *her*. And she's cute. But definitely not your type."

He quirked his mouth to one side. "Oh yeah? What's my type?"

"You want somebody who's soft but tough. Somebody who understands what you do for a living and can live with it. Somebody who wants the same things you do—family, home, job security, community. That girl wants somebody with a paycheck so she can go have her nails done every four days."

That set Michael laughing. "Yeah, I'm afraid you're right about her. As for me … Maybe you're right about me. Everybody keeps saying, 'Oh, Michael, eventually you'll meet somebody who's perfect for you.' But I'm a little afraid. I hear STIs are running rampant in nursing homes, and that's how old I'll be before I find her."

She rolled her eyes. "Maybe not." Then she got a glimpse of her plate. "God, this fish looks amazing."

"Yeah, this steak does too. Their food is really good." He took a bite, tipped his head back a little, and moaned. "Oh, god, this is the best steak I've had in a year."

"You mean your mom doesn't make steak for you?"

He snickered. "No. She's got a repertoire of about eight casseroles, and that's what I'm going to have. Every night. No question. It's just a matter of which one."

"Ah. Just think—you'll move into your house and you can fix whatever you want."

"That's right. I'll have steak at least once a week." He sat there for a second, chewing, before he said, "Oh, god. Yeah. I need to build a patio with a fire pit and an outdoor kitchen. That would be perfect."

"It *would* be perfect," she said in agreement as she took her second bite of fish. It had to be the tastiest fish she'd ever eaten. But as she chewed, something occurred to her.

She was having fun. Michael was a pleasure to be around. He treated her with respect and had good manners, plus he wasn't talking down to her or trying to compete with or impress her. They were having a genuine conversation, and she felt safe talking to him and sharing things with him.

Safe. That was a feeling she hadn't had in a long, long time.

THE NEXT WEEK WAS A BLUR. CARTER ASSIGNED HER several felony cases they hadn't been able to crack, and when she looked over the investigative work, she was stumped. It was solid. They'd done everything right, but they still hadn't managed to generate leads, and that was troubling.

She went back to the scene of the first crime. It was an abandoned meth lab, but it hadn't been abandoned when they'd gotten the original call. Somebody had obviously tipped them off because they were gone when law enforcement got there. Worse yet, it was in an unused barn on someone else's property, someone law enforcement knew had nothing to do with the criminal activity, far enough back from any road or occupied structures for anyone to see them. Added to that was the fact that they came and went through a nearby wildlife refuge property, so there was no one to glimpse them there. Everything in the place had been dusted, and there were no fingerprints. It appeared they'd been wearing full hazmat suits, rubber gloves, and hair protectors, indicating that it was more sophisticated than the locals could usually manage. They couldn't find a shred of evidence.

The second was the site of a fatal shooting, and it seemed the assailant was probably someone from outside the community. It looked like a crime of opportunity. They were coming through, saw lights, stopped and robbed the occupant of the home, then shot and killed him, followed by driving away into the night. There were no surveillance cameras anywhere near the place or on the way to or from, so they had nothing to go on, and ballistics had gotten no hits for use of the weapon in previous incidents. The trail had gone cold.

The last group was the most disturbing, at least to her. It was a cluster of rapes that had taken place over the previous three years with a victim list comprised of younger women of all different ages, and all in a ten-mile radius. In each instance, the investigating officer said he got the distinct impression that the women knew who their assailant was, but were unwilling to tell anyone. After reading the interviews with all seven women, Samara felt the same way. They were afraid, and she wanted to know why.

But the effect it had on her was jarring. In her mind, she went back three years to the moment she'd been over-powered and violated. She'd fought—god, how she'd fought!—but it had been for nothing. He was bigger and stronger, plus he'd plotted for an advantage. The worst part?

She couldn't tell anyone.

Samara knew exactly how those victims felt, and she was sure they were in the same situation. Someone they knew and/or trusted had done that, and her heart hurt thinking about how they must feel. She was climbing back into her cruiser when her phone rang. "Hey there!"

"Hi. I just got off the phone with my mother. There's a lady named Montgomery who lives over on Spring Street, and she has a mobile home on a lot next door to her that she's wanting to rent out. Want the address?"

"Sure!" Samara jotted it down as Michael read it off to her. "Listen, thanks so much. Between gas and the room, I'm not making anything living that far away."

"I hear ya. Hope this pans out."

"Hey, could you … I mean, would you mind …"

"Meeting you there? Of course not. Wouldn't mind at all. I'll be there when you get there."

"Thanks so much, Michael. I really appreciate it."

"You're welcome. See you in a few." And the phone went dead.

Samara used her navigation feature to lead her to the property and, sure enough, Michael's big SUV was sitting there. He was already out of the vehicle, leaning against the side, and she was struck by how nice he looked standing there. He really was an attractive guy, and she wasn't sure why the women around him couldn't see it. *Probably because they grew up with him*, she told herself. That always happened to people. It was why so many kids had boyfriends or girlfriends in adjacent counties. The low-hanging fruit didn't appeal to them. They wanted something up closer to the sun.

She climbed out and took a long look. "Well now, this isn't at all what I expected." Instead of the run-down sixties aluminum and mint green monstrosity she'd been sure she would find, there was an almost-new, well-kept, very attractive park model trailer sitting there.

"Yeah, I was afraid it would be pink and aluminum," Michael said as she walked up.

Samara grinned. "Yeah, me too, but I was thinking mint green. This is nothing like that."

"Okay, so I asked my mom what the deal is. Mrs. Montgomery's mother lived in it until she had to go to assisted living. She doesn't really want to pull it out of there, and she isn't really fond of the idea of renting it to just anybody. When Mom told her it was a deputy who wanted to rent it, she got all excited. Said she'd feel much safer with a deputy next door. Her husband is a truck driver, and he's gone a lot," Michael threw out as explanation.

Samara was ecstatic. "That means it's a win-win." He swept his arm toward the house, so she made her way up the front walk and climbed the stairs with Michael right behind her.

She knocked and the door opened to a short, cute woman in her late forties or early fifties who smiled brightly. "Can I ... Oh, hello, Michael!"

"Hi, Mrs. Montgomery. How are you?"

"Very well, thanks. So are you the lady Marjorie called me about?"

Samara was struck by how sweet the woman looked. "Yes, ma'am. I was wondering about the trailer. I need a place to live and—"

"Absolutely! Let me get the key. Hold on." She disappeared into the house and came back with a key ring that had a tag on it reading *Winner's Chevrolet.* "Here you go. Feel free to go look. Everything's still in it except her clothes and medicine. You're welcome to use all of it, or if you want your own things, I can box it all up."

"Thank you. We'll bring the key right back." She practically skipped down the steps, Michael right behind her.

The door of the trailer swung open and she fought tears. It was beautiful. "Wow. For an old lady, she had great taste," she whispered.

"Yeah. Mrs. Lowry is a great lady. She was my Sunday school teacher when I was little," Michael offered as explanation and pointed to a wedding photo from what looked like the fifties. "This is really nice." She watched as Michael wandered and looked around. "Pots and pans, dishes, silverware. And I bet linens too. Whatever she's going to ask for rent, it'll be worth it."

She peered into the shower. "I'm thinking that too. Oh, wow. Big walk-in shower."

She could feel him right behind her as he looked over her shoulder. "Wow is right. That's really nice."

"Yeah, and how many blocks is this from the office?"

Michael snorted. "Like eight? Nine? No distance at all."

"Uh, yeah. This is mine. I've seen all I need to see."

She locked the door, then she and Michael went back to the front porch. "Well, what did you think?" Mrs. Montgomery asked when she came to the door.

"I'll definitely take it."

Mrs. Montgomery laughed. "I didn't even tell you how much!"

"I have a feeling it'll be worth it. Do you need me to sign something?"

The woman shook her head and smiled. "No, no. I know you're good for it. And if you're not, I can always find Michael." Samara thought that was a weird comment until she spoke again. "I think the two of you will be very happy in it."

Samara panicked. "Oh, no, ma'am. We're—"

"No, no. We're just coworkers, Mrs. Montgomery," Michael damn near shouted. "She's new to the area. I'm just helping her out."

"Oh. I thought you were ... Never mind. You're just such a cute couple," she said with a grin.

Samara still hadn't recovered enough to speak, but Michael added, "That's still a very nice thing to say. Thank you."

"Let me get a pen and paper and write your information down. Just a second." As she stepped away from the door, Michael turned to Samara and shrugged, palms up and wearing a sheepish grin.

That struck her as the funniest thing ever, and it was all she could do to keep from bursting out laughing. "Here we are. Just write it all down." As soon as Samara had written her email address and phone number, she handed the notepad back. "And here's the keys."

"Don't you need a deposit or something?" Samara asked.

"No. That's fine. If you're friends with Michael, that's enough for me."

"Oh! Well, thank you. I appreciate that. When can I move in?"

"Anytime you want. I suppose you'll be helping her with that too, Michael?" Mrs. Montgomery asked and winked at the chief deputy.

"Uhhh, if she needs me to, yeah. I'll help her."

"Good, good. Your mama's raised a fine young man. You two have a good afternoon, okay?"

"Yes, ma'am. Thank you, ma'am," Michael said as she stepped back to close the door.

"Yes. Thank you, ma'am. I appreciate it," Samara added before she spun and headed to her cruiser. When they got far enough away, she whispered, "I got it."

"Yeah. And that's really nice too."

He stopped at her car, so she figured she'd just ask. "Did you mean that? About helping me move?"

"Of course. Be glad to."

"You got a truck?"

He grinned. "Yep."

"Thanks." She wanted badly to ask, but she wasn't sure if she should. Finally, she decided she would. "She thought we were a couple. Would that really be such a bad thing?"

"No. Not at all. Just surprised me, I guess."

"Are the people around here that racist?"

"No, no. Nothing like that. They just ... Nobody thinks I'll ever get married or move out of my mom's house. They all thought I'd marry ..." And he stopped.

Okay, I've got to know, her brain muttered. "Who? Marry who?"

"Nobody. High school girlfriend. That's all." He didn't smile as he spoke, and there was something in his eyes that made her chest ache. "So see ya later? Maybe at the office?"

"Yeah. Maybe at the office. Got some leads to follow up."

"Ah. Well, good luck." He wandered away, but just as he reached his SUV, he turned. "Let me know when you want to see my house."

"I will. Soon." She watched as he climbed in and gave her a little wave before driving away. A glance around told her it was a quiet neighborhood of mostly older people, and that suited her just fine. She'd have to be careful with noise if she got called out in the night, but other than that, she couldn't imagine that she wouldn't fit in.

Amid the thoughts of the cases she was working on and all the other things she had ahead of her, Michael made his way back into her mind. Who had everyone thought he'd marry?

Maybe she'd eventually find out.

CHAPTER 3

MICHAEL BROUGHT HIS TRUCK, and Carter brought his. Carter also signed off on Samara using Gray's department-issued pickup truck for the day. "Moving an employee," he told her. It only took them about four hours and they were finished. Just one trip to Ballard County was all that was necessary. She didn't have a lot of worldly possessions.

Carter had carried in the last box when he asked, "Hey, since you're not really moved in yet, why don't you come over for dinner tonight? Sharla's off today, and she asked me to extend the invitation."

She looked around at the chaos on the floor, the countertop, the table, the sofa, every surface—they were all covered with boxes. "Oh, wow, that would be great. I can't cook anything. This place is too much of a mess."

"Yeah, that was her thinking. Oh, and Michael, since you've been helping, she wanted you to come too."

"Count me in! Your wife's a great cook," the deputy said with a smile that was bound to hurt his face.

"Good! I'll call her and let her know you'll both be there. So, what else do you need me to do?" he asked, hands on his hips.

"Nothing. This is great. Thank you so much. You have no idea how much I appreciate both of you helping me."

"Guess I'll go home and take Angel off her hands for a little while. I know she'll appreciate it. She's been there all day alone with the baby and—"

"Oh, god, I'm so sorry!" Samara chirped. "I never thought about—"

"No, no! Don't worry about it. It's fine. She's just at a really difficult age right now and she's a handful. You'll see when you get there. Six?"

Samara nodded. "Yeah, six is good."

"Works for me too," Michael answered.

Carter waved as he opened the front door. "Good. See y'all then."

Samara moved just enough boxes for both of them to sit down and plopped down on the sofa. "Whew. I don't know about you, but I'm beat."

Michael sat down heavily beside her and sighed. "Me too. I mean, nothing was heavy. It's just the loading and unloading and all that. At least you won't have to do it again for a while."

"Yeah. I certainly hope not." It was right there on the tip of her tongue, and she was fighting to keep from asking, but she was losing the battle. After two minutes of warring with her own thoughts, she finally worked up the courage. "Hey, the other day, you said everybody thought you'd marry ... And then you stopped. Who did everybody think you'd marry?" Michael sat there, staring at his hands, and Samara realized she'd made a terrible mistake. Whatever it was, it was still painful for him, and she was prying. "That's okay. Don't answer. It's none of my business, and I'm sorry for being so nosy."

"No, no. It's okay. Her name is Glenna, and we'd been together since high school. I worked at the big home improvement store in Hopkinsville, and I was a volunteer firefighter too. We had a game every year, cops against firefighters, and we went." For reasons she couldn't understand, the woman's name rang a bell for her. "We were playing and all the spouses and boyfriends or girlfriends were watching. There was an officer who'd been hurt on the job, and he was sitting out. I noticed that he said something to her as she walked by on her way back from the concession stand and in a few minutes, she was back over there, talking to him. I didn't like the way it looked, but I didn't say anything."

Samara groaned. "Uh-oh. I don't like where this is going."

"Yeah, well, neither did I. A couple of weeks later, we were supposed to go have engagement pictures made, but she cancelled the photo shoot. Said the dress she'd ordered hadn't come in yet, so she needed to wait. Then it got to the point that I'd call her like I did every night, and she didn't answer. That's when I started to wonder. A couple of weeks later, one of the guys I worked with said, 'Hey, I saw Glenna last night. Some state trooper pulled her over.' That was the moment I knew she was seeing the guy."

"A state trooper? Somebody I know?"

"I doubt it. That was when we were both twenty-two, so he's probably long gone by now, especially if he kept hitting on other people's wives."

"So what happened to her?"

"Oh, she married him. But that didn't make him faithful. He's fucked around on her all over the area and she just keeps letting him come back."

A knot was growing in her stomach, and with that last sentence, it grew spikes. It couldn't be. It just couldn't. "What's his name?"

A sensation like the floor liquefying under her feet made her heart drop into her gut when he answered, "Alex Stadler."

For a split second, it was hard to breathe. She could feel her body trembling, and she didn't know how to make it stop. Alex Stadler. The man she wished dead every night before she finally managed to go to sleep. The asshole she wanted to put a bullet through. The guy that even being burned at the stake wouldn't be good enough to suit her. A voice cut through the shrieking in her head. "Samara? Hey, Samara, you okay?" She shook her head. "You don't look right. Look, let's …" There was movement all around her, and she felt herself falling backward, but her head landed on a toss pillow, and she felt her feet rising until they were on the sofa. "There ya go. Lie down for a minute. Let me find a glass and get you some water. Probably just pushed a little too hard today."

"I'm fine. Really. I'm fine. It's okay," she called out blindly, but it wasn't. It really, really wasn't.

"No. You're not. Looks like your blood pressure bottomed out or something. Here, sit up just a little and take a sip." She felt him lift her head slightly, so she did her best to rise, propped on her elbows, and took a sip of water. All that accomplished was making her feel nauseous. "Just take a deep breath and calm down. What's going on?"

"Nothing. I think you're right. I think I just pushed myself a little too hard today. I think I'll lie here for a bit and catch a nap before I go to Carter's house. You should go on home and get a little down time too." He opened his mouth to argue, but Samara stopped him. "No, go on. I'll be fine. If you get there and I'm ten minutes late, come looking for me. Otherwise, I'll see you then."

"If you're sure …"

"I'm positive. I'm fine. Just go on. And thanks again."

"You're very welcome. See you in a bit." She watched as Michael wound his way through all the boxes and opened the front door. It wasn't until she heard his truck drive away that she felt like she could breathe.

Alex Stadler. Kentucky State Police Trooper Alex Stadler. That's where she'd heard Glenna's name. She wondered if Glenna had any idea what kind of shit he was up to. Did she know all the things he did? Did she know what a reprehensible, barely human asshole her husband was?

And then everything tumbled around until it was in pinpoint focus. She thought about the rape cases she'd inherited. There was one thing they all had in common, only one. Every one of those young women was terrified to name her attacker. Samara knew how that felt.

Because five years into her job as a trooper, Alex Stadler had raped her.

SHE SPENT THE REST OF THE TIME BEFORE SHE HAD TO BE at Carter and Sharla's trying to figure what, if anything, to say to Michael. She felt safe around him, but if she had to tell him something like that, she'd better have a way to back up her allegation. So she hatched a plan.

On Monday, Samara would start calling other departments in the Post 1 area to see if they'd had similar reports. It was almost a sure thing that if he'd done it to women in Trigg County, he'd done it in surrounding counties too. Did he live in Trigg County? The thought made her queasy. If she had to deal with him, she didn't know what she'd do. But if she could convict him, she'd be thrilled, even if her own situation had to be brought to light.

She wasn't sure what she was expecting Carter's home to look like, but she was a bit surprised. It wasn't large, just big enough, and modest. That puzzled her, given that she had some vague knowledge of what he made, and she knew his wife worked too. They could surely afford a bigger, nicer house, but then she remembered the teenagers in his pictures. If they were in college, that would explain their thriftiness.

Michael's truck was already out front, so she got out and strolled up the front walk, looking at the landscaping as she went. Very nice. It was obvious he kept things up and tried to keep it all looking pretty. The front door opened and Michael stepped out, letting the storm door close behind him. "You okay?" he asked quietly when she'd taken the three steps up to the porch.

"Yeah. I'm okay. Just pushed a little too hard, I guess."

"Good. You had me worried for a minute there. I didn't know what was happening."

"I'll probably be fine once I've had a good night's sleep." He held the door for her and she glanced around once she was inside. Spacious and well-appointed. Beautiful furniture, classy artwork on the walls, expensive drapes. And a portable crib turned playpen on the far side of the room. Yep. There was definitely a baby there somewhere. "Hey, y'all," she called out as she stepped into the kitchen.

"Hi! I'm Sharla," a very, very attractive blond said. The woman made a beeline straight to Samara and hugged her. "It's so good to meet you! The guys have said some very flattering things about you."

"Oh! Well, that's nice. What kinda lies did y'all tell on me?" she asked, grinning.

"Not a single one. We were talking about how well you've just fit right into the department," Carter answered.

Michael nodded. "Yeah, and what a good officer you are." Thoughts of the rape cases started swirling in her head, but she fought to keep a lid on them.

"Well, thank you, both of you. That's nice to hear. So can I help in any way?"

From somewhere in the house, she heard a shriek. "Uhhh, do you like kids?" Carter asked, a look of desperation clouding his face.

"I love kids."

"Then first door on your right down the hallway. She probably needs changing. Been napping. And she'll be blowin' and goin' in a couple of minutes, so time is of the essence."

"Gotcha. Be right back." She dropped her purse on the sofa as she darted by and tiptoed down the hallway. When she came to the first door on the right, she peeked in, but she wasn't sly enough.

The baby heard her and began to shriek again. "It's okay! It's okay! Come here, sweetie," she said and lifted the little thing. The cutie was a chunk! "Hey, hey, hey, it's all good, baby girl. Let's get you changed so you can go see Mommy and Daddy, whaddya say?" The infant stared at her for a minute, then touched her hair. "Yeah, probably never seen anything like that, huh? Wait. You've got a brother whose hair looks like this," Samara said with a chuckle. "Okay, where are ... There they are. So let's get it done, shall we?" she asked as she placed the baby on the changing table and reached for the wipes.

A presence behind her startled her just a little, but her training kept her from jumping. "So you know all about babies?" she heard Michael's voice ask.

"My little sister is about eleven years younger than me, so I helped out with her a lot."

"Oh. Well, I know nothing about babies. Nothing at all. But you look pretty proficient there."

"That's because I am." She sprinkled some powder on Angel and inside the diaper, then pulled the tabs and stuck them down to hold the diaper on. "There we go! Now, let's go find Mommy and Daddy." Michael stepped back with a grin on his face as she made her way back toward the kitchen. "All cleaned up and prettified," she announced.

Carter chucked the infant's chin. "Hey, sweet girl! Mommy's almost finished here. Do you wanna play in your play yard? Your toys are in there."

"I can sit here and hold her if that'll make her happier. I don't mind," Samara told Sharla.

"That would be great. I'm afraid if you leave her in

there, we'll either have to go sit in there or you'll wind up bringing her back in here. She wants to be where she can see what's going on."

"How old is she?"

"Almost thirteen months. She'll be walking pretty soon. She's been pulling up and standing for at least four months, but she just won't turn loose and take those first few steps," Carter said from behind the rim of his beer bottle.

"Awww, she'll start soon enough and you'll wish she was still six months old so she'd stay where you put her," Samara said, laughing.

Sharla laughed. "Oh, I know that's right."

Michael clapped his hands loudly. "Okay, what can I do to help?"

"You can come with me and be the assistant grill master," Carter said, handing him a beer.

"No matter what I do, I'll always be one step under you, am I right?"

Carter laughed. "Yep. I plan to keep it that way until I'm old enough that I just don't care." Both men were laughing as they disappeared out the back and when the storm door closed, she got the full aroma of whatever was cooking on the grill. The growl her stomach let out would've been embarrassing if anyone had been close enough to hear.

"So how are you liking it here?" Sharla asked, never turning around.

"I like it. Everybody's been really nice—coworkers, members of the community, everybody. And finding that trailer was some luck."

"Yeah, that's what Michael said. Good thing he asked

Marjorie. That woman is like a dog on a bone when she wants something. I bet she called everybody around here who has so much as a porta-potty."

Samara laughed. "Yeah, probably." Should she? *Oh, what the hell. Go for it*, she told herself. "So, how does Carter feel about his employees seeing each other?"

"Uh-oh. Who's fooling around with whom?" Sharla asked, spinning to look at Samara. "Oh, you're talking about yourself. Ah. Sorry. Um, he doesn't care as long as it doesn't affect their jobs. And that's a tough tightwire to walk."

"Yeah."

"Who is it? Justin? Oh, the new guy, what's his name ... Anand Chadha? Indian, right?"

"Yeah, uh, no. It's not him. He's married."

"Oh. That's right. There are only eight more officers. Who in the world is it?" Samara cut her eyes toward the back door. "But Carter ..." She could tell the moment it dawned on her hostess. "Michael?"

"Yeah."

"Seriously?"

Samara wrinkled her brow down and dropped her chin. "Well, yeah. What's wrong with Michael?"

"Nothing! I mean, nothing is wrong with Michael. I've just never known him to, um, date."

"What does that mean? Does he hire hookers?"

Sharla giggled. "Not that I know of."

"Yeah, well, I heard all about his ex-girlfriend."

Sharla leveled her gaze at the younger woman. "Is that so? Because nobody knows that story. Nobody. Nobody's ever said anything."

"Well, if you've known him this long and he hasn't confided in you, I don't feel like I can say anything."

"No, no. I wouldn't want you to betray his trust. He has an ex-girlfriend?"

"Yeah. And apparently she hurt him pretty badly."

Sharla sighed and leaned back against the countertop. "So that's why he doesn't date. How long ago was this?"

"I don't know. I just know it's been more than three years."

"Probably much longer than that." Sharla turned back to the sink, rinsed a spoon, and placed it on the drying rack. "Poor guy. Probably why he's stayed with his mom all these years too."

"Nah. Part of that was so he could pay for the house."

"Oh. Got it. Well, that was wise on his part."

"Yeah. It's paid for, and he's paying for the renovations as he goes."

"Oh!" Sharla spun back around. "That's pretty amazing. So he doesn't have house payments? Lucky him."

"No, just lots of hard work. And part of his dad's insurance money."

"Yeah, that's right. I haven't lived here long enough to have known him, but everybody says Wilson was a great guy."

"Where did you live? I mean, before you and Carter—"

"Hopkinsville. Once we got together, I moved here. The kids were already out of high school, so it didn't bother them. But everybody speaks very highly of Michael's dad."

"So I've heard." The baby was playing with a little stuffed toy Samara had handed her from the floor, and she squealed and threw it down. "You've been so good. Why you gotta act a fool now?" she asked the infant.

"Eh-eh-eh," Angel babbled. "Ummm-ummm-ummm gah."

Samara laughed. "Is that right?" Angel reached up and slapped Samara's nose. "Oh, I see how you are. Bully." She kissed the top of the baby's head and kept laughing.

"She's a handful. So Michael's going to ask you out, you think?" Sharla asked.

She's not going to give this up now, Samara told herself. *I shouldn't have said a damn word.* "No. I doubt it. So I'm going to ask him."

Sharla nodded. "Solidarity, sister."

"That's what I'm talkin' 'bout. This is the new millennium. We can do whatever we want."

Sharla laughed. "Hell yeah."

Samara and Sharla kept chatting, and the longer they talked, the more Samara liked the sheriff's wife. She was funny and smart, and she seemed to enjoy both her job and her family. They talked about what had happened with Tamara, and she was surprised to see so much pain still on the gorgeous woman's face. Sharla didn't exactly blame herself, but she also didn't let herself off the hook, and Samara felt sorry for her.

But dinner … It had been years since she'd had such a good time. The four of them laughed and told stories on themselves, plus Carter told stories on Michael, which wasn't uncommon, except for one thing.

Never, at any time, did it feel like he was making fun of Michael, and she loved that about her boss. While her superiors in the KSP would've embarrassed the hell out of anybody and everybody every time they got the chance, Carter wasn't like that. His ribbing of Michael was more like a dad telling funny stories about his kid, and it struck her for the first time how much Michael must miss his dad. Anyone with eyes could see that he respected and trusted Carter and, yeah, maybe even loved him as a friend. The three people there with her seemed to have very, very healthy relationships, and that was different from most of the world around her. It was refreshing.

At the end of the evening, she insisted on rocking Angel to sleep, watching the baby's little lip quiver as she slept. She was beautiful and perfect. Maybe someday … Nah. Probably not.

Samara stood in the kitchen doorway, her hands clasped together in front of her. "Guess I'd better get home. I'm not even sure there are sheets on the bed yet. Matter of fact, I'm pretty sure there aren't. And I'm beat. But thank you so much for dinner. I would've had to find something for the microwave at the grocery if you hadn't invited me over. I really appreciate it."

Carter smiled. "We just wanted to help."

"Well, you did. You not only gave me food after I'd helped all day, but you gave me somewhere to go without having to deal with my mother. That's worth everything," Michael said with a sour chuckle.

Carter laughed. "Escaping Marjorie *is* worth everything, and I should know. Sharla's saved me from Wilda Fern a million times."

Sharla gave him a peck on the cheek. "Yeah. You owe me big time."

"Oh, I intend to pay you back. Trust me." Then he slapped Sharla's ass.

Michael snickered. "On that note, I think we need to go. Carter, thanks again," he said and extended his hand.

Carter shook it, then shook Samara's. "You're very welcome. See you ... Well, I hope I don't see you for a couple of days, but you know how that goes."

"Oh, yeah. Hopefully not. Thanks again." Samara opened the door and headed out, Michael on her heels. As they walked, she giggled. "Did we just escape a sheriff and wife make-out session?"

She heard Michael let out a little laugh from somewhere behind her. "Yeah. I think so."

"Good. Don't wanna see that." When she reached her car, she turned and leaned against it. She wondered if Michael would just keep walking, but he didn't. Instead, he stopped in front of her. "Tomorrow morning I'm going to get up and work like hell to get stuff put away. Want to come over tomorrow night for dinner?"

"Sure? That's a lot of work to then cook dinner."

"I can handle it."

"I've got a better idea. How 'bout I pick up something at the Cadiz Diner and bring it over?"

"You wouldn't mind?"

"Not at all. They have a different special every day, so I'll give you a call when I get there and find out what they have, and you can tell me what you want. Does that sound good?"

"Sounds great. Okay. It's a date." She hadn't even realized what she'd said until she got a look at Michael's face. "What?"

"A date?"

"Yeah. Do you not want that?"

"I-I-I-I-I didn't say I didn't."

59

She cocked a hip and folded her arms across her chest. "So you don't want a date with me?"

"I didn't say that either."

"Are you the least bit attracted to me?" She couldn't wait to hear his answer.

"Uh, yeah. I am. Very." He stood there for a second and stared at her. "You're not playing a trick on me, are you?"

"I wouldn't do that. Why would you think I'd do that?"

"Sorry. I'm just not used to … women wanting to … spend time with me."

"Women have been overlooking you. That's been their mistake. But I'm not like most women. I've …" She wanted to tell him what she'd survived, but she couldn't. "I've lived a different life than most women. I don't know if this will work. It may flop. But it may fly. Do you want to find out? Or do you want to forever wonder, 'What if?'"

"I don't want to wonder. I'm in."

"Okay. Call me tomorrow when you get to the diner and let me know what they've got. And I'll see you when you get there."

"What time?"

She opened the car door and put her right foot on the floorboard with her hands on top of the door. "I'm going to be there all damn day. Doesn't matter. Just whenever you want."

His smile was shy but bright. "Maybe sooner rather than later?"

"Sooner rather than later is my favorite."

"Good. See you then. Be careful driving back."

"You too. Night."

"Night, Samara."

She slid behind the steering wheel and watched as he did the same. As soon as she started up her Jeep and pulled out, he pulled in behind her and followed her until she got to the trailer. When she pulled into the drive, he tooted his horn and drove on. He was making sure she was safe. It had been a long, long time since anybody had given a shit whether she was safe or not. But he did.

He couldn't possibly know how happy that made her.

"OH MY GOD. OH MY GOD. *OH MY GOD.*" MICHAEL DROVE along the dark highway, but there was a blinding light in his heart. He'd been trying to figure out a way to ask her out, or to at least let her know that he liked her, and he'd never dreamed she'd feel the same way. All his life, he'd been told he was too sweet, too kind, too shy, too quiet. The first time he'd dropped a suspect to the ground and cuffed them, he'd felt like he was showing the world what Michael Edwards was really made of. Of course, Glenna hadn't seen that. She was already gone.

That had been part of his motivation for becoming a deputy. He wanted a way to eventually get to Stadler and stop the asshole in his tracks, and the only way he could do that was to become a cop himself. What he'd found amazing was how quickly he made it through the academy. He was afraid he'd never pass, but he had come out at the top of his class instead. Something about police work came easy to him. He had zero trouble remembering statutes and ordinances, and learning the codes they used was simple. It all made sense to him, and he loved it, not to mention the fact that he got to help people. There was no way he'd try to get a position with KSP. Stadler would figure out pretty quickly who he was. But being hired at Trigg County and working for Carter had been the best thing that had ever happened to him. He was back in his hometown, back with his family, in a place where he felt welcome and safe, working for a guy who always had his back, and finding a house to turn into a home. There was only one thing lacking.

Now he had a chance to drop that missing piece into the puzzle. Samara was strong and capable, but there was something about her that told him she had a vulnerable spot, something that needed to heal. What was it? Maybe she'd eventually tell him. He certainly hoped so. In order to do that, she'd have to trust him, and he could be that person. If anyone could take her pain, keep it to himself, and help her be rid of it, it was him. He could do it and be quiet and calm about it. Whatever was bothering her, he wanted to know. He wanted to fix it if he could. But most of all, he just wanted to be there for her.

It looked like he might get a chance to do exactly that, and he had to be careful. Blowing it was not an option. If he played his cards right, the next evening would tell him if it was a waste of time or if he stood a good chance of finally having what he longed for. To most people, that seemed simple, but to Michael, it had seemed impossible.

All he really wanted was someone he could love. And someone who'd love him back. Maybe it wasn't so impossible after all.

By the time he got home, he was exhausted, and he thought he'd go straight to bed. But just like the evening of the first time he'd seen her and every evening since, his body wouldn't let that happen. Never had a need so consumed him, and he wanted her. The connection he'd had with Glenna had been nothing like what he felt when he looked at Samara, and he hadn't even known her that long. Hand wrapped firmly around his hardness, he stroked himself slowly, thinking about her eyes, her dark hair, and that skin as soft as flower petals and the color of burnished saddle leather, a warm, rich hue with lovely reddish undertones. What he wanted more than anything was to hold her, to touch that lovely face and feel her warmth against him. His body gave in, turned loose, and he whispered her name. "Samara. Oh, god, Samara."

The next thing he knew, the room was aglow with early morning light and he could hear his mother puttering around in the kitchen. After he managed to stumble to the bathroom and clean up, he looked at himself in the mirror and smiled. He wasn't sure what she wanted, but if it was security and love, he had it to give.

His thoughts were pierced by that tinny voice. "Mikey! Breakfast!"

"Coming." Brush in hand, he tamed his unruly head of hair and followed the sounds of her early morning rattling.

"Mikey! You're not even dressed! Aren't you going to church this morning?"

"No, Mom. I'm not."

She stared at him, her head cocked to one side. "Of course you are."

"No, Mom, I'm not. I've got somewhere else to be."

"What could be more important than going to worship our Lord and Savior?"

The sigh he let loose sounded appropriately irritating. "I dunno, Mom. Maybe my life?"

"What's that supposed to mean?"

He rolled his eyes and dropped his head. "I really have no idea. It's seven o'clock in the morning on one of the only days I have off, and I don't think I can answer questions right now."

"Well, eat your breakfast, clean yourself up, and get dressed. Mabel's daughter is here visiting from South Carolina, and I'd really like for you to meet her. I hear she's a lovely woman, and you could maybe—"

"No, Mom. I'm not letting you fix me up with somebody. Besides, I already have somebody I'd like to start dating."

"Who on earth could that be?"

"Somebody you don't know. Somebody who's new to town."

"What's her name?"

"No, Mom. I'm not going down that road with you. I'm just not—"

"Are you lying to me, Michael Wilson Edwards?"

"No. I am not lying to you." That was it. He'd had all he could take, so he stood and pushed his chair back from the table. "I've got somewhere to be."

"But you haven't even eaten your breakfast!"

"That's fine. I'll get some somewhere. Go on to church. Don't wait for me, because I'm not going."

"Mikey! Mikey, you come back here and …"

He let her ramble and grabbed a towel and washcloth, then walked straight into his bathroom and closed the door. All he really wanted was some hot water and a semi-trailer load of peace and quiet to go with it. It only took him a couple of minutes to shave, and he climbed in, sighing with relief as he stood under the hot spray. God, it felt good to stand there and not have to hear her droning on and on. And right there, that minute, he made his decision.

The water was on in his house. So was the electricity. The HVAC unit worked fine. He'd have to move stuff again to put the flooring in, but until then, he could sleep on a mattress on the floor. The closet didn't have doors, but it had a rod and a shelf, so he had somewhere to put his clothes. All he really needed were some towels, sheets, pillows, a blanket, a mattress, and a few dishes, and he could move right in.

As soon as he was dressed, he'd get in the truck and drive into Hopkinsville. He could get everything he needed there, including a mattress, and take it all back to the house. By evening, he could be moved into at least the bedroom and en suite bath, and he'd never have to listen to that poking and prying again. If he came to visit and she started, he could just walk out. That would suit him fine.

Three hours later, everything was in his truck. He tied down the mattress and headed back to Cadiz. He'd stopped on the way to town and gotten a bacon, egg, and cheese biscuit and some coffee, but it was almost lunchtime, so he picked up a pizza and drove straight to the house. It only took him a couple of minutes to put the pizza on the counter so he could start unloading.

On his last trip back in, a voice called out, "Hey, whatcha doin', Michael?"

One look told him it was his neighbor, Danny. "Moving in. Not completely, but enough to stay here."

"Marjorie driving you nuts?" the man asked. Yeah, his mother was a legend around town all right.

"Yep. You got it. But no more. It's almost done anyway, so I figured I might as well take advantage of it."

"That's the spirit! Need some help with that mattress?"

Michael looked at it, then turned back to Danny and smiled. "You know, that would be nice. I'd really appreciate it."

"Okay. Let me go get Mitzi and ... Oh, I'm just messin' with ya! Come on, I'll help you."

"I'd offer you something to drink, but I've got nothing right now," Michael said when they'd gotten the mattress into the bedroom. He'd have to take the sheets to the laundromat to wash them, but that was doable.

"That's fine. Hey, let me go get you a soft drink. How's that? Since you don't have anything here."

"That's okay, but thanks a lot. And if I can ever help you with anything, just let me know," Michael told Danny as the two men shook hands.

"Will do. I'd better get back over there. By now she's figured out that I'm not in the den and she's been talking to thin air. That has a tendency to aggravate her, if you know what I mean," the older man said with a pat on Michael's shoulder.

"I do! Thanks again." He waited until Danny had shown himself out before he started opening packages and putting things away. In an hour, he'd hung the shower curtain and liner, stacked up the towels and washcloths, put down a couple of rugs, and stored all the newly-purchased cleaning supplies under the kitchen sink. At some point he'd have to take the blinds down to paint, but for at least the time being, the windows were covered. The drapes could be bought and hung after the painting was finished.

His phone rang and he almost didn't look at it. He

figured it was his mom having a fit about him not going to church. Instead, it was Carter. "Hey there."

"Did I just see you dragging a mattress into your house?"

Michael started laughing. "You absolutely did!"

"Just couldn't take Marjorie anymore, could you?"

"How'd you guess?"

"Because I have a Marjorie, but her name is Wilda Fern," Carter said with a snort. "Need any more help?"

"Nah. My next-door neighbor helped me get it inside."

"Good. So what are your plans with Samara tonight?"

"I'm supposed to … Wait. How did you know about that?"

"Lucky guess. I mean, you asked how I felt about employees dating the day we offered her the position, and then Sharla told me Samara was quizzing her about you. So you worked up the courage to ask her out?"

Michael thought he'd heard wrong. "Samara was asking about me?"

"Yep. Sure was."

"She actually asked me out. Or, I should say, to come over. I'm bringing dinner with me."

"Sounds promising."

"I hope you're right."

"Really, you'd make a cute couple," Carter said.

"Funny you should say that. When I took her to lunch that first day, the girl at the restaurant thought we were a couple and she said the same thing. So did Samara's new landlord."

"See? It's true. So you guys have fun and make sure

you're both not dragging in tomorrow morning or everybody in the office will know."

"Yeah, yeah. We'll behave. Thanks, Carter."

"Any time, bud. Talk to you in the morning."

"Yep. Bye." Holy shit. He'd better be on top of his game in the morning. She'd better be too. Otherwise, everybody in the office would think they were sleeping together.

And nothing would make him happier than to make them right.

CHAPTER 4

SHE BROKE down the boxes as she emptied them, and pretty soon, she had a huge stack of them outside the front door. Maybe Michael could take them in his truck and get rid of them. The washer was humming, and so was the dryer. By the time she could get everything put away, both would be finished and she could start another load. The few pieces of artwork she owned had found homes on the walls and shelves, and her favorite coffee mugs sat on the counter. As she worked, she wondered when Michael would call.

The worst of it was done, and she stepped into the shower, enjoying the feel of the warm water caressing her skin. She'd managed to soap up and load her hair with a great-smelling Argan oil-infused shampoo when the phone started ringing. Shampoo dripped down her face and hit her left eye as she scrambled. "Owwww! Coming! Hello?"

"Hey. You sound—"

"I'm in the shower."

She couldn't remember his voice ever sounding that

deep or gruff when he quietly answered, "Looks like I'm a little late."

"Oh, ha-ha-ha. But seriously, shampoo in my eye and—"

"Call me back when you're done. Take your time. No rush."

"Yeah, okay. Bye." She could hear him chuckling as she hung up. "Damn, poor timing," she said aloud to no one. Then she thought about what he'd said.

The idea of him there, in the shower with his hands on her soap-slicked body, made her shiver. A lot of time had passed since the last time she voluntarily let a man touch her, but she felt safe with Michael. Everything about him screamed honesty, integrity, respect, and dignity. She hadn't so much as held his hand yet, and all she wanted was to feel his arms around her. To be held. Sheltered. Loved.

"Shut that down right now, girl," she muttered to herself as she rinsed the shampoo from her hair. Love. Yeah, right. Men didn't love women. They just used them. And yet she couldn't shake the feeling that she was wrong, at least when it came to Michael. He'd loved a woman, but she'd tossed him aside for the likes of Alex Stadler. What did that say about that bitch? That she was shallow and stupid? Yeah. That pretty much summed it up.

Her supply of conditioner with avocado oil was getting low, so she spoke to her electronic assistance device and made a note in her shopping app to pick some up. After she'd loaded her hair with the leave-in product, she ran a brush through it gently, letting it untangle itself instead of pulling at it. God, she'd hated it when her mom had brushed her hair! Being six years old and having someone yanking your head as they aggressively brushed your hair was no fun, but back then, they hadn't known any better. Hair care had become much easier with the products they had available. When she'd finished brushing it upside down, she stood and brushed it again, then started finger-curling it. Her hair was nice, but it wasn't super thick, and that meant it didn't take quite as long to curl or dry. Once she'd gotten it the way she wanted it, she used her blow dryer with the diffuser and dried it as best she could. It hung almost to her shoulders in small spiral curls, like a headful of storm door springs, and she loved the way it looked. Yeah, she wore it up when she worked, but down was her preferred style.

The little sundress looked like the right choice. She didn't have a lot of clothes, but what she did have, she'd chosen with care, things that were casual but could be dressed up with a jacket. Her shoes were the same way, not very many but all very versatile. She wasn't fancy, but she was pretty sure fancy wasn't what Michael was looking for.

One look in her lingerie drawer and she was a bit depressed. Most everything in it was functional, not pretty. Her breasts weren't especially big, but she hated the feeling of them flopping up and down when she ran, so she usually opted for a sports bra. She had one pretty bra, a convertible, but it hadn't been washed, so she just opted to go without. *Wonder how he likes granny panties?* she mused as she pulled out a pair. That was all she bought. They were a lot more comfortable than a lacey thong while she was working.

Dressed and ready, she picked up her phone. He answered on the first ring. "All done?"

"Yeah. Squeaky clean."

"Good for you! I called the diner. They've got fried chicken, tuna steaks, and meatloaf today."

"Meatloaf."

"Okay, vegetables ..." He read the whole list off to her. "What'll it be?"

"I'll take the mashed potatoes with gravy and home-style green beans."

"Sounds like a winner. I'll see you in a few."

"Okay. Bye." Samara sat there after the phone went quiet and thought about what was happening. Was that really what she wanted? Early in her life she'd identified men's forearms and hands as something she found extremely sexy, and his were, especially his hands. She'd watched him check his weapon, write reports, and run his fingers through his hair when he was frustrated. Those hands looked positively magical, and she trembled at the fantasy of them on her skin.

She'd put away the last of the towels from the dryer when she heard a car door out front. Through the sheers over the front windows, she could see him get out of the truck, then round the front end and take the food from the passenger's side. Both hands full, he pushed the door closed with his foot and turned toward the trailer.

Samara opened the door when he reached the landing on the porch. "Hey. I can smell it from here. Smells really good."

"They have great food, and it's not expensive. My favorite place to eat," he said as he set everything on the countertop.

"I thought that would be one of your mom's casseroles," she quipped.

"Oh, yeah. Wonder what it'll be tonight? I don't care, because I won't be there," he said with a grin. Then he looked around. "Wow. You've gotten a lot done. Looks nice. And it looks like you. It has your personality."

"Yeah? How so?" She couldn't wait to hear that answer.

"Pretty without being too frou-frou. Nothing bougie."

"Bougie? That's a term you know?"

He laughed. "Yeah, I've heard Chelsea say it. Sharla too."

"Do you know what it means?"

"Of course I do! Like, 'All those ladies in Lexington are so bougie.' Meaning they want to live like the Kardashians."

She nodded and gave him a nasty smirk. "Yeah, that pretty much sums it up."

"You think I don't know these things?" She laughed. "Okay, so that right there," he said, pointing to a wooden puzzle clock she'd put together, "that's sick." Samara laughed loudly. "It is. Very cool. Does it really work?"

She stepped over to it and touched it. Something inside it started to whir, and instantly, the minute hand started to sweep around. "Whaddya think?"

"It does work! I like it. I've been seeing those on the internet and wondered if they really worked. Might have to get one. Got some plates? Want to use paper plates?"

"Paper plates are sick," she said as she grabbed a few from a stack in the cabinet.

"Oh, I see. You've got it too?"

She placed the plates on the table. "I sure do."

"You woke too?" he asked with a laugh.

"According to my younger sister I'm not."

"How so?"

"I had to set her straight. She was saying, 'No black woman should have to cook. We need to stay the hell outta the kitchen.' And I said, "Yeah, well, what if she likes to cook?' So she said, 'Ain't no black woman wanna cook.' And I said, 'If she wanna cook, she should cook.' She looked at me like I was crazy." Samara was chuckling under her breath. "My mama said, 'Girl, you couldn't boil water, so you ain't got no say.'"

"To you?"

"No. To her. I can damn well cook," she informed him.

"Oh. Well, glad we cleared that up."

"I said I *can* cook. I didn't say I *like* to cook. There's a difference."

"Boy, I hear ya there. I like to eat, but I don't like to cook. Difference there too."

"Uh, the biggest. And I don't mind the cooking, but I hate the cleaning up."

He grinned. "Me too. That's the least fun part of the whole thing."

"Then we should have fun because we don't have anything to clean up here. What do you want to drink?"

"Got any tea?"

"Do I got any tea? Do corn got rows? You damn straight I got some tea." After she'd filled two glasses and set them on the table, she grabbed a stack of napkins and laid them on the table's corner. "Anything I've forgotten?"

"Ketchup."

"Ah. Yeah, all good meatloaf gotta have ketchup." She plunked down a brand-new bottle. "That enough?"

"It had better be or I'll go into diabetic shock."

She stared at him. "You diabetic?"

That made him laugh. "No. But if I eat enough of that stuff, I will be!"

What commenced from that point was the most fun Samara had experienced in a long, long time. They talked and laughed and before she knew it, two hours had passed and they were still sitting there. Then she thought of something. "Oh, shit. I didn't get anything for dessert."

Michael immediately asked, "You like ice cream, right?"

"Oh, lawd, yes. Love me some ice cream."

"Let's go to the drive-in down by the interstate and get some ice cream. Or a shake. Or whatever you want."

"Oooo, yeah! Sounds good."

An hour later, they were back and on carb overload. "Oh, god, that was good, but I'm stuffed."

"Yeah, when they make a sundae, they go all out," Michael said with a groan. "You know what sounds good right now?"

"What?"

"One of two things. Either a movie or a nap. Which sounds best?"

"Ummm ..." She sat there for a second before she answered. "We could really take a nap?"

"Hell yeah. We're grownups. We can do whatever we want."

"I vote for a nap."

"I was taking the poll, so I don't get a vote. Nap it is." Michael stood and swept his arm toward the bedroom. "After you."

"Thank you, sir." As she headed that direction, she made sure to give her hips a little extra sway and hoped he noticed. "You pulling anything off?"

"Do I need to? I'm in a tee and jeans. It's not like I'm going to mess up my clothes."

"Okay. Just wondered."

"You?"

"Nah. All I've got on under here is a pair of underwear. Nothing to mess up."

"Do you want to go get something to eat later when we get hungry?"

She thought for a minute. "Yeah, I might."

"Then take off the dress and put on a tee. That'll keep your dress fresh."

"Good idea." Instead of heading to the bathroom, she pulled open a dresser drawer, pulled out a tee, then dragged the dress off over her head and pulled the tee on. The mirror was right in front of her, and she knew he had a good view of her breasts. She could see him grinning just a little as she smiled at his reflection. "What?"

"Trying not to ogle."

"Did you succeed?"

He laughed. "Not completely, but I was hoping I wasn't *too* obvious."

"I'd call that look on your face interested but not creepy," she replied, laughing.

"Oh, interested but not creepy, huh? Get on this bed. Your suggestion, and now I'm sleepy."

Samara was still laughing. "Like a baby. Feed 'em, burp 'em, and put 'em down for a nap."

"Hey, it was your idea! Don't be blaming me!" He was already on his back, fingers interlaced behind his head as he lay there, and when she lay down, she rolled to her side, her hands folded under her face on the pillow, and watched him. He gave her a quizzical look. "What?"

"Nothin'."

"No, it's something. What?"

She blinked deeply and shrugged against the mattress. "It's just … You haven't made any attempt to touch me. Unless you really don't …" She just couldn't say it.

"Want to?" She wasn't sure how she was supposed to respond. Besides, she might really embarrass herself. In answer, his hands came down from behind his head and he rolled to face her. He swept the knuckles of his right hand down her cheek. "Oh, I definitely want to." His index finger slid until it was under her chin, and pressed toward the headboard until her face was even with his. "I think I've wanted to do this since the first minute I saw you."

A fluttering burst into being in her chest when his lips touched hers, and she felt her body, dormant for so long, come to life. Nerves she'd forgotten she had buzzed like live wires and gooseflesh popped up on her arms. When her palm came to rest on his cheek, she knew she was gone. That kiss lasted forever but not long enough, and when he pulled back, he smiled into her eyes. "Oh, god, Michael, is … is this real?"

"As real as it gets. Now let's take that nap. The first time we're joined together, I don't want it to be two ice cream-drunk idiots groping each other." Then he leaned in and kissed her forehead.

Samara melted into him and never wanted to be anywhere else. To his coworkers, Michael seemed green and a little slow, but there was nothing slow about him. He was deliberate, confident, and smart as a whip. She'd noticed it right away, how even when he was under stress, his demeanor never wavered, his hands never shook, and he never got frazzled. That was what she needed, someone steady and sure, not high octane and combustible. As soon as she pressed herself to him, his arms wrapped around her and squeezed. It was heaven.

"Damn, your hair smells good," he whispered.

"Thanks. Argan and avocado oils."

"Hmmm." She felt him settle into the pillow and he held her tightly against him. "This is nice. Really, really nice."

"Yeah, it is." She snuggled into him even tighter, and then she noticed something pressing up against her. "Um, are you …"

"Yeah. It's fine. It'll go away."

"Do you want it to go away?"

"Right now? Yeah. But it can come back after dinner if you want."

"Oh, can it?"

"I'm pretty sure I can make that happen. I could be wrong, but I haven't been. About that, I mean." He pulled back just a little and his brow furrowed. "I thought you wanted to nap."

"I do. Sure you don't mind?"

He laughed softly. "Do I look like I mind? Or sound like I mind? No. I don't mind at all. I'm not some voracious animal who can't control himself."

The minute the words were out of his mouth, she could feel herself stiffening and trying to pull away, even though she didn't want to. Every inch of her body was on high alert and out of her control as memories tumbled through her mind like a waterfall roaring. Her pulse was doubling and her heart pounded so hard that she could feel it under her skin.

His hands were on her upper arms and he was staring

into her face. "Samara? What's happening? Hey, what's going on?"

Hands. Those hands, gripping her as she fought against him. "Let go of me! Let go! Stop!" Wiggling and squirming, she broke free and felt that relief.

Until she looked into Michael's face.

Shame washed over her, and she could feel her cheeks burning. "Oh, god, I'm so sorry. Really, I—"

He wasn't touching her. Instead, he'd sat up on the mattress and was staring down at her. "What the hell was that about? I mean, what is … Did I … I mean, I'm sorry if—"

"No, no. No. It's not you. It's me."

"Oh, is that like the old saying, 'If they say it's not you, it's me, then it's definitely you?' Because if you don't want this, you shouldn't have—"

"But I do!" She couldn't stop the tears. She wasn't prone to crying, but the adrenaline rush had passed and the drop that followed made her shake. "I didn't mean to do that! I'm so, so, so sorry. Oh, god, Michael, did I hurt you?" She knew she'd been fighting pretty hard, and if she'd injured him, she'd never forgive herself.

"No. You didn't hurt me. But I'm pretty fucking confused right now." There was no malice in his voice, no frustration or anger, and she was thankful for that.

"Long story. I'm sorry." She rolled with her back to him. "I won't blame you if you want to go."

"Oh, no. You're not getting out of this that easily. We need to talk about this."

"I don't want to talk about it."

She heard him sigh before he spoke. "Samara, normally I would say that was fine. Give it time. Do it when you're ready. But not this time. If we can't talk this out, if you can't explain, then we can't move forward. I don't want to hurt you, and I don't want you to accidentally hurt me. And I don't want to be responsible for making you feel worse instead of better. I want to move forward. Do you want to move forward with me? Or do I remind you too much of someone else?"

That made her sit straight up on the bed. "No. You do *not* remind me of someone else. It was … It was …" She couldn't finish.

"What? What did I say?" Just from his expression, she knew he was running through everything he'd said, trying to find the key to a door she wasn't sure she wanted to unlock. "The last thing I said … I said I wasn't some animal with no self-control." Just the words made her flinch, and his whole countenance changed. "When? When did it happen? Talk to me, babe. Just talk to me. I'll do whatever I can to help you, but you've got to trust me. If you can't trust me enough to talk to me about this, there's no hope for us."

Shame was drowning her, and she knew her face was fire-engine red under her dark skin. "I haven't told … Nobody knows that …"

"Yeah, well, I've done enough interviews with victims to know what's going on here. I just need to know who and when."

"No. It was three years ago, and I … I can't tell you who it was." She was shaking again, but that time, it was with pure fear. He was getting close to the truth, too close, and if he found out … It wouldn't be good. She was sure of that.

"While you were KSP?" She nodded. "A perp?" She

shook her head. "Friend?" Another head shake. He sat there for a few seconds, and then his face fell. "A fellow officer?" When she didn't respond, his eyes went wide. "It was a fellow officer? Who the hell was it?" Her lips wouldn't move, and her throat wouldn't make sound. "Samara, you've got to tell me. If he did that to you, he's a threat to every woman he comes in contact with. If a fellow officer couldn't fight him off, civilian women don't stand a chance. He could keep doing it."

Through her sobs she stuttered, "I-I-I-I think he al-al-already has."

"Jesus, babe! Why didn't you say something?"

"Because! Because I knew he'd come after me! Because I knew my life would be in danger! He'll kill me if I ever talk, Michael. You know he will."

"You don't know that. And I don't know that, because I probably don't even know him." Samara struggled, but she knew her face was giving it away. "I know him? I don't know that many state troopers. Just a handful. A couple of guys I met at some special trainings at the academy. One from a charity event we helped Post 1 with."

It was only a matter of seconds and he'd figure it out as she cried harder and harder. Couldn't he leave well enough alone? What would he do when he figured it out? Every inch of her body was trembling with fear. And then her worst nightmare became reality.

"And that fucktard, Alex Stadler."

Every second of horror, grief, and shame bubbled up in Samara's throat and she couldn't stop screaming. She screamed the same way she had that night, the way she had when he'd first grabbed her, the way she had while he was violating her, and it had done no good, but she still screamed. She screamed until her gut hurt and she doubled over. When the screams subsided, she couldn't stop wailing and sobbing. Michael wouldn't want her. No man would want her.

A voice cut through her pain. "Samara? Samara, was it Stadler? You need to tell me, babe."

Gasping for breath, she managed to sit up, her face soaked and her nose running. "God, please, Michael, don't say anything. Please don't. He'll kill me. You know he will."

"Not if I kill him first."

"No! No, you can't do that!"

"That's a knee-jerk reaction, babe. I wouldn't. I can't. But I can definitely arrest him."

"No, you can't. There's no evidence."

"Then we'll get some."

"How?"

"I have no idea."

Would he go for it? Could she convince him she could do it? "I may have a way."

"Did … you … save something? Keep it all this time?"

"No. But there's been a string of rapes in this county."

His eyes widened. "You're right. There has been."

"What if it's him? What if he's doing it? What if he did it to another police officer and I just don't know about it? What if we can catch him that way?"

"Honey, I worked some of those cases. None of them reported it until it was too late to collect evidence. In every instance, someone else called, a mother, a sister, someone who'd realized something wasn't right. And every one of them—"

"Wouldn't say anything."

His eyebrows shot up. "Like they were afraid."

"Exactly."

He sat there for a minute, and she couldn't imagine what was going through his mind. Finally, he said, "Could you look at a picture of him? Would it trigger you?"

"I have no idea. What are you thinking?"

"If you can stand it, I'm thinking that you should go back to every one of those rape victims. Take a picture of him with you and when you show it to them, watch their response. You'll be able to tell."

He was right. That was the most basic of detective work. She'd intended to look the cases over to see if there was any pattern, but his idea was better. "Yeah. You're right. Oh, and I decided maybe I'd better check with some of the other counties around here, see if they've had the same thing happening. I'll ask around the counties in Post 1, then I'll move on to the Post 2 region. If there are none there, we'll know it's confined to Post 1."

"Good thinking." He took her hand, and that simple action released a flood of relief flowing through her soul. "But to answer your unspoken question, no. It doesn't matter to me at all. Your history is yours, and mine is mine. But this is the here and now, and none of that stuff should matter."

"It doesn't matter to you that the same man … both of the women you've …" She couldn't even finish the sentence.

"No. It does not. Besides, it's one thing to be Glenna and be stupid enough to stay with him. It's totally another to have no say in the matter. Baby, you know that. Glenna messing around with him? That was sex. What he did to you, that's not about sex at all. You know that too. It's about power and intimidation, and a lack of self-control. It's about inflicting pain on another human being because it gives him a power trip to do so. Totally different. Totally."

She squeezed his hand, and he squeezed hers back. "I'm sorry. I'm sorry for what happened a few minutes ago, and I'm sorry I didn't tell you."

The smile he gave her put her heart at ease. "Well, first off, that wasn't your fault. And I can work with that. Second, quite frankly, I would've been surprised if you'd told me the first time we had a meal together, 'Oh, and by the way …' That would've been rather unusual."

"That's a good term for it. Besides, the first time we had a meal together was in a restaurant. That would've been super awkward."

Michael laughed, and the tension in the room disappeared like smoke. "Yeah, super awkward. But there is one thing I think we need to do."

She hung her head. That would be hard. "Tell Carter."

"Yes. He needs to know. He would want to know. And I can tell you that he'll support you in anything you try to do to make this better, babe. That's just Carter. It's how he operates. But I'll tell you now, if you want to work through this and try to put Stadler away, you've landed with the absolute best team in the area, and maybe even in the state. Every one of these guys will support you, believe me."

"Even Watson?"

He snickered. "Yeah. Even Watson. He may be mad about my position, but he won't take that out on you. Justin's kinda stuck on himself, but he's not a bad guy. You need him, he'll be there. Carter would accept no less from any of his officers. Now, come here." Michael opened his arms.

Samara fell into them and let him pull her against him as they sat there on the bed. Everything he'd said to her was reinforced by his touch. He was the man she'd been looking for, the one who'd give her shelter and help her find justice.

And she had every intention of doing just that.

THE PAIN HAD BEEN LIKE A KNIFE IN HIS CHEST, BUT HE thought he'd hidden it pretty well. She didn't need him coming unhinged. She needed him to be strong for her, and he wanted to be that guy, the one she could lean on.

At least he knew what he was dealing with. It was going to be a balancing act between being careful and gentle with her while also not treating her like she was breakable or defective. That would be a hard line to walk, but he could do it. He knew he could.

She'd finally quieted, but he kept holding her, hoping she'd say something, anything, that would let him know she was still interested in being with him. When she did finally speak, he was stunned. "I haven't felt this safe in three years."

Her hair tickled his nose as he kissed the top of her head. "Good. I'll keep you safe. That's my job."

"I'm a police officer too."

"Yes, I know that, but you know what I mean. You may know how to keep yourself safe on the job, but if you'll let me, I'll keep your heart safe."

She tipped her head back and smiled up at him. "I'll keep your heart safe too." Then she leaned in.

He didn't meet her. It was her move, and he was going to let her do it and not rush in. The minute her lips touched his, however, he was in charge. What she'd said about feeling safe? He could *feel* it in her kiss. She meant it. And he'd meant what he said too. When she pulled back, she smiled again, and it seemed to him that everything was going to be fine. "Do you think you could stay here tonight? I'd feel better if I wasn't alone."

"I can, or you can come to my house. I moved in this morning."

"What?" She sat up and slapped his left pec with her hand. "Look at you! You moved into your house! That's awesome. I haven't even seen it yet."

"Let's go over there and I'll show you around. I don't mind staying here, or you there. Doesn't matter, as long as we're together."

"Same. I'll go to the bathroom and splash some water on my face. It'll only take me a minute."

"Okay. I'll just wait in the living room." He needed to go too, but he'd wait until she was finished.

By the time he'd gotten rid of the tea he'd had earlier, she'd changed back into her dress, had shoes on, and was waiting with her bag on her shoulder. "Ready?"

"Yeah, I just need to …" He pulled his phone from his pocket and looked at it. "Dear god, she's called me like ten times."

"Who? Your mother?"

"Yes. She's like a dog on a bone. I guess I should call her or she'll keep calling."

Samara was grinning at him. "Did you put your phone on silent?"

"Hell yeah. Of course I did. She'd drive me crazy if I didn't. And please, don't say anything. I want to tell her about you when it's time, not have her find out accidentally, okay?"

"That's okay. I get it."

"I doubt you do, but you will. Just wait." He hit the button, then put it on speaker and waited.

She didn't even say hello, just barked into the phone, "Mikey, where are you?"

"I'm at a friend's house, Mom. Whatcha need?"

"I opened your door and—"

"Yeah. A lot of my stuff is gone. I moved into the house this morning."

"Why on earth would you do that? I mean, why would you want to leave here? It's a nice place, and it's not costing you anything." *Except my sanity*, he mouthed to Samara and she pressed her hand to her mouth to stop her laughter. "Why would you want to go?"

"For my privacy, Mom. I kinda need that."

"Now, son, I haven't walked in on you when you're in the tub since you were twelve and I did that and you were—"

"Mom! Stop! I've moved out. It has nothing to do with you," he said, and he could see Samara out of the corner of his eye, shaking with pent-up laughter. "It's just way past time and I really need to do this."

"I know what you're doing. You're trying to find a woman. And how did that work out last time?"

"Hanging up now, Mom. Gotta go."

"You know what I'm saying. You move out, you have a dangerous job, you're looking for a woman to—"

"Mom! Going! Bye!" He hit END on the phone's screen and waited. Sure enough, Samara shrieked with laughter. "She's gonna be the death of me yet," he muttered.

"She walked in on you beating your meat?"

"I was *twelve*. And it was the slapping sound of the water. She said she thought I was drowning and struggling to get out."

"Of the *bathtub*?" Samara said, still laughing so hard she could barely breathe.

"Yeah, that was her excuse. She's just nosy."

"Baby, I swear, if you are in the bathtub and I hear slapping sounds, I will *not* check on you. I'll just let you drown." She'd almost quit laughing—almost, but not quite.

"You do that. Didn't your parents ever do something that embarrassed you?"

"Yeah. I was eight, and I'd stolen a bra from my older cousin. I had it on and I was trying to find things to stuff into it when my mom walked in."

He laughed. "What did she say?"

"She said, 'Gurrrrrl, one-a these days you gonna wish you had them little titties back.' I said, 'I don't think so, ma'am.' And she said, 'Oh, it's true. You wait. Have them big ol' tits and hafta wear slingshots to keep 'em in line. It ain't no picnic.' I was so embarrassed. And she made me take the bra back to my cousin and tell her what I did. That was totally humiliating."

"Your first brush with the law. I like it! So, was she right?"

"About my boobs? Hell no. I'm proud of these girls. They look pretty good compared to some I see."

"And where do you see boobs?"

"Porn."

He laughed again. "You watch porn?"

"Well, yeah. Don't tell me you don't."

"I don't."

She glared at him. "That's not true."

"Okay. Maybe I do, but just—"

"Oh, no. No, no, no. Now you gotta tell me what you like. Schoolgirl fantasy? Stripper? Ménage? BDSM?"

"Mostly ménage."

"Is that right? Two women?"

"No. Two men."

"Ah. *Now* we're gettin' somewhere."

"No. We're not. But we need to. Am I staying tonight?"

"I dunno. Depends on your house."

"Okay. We should go look around, I suppose."

"Yeah. I mean, I been standin' 'round here for ten minutes, waitin', talkin' 'bout porn."

He shook his head and laughed. "Then let's go."

CHAPTER 5

HE COULDN'T JUST COME out and tell her, but he was excited. She'd liked the house. She'd also said she didn't want to stay there until the bathroom had a door. Her exact words were, "I ain't no prude, and I know everybody poops, but I really don't think I have the need to do it in a bathroom without a door." That had been fair enough.

They stopped for dinner at the barbecue place and then headed back to the trailer. While they were at the house, he'd packed a go bag so he could get ready there the next morning. There was just one question he needed answered before they were in for the night. "Got a question. Do you think I need a box of condoms?"

"I hope you need a box of condoms. This ain't no scouting sleep-over. And I'm on the pill, but still ..."

"Got it. I'll just stop up here at the pharmacy." He whipped into a parking space, got out, and headed for the door, trying hard not to run. How immature would that look? He grinned to himself until he got to the door.

Inside, plain as day, there was a guy holding a gun,

pointing it at the pharmacist and the pharmacy tech. Michael looked around the parking lot. Yeah. That was probably the car right there. It had Lyon County plates on it. Most likely trying to steal stuff to make meth. He hustled back to the car. "This is gonna take me a few minutes."

She gave him a weird look. "Long line at this time of night?"

He reached into the pickup's back seat and took out a Heckler & Koch .45 caliber, slammed a magazine in, and racked a round into the chamber. "No. Dumb sumbitch robbing the place."

"Jesus! I don't have a weapon on me!"

"That's okay. I'll only be a second." He walked back toward the door and stood there, watching the guy still doing the same thing. If he was actually doing meth, that could be bad, but he was probably trying to get drugs to make it. Or he could be stealing oxy. They had as much trouble with it there as they did everywhere else.

Michael opened the door as quietly as possible and stepped into the store, careful to avoid the big convex mirrors at the ends of the aisles. He crept slowly up an aisle until he was within ten feet of the robber and lifted his weapon. "Law enforcement. Drop the gun. Now. DO IT NOW," he growled. When the man hesitated, Michael added, "Do not make me shoot you, because I will. Put it down. Slowly."

The man stooped until he could drop the gun to the floor, then rose. "On your knees, hands out to the sides." As soon as he dropped, Michael kicked the gun away and barked at him, "Clasp your hands behind your head." In seconds, he had the man's wrists bound with a zip tie he always carried. He pulled his phone out and hit the emergency button.

"This is nine-one-one. What is your emergency?"

"Karen, this is Michael Edwards. Send a unit to Pharless Pharmacy. I've got a ten seventy-two. Armed robbery."

"Got it. I'll send them. I thought you weren't on duty tonight."

"I'm not. Stopped at the pharmacy and this asshole was waving a gun around. Oh, and run this plate. L-V-R ..." He read the numbers off slowly. "Lyon County plate."

"Let's see here. Ask him if he's Wayne Golightly."

"You Wayne Golightly?"

"Who wants to know?" the scumbucket asked.

"Yep. I'd say he is," Michael told Karen.

"Got two outstanding warrants out for him. Lewis should be there in just a minute."

"Thanks. Bye."

Sure enough, the sound of a siren was getting closer, and in a few seconds, Gray walked through the door. "What the hell? You're not even supposed to be on duty."

"Yeah. Can't stop at the pharmacy for a simple box of ... Band-Aids." He'd almost said condoms. That wouldn't do.

"Okay, idiot boy, let's go. Know who this one is?"

"Yeah. Name is Wayne Golightly. Got a couple of outstanding warrants. Just take him to the jail and I'll write up the reports in the morning."

"Outstanding warrants? Oh, this is gonna be fun for sure. Thanks, Michael. Have you Mirandized him?"

"Nope."

"Got it. See you tomorrow."

"Yep. See you then. Thanks for coming out."

"My pleasure."

Gray disappeared out the door with the robber and Michael sighed. All he'd wanted was a box of condoms. That was all. And he wound up doing something like that. It took him a minute or two to figure out where they were, and on his way to the register, he spotted a vase of roses, individual long-stemmed ones. He picked out the prettiest of them and headed for the counter.

When he slid back into the car, he sighed. "Holy shit. Can't even go to the fucking drugstore."

"I saw Gray. Did he say anything about me?"

"No. Think he saw you?"

"I don't think so."

"By the way, I got this for you." He handed her the flower. "I figured it was the least I could do since I spent time with a gun in my hand when I should've been holding your hand."

Her smile was gentle, and she leaned over to give him a kiss on the cheek. "That's so sweet. Thank you. For the record, I saw the long gun back there and I almost grabbed it and went in, but I figured you had it under control."

"I did. I told you I'd keep you safe. Do you believe me now?"

"I believed you when you said it."

"Good. Let's go."

The drugstore was only a mile from her trailer. He wondered how long it would be before someone saw them together and let it slip to his mother. That wasn't how he wanted it to go. Talking to his mother first would be the best way. Otherwise, there was no telling what Marjorie would say in front of Samara.

There was no point in rushing. It was still a little early, barely eight o'clock, so he carried the condoms into the bedroom, then came back to the kitchen. She'd already sat down on the sofa and taken her shoes off. Instead of sitting down, he asked, "Want something to drink?"

"Yeah. I think I've got some wine coolers in there."

He opened the door. "Want peach or wild cherry?"

"Wild cherry sounds good."

"Got it." He looked around a bit more and found a can of soda. But when he got back to the sofa, she stared at him. "What?"

"You're not having a beer?"

"Nah. Don't really feel like one."

"You do drink, right?"

"Oh, yeah. Remember, I was drinking beer over at Carter and Sharla's."

"That's right. I forgot."

He sat down beside her and threw his arm over her shoulders. To his delight, she snuggled up against him. "Wanna watch something on TV?"

"Nah. I'd rather just sit here and talk or go to bed."

"Would you rather sit here and talk, or would you rather go to bed?"

"Honestly, I'd rather go to bed," she said with a little grin.

"Then drink your wine cooler."

They sat there side by side, quietly downing their drinks. Finally, Michael asked, "What about your people? You've never really said. Except the thing about the tits."

She laughed. "Yeah, I haven't, have I?"

"Nope. So what does your dad do?"

"My dad is an electrical engineer. He worked at the

TVA steam plant in West Paducah. That's why they live in Ballard County. Mom is a nurse's aide at a long-term facility over in Cairo. Got a sister, Marita, who's three years older than me and works in Alabama at a car factory as an analyst, and another sister, Relena, who's two years older than me. She lives outside Cleveland and she's married to a doctor. My little sister, Kendra, is eleven years younger than me and she's finishing up her doctoral degree at University of Tennessee Knoxville. My brother, Kenyan, is four years younger than me. He's a stockbroker, and he and his husband live in Sausalito."

"And you're the kid in the middle."

"Yep. The one who refused to do anything with her life."

"Aha. I see. I didn't even think to ask you earlier … Have you been married?"

"No. Dated a lot. Engaged once."

"What happened?"

"Cheating. Ridiculously common."

"So I hear. And before you were an officer?"

"I went to college. Getting a degree in criminal justice. Was thinking about getting my masters when I decided on a whim to sit for the test at the academy and got in. And that's what I've been doing ever since."

"So you're, what, thirty-four?"

"Thirty-five. And you told me you're twenty-six. My birthday's in April."

"Mine is in late June, so I'm almost twenty-seven."

"So I'm eight years older than you. Ever date an older woman?" she asked with a chuckle.

"Yep. I dated a woman who was in her early thirties when I was in community college."

Her eyes went wide. "Yeah?"

"Yeah. Good times, those."

"For a kid that young? I bet."

"Yeah. Taught me a lot, I'll give her that."

"All the right kinds of things, I hope."

Michael nodded. "Oh, yeah. All the right kinds of things. I mean, *all* of them."

"Not *all* of them."

"Oh, yeah, definitely all of them." He snorted a little. "Yeah, I think most of the guys think I'm a virgin."

She drew back, looked up into his face, and peered at him from under her furrowed brow. "Why the hell would they think that?"

"Because they've never seen me date anybody. When I first started there ... Remember 'The Fergs' from *Longmire*?"

"Yeah."

"They thought I was Ferguson. At least that's how they treated me. Like a larger version of Barney Fife."

"That sucks."

"Yeah. I just didn't want to go out with any of the women my mother pushed me to date, and there aren't that many around here. Plus I went to school with a lot of them, and I didn't really want to date them. The dating pool around here is very, very shallow."

"I got that impression." She drained the bottle and set it on the coffee table. "You about done?"

"Yeah." He polished off the last of the soda and sat there. "So let me say this. Knowing what I know now, we're gonna take this at your speed. I won't push. But that means you're going to have to communicate with me. I can't read your mind, so whatever you want, you have to tell me. I'm not going to treat you like you're made of glass, Samara, but I don't want to push you too far either. Comfortable—I want you comfortable with me. And then once we get to know each other better, I'll have a better idea of what you want and when. But until then, I really need some guidance."

She sighed and nodded. "Yeah. I can do that." He could see a hint of pink spread across her cheeks. "Thank you for ... understanding."

"I'm not going to lie to you. I could *never* truly understand. But I want to. I really do. And I want you to always feel safe with me. Always."

"I do. You haven't done anything that's made me feel uncomfortable. Nothing." He hated the sad look on her face when she said, "I just want to feel normal."

Michael shook his head. "Honey, none of us feel normal. That's just life."

"You don't feel normal?"

He rolled his eyes. "No. I'm an almost-twenty-seven-year-old deputy sheriff whose mother is driving him crazy. Does that sound normal to you?"

"A mother driving you crazy? Yeah. That does. And most people would agree," she said and giggled.

"Yeah, you got me on that one. But you know what I mean. Life is about ups and downs, but I have to believe it would be easier if you had somebody's hand to hold while you were on that wild ride."

She nodded and leaned against him again. "I think so too."

"And I had a great role model. Until the day he died, my dad was in love with my mom. Didn't just love her—adored her. Flowers about every other week, big fuss over special occasions, date nights out, things like that."

"Yeah, mine weren't that lovey-dovey, but you could tell they were a partnership. They backed each other on everything. It was always a unified front."

"That's the way it should be. I want somebody who'll partner with me, not fight against me. I mean, if you don't trust the person you're with to make decisions and can't trust their judgment, you're in trouble before you begin."

"I agree." She leaned out and set the bottle on the coffee table. "All done."

Michael did the same with his can. "Me too."

Her head tipped toward the bedroom. "I'm going into the bathroom to get ready for bed. When I get out, you can have a turn."

"Sounds good to me. I'll take these and throw them away."

"Okay." Samara leaned in and gave him a peck on the lips before she stood and wandered toward the bedroom, those beautiful hips swaying under the thin cotton dress. Michael took a deep breath and let it out slowly, then picked up the bottle and can and headed to the trash bin by the laundry room door.

The back door went out of the laundry room, so he opened it and looked out. The yard looked more like a jungle, but not an unruly one. It was obvious Mrs. Lowry liked plants because they were everywhere—big ones, small ones, bushy ones, every kind of plant imaginable. *Are those banana trees?* he asked himself, because that was sure what they looked like.

As he stood there looking out over it, he thought about

the woman in the other room. He felt lucky to have found her. Was she playing him? He didn't think so. After all, being the girlfriend of the chief deputy of Trigg County wasn't exactly a position of great esteem, even if she did work there. More than that, she ticked off every box on his list for what he'd want in a partner. Over the short time she'd worked for their office, they'd worked well together, and comfortably too. It didn't seem too much of a stretch to think she'd be the same way in a relationship.

It was time to put up or shut up, and he intended to make it the best experience he possibly could. That meant being conscious of her needs and sensitive to the things she said and did. He could take a lot of clues from both of those. He knew women weren't usually good at asking for what they wanted, mostly because they'd either been turned down or ridiculed for being "too sexual." That wasn't going to happen with her. He'd make sure of it.

By the time he closed and locked the door, then turned off the lights in the kitchen and living room, he'd managed to talk himself down off the ledge. It wasn't like he didn't know how to have sex. Glenna had seemed pretty satis-fied ... until that asshole had come along. *Don't let him ruin this for you!* a voice in his head shouted. She'd left him for what she thought would be a more exciting guy. He remembered the first time she'd seen him in the store in his uniform. He'd pretended that he didn't see her, but she'd stared a hole through him, and he'd laughed all the way to the car.

It took some work, but he pushed it all out of his mind and went back to his thoughts about Samara. By the time he crossed the room, he could feel his body readying. She was already in bed, under the covers, the sheet tucked across her chest and a smile on her face. "Hello, beauti-ful," he said and knelt on one knee on the bed to lean down and kiss her. "I'll only be a minute."

"Hey, can I tell you something?"

He stroked her cheek. "Of course."

"I don't have any pretty lingerie. Nothing like that. Granny panties and sports bras. That's about it. So I'm nothin' fancy under here."

"Do you have on *anything* under there?"

A low, throaty laugh bubbled up from her throat. "Um, actually … nope."

"Good. I like that best. Be right back." The bathroom door closed with a *click*, and he started shucking clothes. When that was done, he grabbed a washcloth and wiped himself down as best he could. That would have to do. He had his clean clothes for the morning, but that was it. *Should I go out there in my boxer briefs? Or bare?* The boxer briefs, definitely, but not his shirt. That was good enough.

Then he looked down. There was no hiding it. He was hard and ready, already aching and almost panting. Would that be too much for her, seeing him like that? *Look, Edwards, you're all man. She knows that. It's not like she's never had sex before. She hasn't since, well, but … Stop overthinking everything and just get out there.* He smashed a little toothpaste on his finger, ran it around all over his teeth and tongue, then washed his hands and spit the tooth-paste into the sink. Why the hell hadn't he thought to bring his toothbrush into the bathroom? It was out there in his bag, and that wasn't helping him any. *Why the fuck am I so nervous?* he asked himself.

When he opened the bathroom door, she'd turned

down the lights and lit a candle. The whole room smelled like some kind of incense, and it made him throb just thinking about all the erotic and exotic promises that scent made to him. Then he thought of something he should've taken care of before. When he opened the door into the hallway, she asked, "Where are you going?"

"Just a second." There was bottled water in the refrigerator, and he brought two bottles back, placed one on her nightstand, and carried the other one to his. "We might want these."

She smiled. "We might need them."

Thumbs hooked in the waistband of his briefs, Michael dragged them down and stepped out of them, then slid between the sheets. When he reached for her and pulled her against him, the sensation of her hardened nipples against his chest took his throbbing to a burn. As he kissed her, he tipped his pelvis toward her, and he knew she could feel his hardness against her skin. Michael took the kisses from her lips, down her jaw, down the side of her neck, and onto her collarbone, before he finally pulled the sheet away.

Beautiful. There was no other word to describe them. "God, babe, your tits are amazing." He didn't give her a chance to respond before he latched onto one with his teeth and gently nipped it.

"Amazing?"

"Yeah. So beautiful." No more talking, at least not right that minute. He wanted to see if he could get her to squirm a little before he went any farther. The sensation of her nails scratching his scalp under his hair made him moan against her skin, and he dragged his free hand up her ribs until he could tweak the other nipple. It took a few seconds, but she finally gave a little wiggle, and he knew she was feeling it. Still pinching and pulling just a little, he lifted his head. "Does that feel good?"

"Oh, god, yeah. Oh, Michael …" The words had no more than slipped from her lips when he flexed his pelvis and dragged his cock up her leg. "Oh, god …"

"That's how bad I want you, Samara. I want you so bad, girl. I'm so fucking hard for you, babe."

The sheet billowed as she threw it off, giving him a view of that supple, smooth belly. She surprised him by grabbing his free hand and dragging it down her torso. "Oh, god, Michael, touch me. Please touch me? I need it so bad."

His lips left her nipple and claimed her mouth again as his fingers opened her slit. The second he touched that little bundle of nerves, she cried out, "Oh! Oh, god, Michael, please. Please?"

"What do you want, angel? I swear to god, you're the most beautiful thing I've ever seen. Want me to stroke you?"

"Yes, oh yes. Until I come. Make me come. Please make me come."

"Tell me if I'm going too fast." His finger quickened, and he could feel her pelvis rocking.

"Ohhhh. Damn, I need this."

"Scratching your itch?"

"Yeah, babe. Definitely. Ohhhh," she moaned again and thrust her pelvis upward. "Damn, Michael, you know what you're doing."

"Yeah?" He kissed her cheek, then kissed downward again until he was back at that luscious nipple. "I want you to fly, girl," he whispered before he sucked it between his lips again. Between his teeth and tongue and the stroking he was giving her clit, she was growing more worked up by the minute. He almost stopped to ask her if she was okay, but he decided not to. The bud between his lips was like velvet, and the pearl in her slit was swollen. He dragged his finger deeper between her lower lips, then used her juices to keep her nub slick. *It's time*, he told himself.

As he ramped up his stroking, he was careful to get it just right, watching her belly until it quivered, knowing her core was heating up and blood was pooling below her navel, making everything inside her feel heavy. His nips and sucks grew more insistent, and he trapped her nipple between his teeth, then pulled outward to stretch it. "Oh, god, babe! Oh, please, Michael, I need to come. God, I want you. I want you so damn bad. Please make me come. Please. Oh, god, please."

Michael propped himself up on his elbow, letting his finger and thumb grip her nipple, and looked down. Every muscle in her belly was tight, and her hips were pumping. Watching his finger moving against her clit, he picked up the pace just a little and tried circling it. That coaxed another cry from her lips. "You're getting close, angel."

"No. No, I want you inside me when I come. Please? Please, Michael? Please? Oh, damn. Damn, damn, damn." That was not what he thought she was going to say.

"You sure you're ready?"

"Oh, god, yeah. Please."

It took him a whole two seconds to grab a condom and roll it on, and he crawled between her legs and braced himself over her. "You sure you're ready? Because you need to understand, I do this, you're mine. There won't be any seeing other people. It'll be us, the two of us. That's how it has to be."

"Yes. That's what I want. Please, Michael? Make me yours."

There were no three words she could've said that would've lit a hotter fire in Michael Edwards' soul. The head of his hardness pressed against her warmth, and it only took a second for her to relax enough to let him in. Halfway there, he whispered, "You okay?"

"Yeah. This is amazing. Damn, you're long and hard. I need you all the way in, babe. Please."

"You got it." When the tip of his shaft hit the bottom of her channel, he thought he heard angels singing. She was warm and wet and plenty tight enough. He moved until his knees were barely under her ass and told her, "You need to grab the headboard and hang on, precious. I'm lighting you up."

Looking up the length of her body, Michael was stunned. She was easily the most beautiful woman he'd ever seen. There was something about being able to gaze on the underside of her breasts as his balls pressed against her that made him harden painfully. As soon as he was in and still, he started to stroke her nub again, watching her twitch and moan. Every muscle in her channel gripped him tightly, and he wasn't sure how long he could hold out. She'd had her feet flat on the mattress, her legs bent, but to his surprise, she let her knees fall outward, and she was totally open to him. There was a little rhythm to the way he pressed into her, not stroked, just pushed slightly, just enough that she could feel it, and she shocked him by playing with her own nipples. "That's it, babe. Enjoy the ride." He knew he sure was.

She was almost there, he could tell, so he stroked a little faster. "Babe, let go. Just let it take you. It's okay. I'll take care of you. You know I will. I want you to grip me hard. That's it, that's it. Damn, girl, you—"

Samara let out a shriek. Her back bowed and her whole body jerked as she convulsed forward, her channel pulsing around Michael. He kept going, waiting for her to tell him to stop, but she didn't. It only took a few seconds before she arched her back, her legs stiffening and shaking as she grabbed the headboard and screamed out her pleasure.

Breasts heaving, she gasped for air as he stopped and stared at the beauty before him. It had been a powerful moment, and he couldn't remember any woman reacting that way to him before. Thoughts almost paralyzed him until she grabbed his hands and pulled him down to her. "I need you to move inside me, Michael. Please, god, please. I need you to move. I need it, I need it, I need it."

His hips drew back of their own accord, and he plowed into her with every ounce of passion he felt for her. The guttural sound that came from her throat told him he was right on the money, and he stroked hard, his balls slapping her ass, listening to her cry out, feeling her squeeze his biceps. He felt strong and powerful, giving that woman what she wanted and taking his pleasure from her in return. "Oh. Oh, oh, oh, I'm gonna do it again. Oh, god!" Her pussy gripped him so tightly that he saw stars, and he began to pound her even harder. "Yeah, that's it. Oh, god, yeah. Oh, Michael, yes. Yes. That's what I want. Give it to me, baby, please."

"Girl, I hurt for you. I'm so damn hard … Samara, baby, I need to let go. I wanna last longer, but I need to … Oh, god, yeah. I need to come. I just … Ohhhh. Damn, baby." His mind spun away and he moved instinctively, the length of his shaft forcing her open and then retreating, over and over. He gripped her breasts with both hands and squeezed hard as he pounded into her, and he felt her muscles ripple again, gripping him tighter and tighter. "Oh, damn. I'm … I'm … Ohhhh, yeah, baby. Oh yeah." Heat flooded the condom and he knew that was it. He was done but, by god, he'd given her a good ride too.

He stilled inside her and leaned down to kiss her. As soon as her arms wound around his neck, he pressed his full weight on top of her and deepened the kiss. When he finally pulled back, he smiled down at her. "Did I give you what you needed?"

She let out a little huff. "Damn, baby, I've never come that many times in my *life*. What the hell, boy? You magic or somethin'?"

"Yeah." He held up his index finger. "This is the magic right here."

"That's not the only magic you've got. Shit, I thought you were gonna split me wide open. You feel good in there."

"And you feel good around me. Wow." He didn't really want to pull out of her, but he was exhausted, and he fell to the mattress beside her, then drew her to him. "Oh, god. That was … I don't have a word."

"Sexy as hell. That's what it was. It was sexy. As. Hell. Babe, I ain't never been fucked like that before. I don't know who that older woman was, but you were right. She taught you well."

"I tried to tell you. I may be kinda goofy and inept, but by god, I know my way around a woman's body, and yours is exceptional."

"Why, thank you! Yours is amazing too. That dick right there is pretty damn special."

"Oh, my dick's special?"

"Yes. It is. The minute you buried that thing in me, mmm-mm-mm-mmmmm. Oh, yeah. My belly's never felt that heavy before. Damn. I needed that."

"Good. Glad I could deliver." Her head rested on his pec, and he stroked her face as he committed every line and shadow to his memory. "You are beautiful, Samara. The most beautiful woman I've ever seen."

"Now I *know* you're lyin'!" she said and laughed.

"No. I'm not. Damn, I wanna be inside you again. That was … You were … Well, fuck."

"What?"

"I'm getting hard again."

A soft palm stroked up his length. "Well, you sure are, baby. And I want some-a that."

"Oh, yeah?"

"Yeah. I've gotta have it. Give it to me," she said and rose up to kiss him—hard.

"You want more of my cock, I'll make that happen. Need a new condom, though. Hang on. Let me get rid of this one." The old one was rolled off and thrown on the floor. "Just don't step on that in the night." That made her laugh as he rolled on the new one.

He'd stroked himself a couple of times when she pressed his shoulders back onto the mattress and climbed on top of him. "I'm gonna ride you. You mind?"

"Oh, no, ma'am. I do not mind. Not one bit. You ride as far and as long as you want." Michael flattened his hands behind his head, clasped his fingers together, and lay back, watching her rise and fall, watching those beautiful tits bounce with every stroke. He thanked the heavens that he was a man. The woman on top of him with his shaft as far up in her as it would go was a wonder to him. She rode him until she was weak, until she'd come twice, and the third time, he stroked her clit until she screamed and shook, then rolled her to her back and pounded her. She screamed and squeezed his arms, her breasts shaking, those nipples as hard as flint. He finally just gripped her ass, leaned down, and fucked her for all he was worth, listening to her beg him for more the entire time.

"Oh, damn!" he shouted out as he came inside her. "Damn, woman! Your pussy has teeth, I do believe." Once again, he dropped to the mattress beside her, heaving in air. "Shit, I'm beat. You've completely drained me."

She giggled. "I bet I could get it up again if you—"

"Noooo. I'm not as young as I used to be. You're gonna have to give me time to work up to this."

"Lightweight," she said, and she tweaked one of his nipples as she stood and made her way to the bathroom. "I think I need a shower. Coming?"

Coming indeed. What took place next was the thing fantasies were made of. The hot water beat into his shoulders as he hunched her from behind, listening to her begging him for more. His cock pierced her over and over, and he didn't know how long he could hold out, but he knew she'd already come. As soon as his release came, he pulled out, grabbed the soap, and washed everything between her legs tenderly, like a parent caring for a child. They stood, their lips locked together, under the hot water. It was like a dream come true.

When they were both dried off, he took her hand and led her back to bed. Her body curled against his and he absentmindedly toyed with one of her nipples, loving the sigh she breathed out. If nothing else, the day had told him one very important thing.

He was exactly where he was supposed to be.

———

Samara molded herself to Michael's side and let out a deep, leisurely sigh. He was everything she'd ever wanted. He was smart, funny, resourceful, sweet, gentle, self-confident, and considerate. The best word she could find to fit was … gentleman. He treated her like a lady, but not like a helpless, fragile flower, and she loved that.

She could feel him relax, and that let her relax too. Even sleeping, his arms were still locked around her, and she felt safer than she'd felt in … She didn't want to think about that. It was in the past. Michael was her future, and from where she lay, it looked pretty bright.

He eventually rolled to his back and threw his right arm out to his side, but his left arm was still under her, and she could feel his fingers cup her back. It was time to try to sleep, but she just couldn't help watching him, so peaceful and relaxed. If anyone had earned a rest, it was him. He'd moved that morning, and when she'd looked around his house, it was obvious that he'd been putting in an enormous amount of work in time that he really didn't have to spare with their call-outs. It had meant late nights, entire weekends, any time he could find, but he still tried to do it right, and it showed. The house would be beautiful and even more solid when he was finished.

She just snuggled down beside him and closed her eyes. What a perfect day it had been! She knew work would be difficult the next morning, but that was okay. He'd be there, and she'd be there. Not only would she be working with and for him, but he treated all of the people in the office as his equal. She'd watched as he assumed the role of chief deputy, and he was fair but frank. Carter had told him to flex his authoritative muscles, and if he wanted someone to do something, he expected them to do it. The first three days she'd been there, she had watched Justin finally accept Michael's authority and begin to work with him when he realized Michael didn't want to be his boss. The man beside her in bed wanted to be a coordinator, a manager, and a sounding board. His door was open to everyone in the department, and that let Carter close his from time to time. Poor guy. The sheriff worked his ass off.

The next thing she knew, there was a crazy sound, and she sat straight up in bed. "What's that?"

"It's my phone. What the hell time is … Fuck. It's after three o'clock."

"Mine's going off too."

Michael punched the phone's screen. "Shit, that can't be good. This is not a drill of any kind." He answered it with, "Chief Deputy Edwards."

She answered hers in the next second. "Detective Futrell."

"Samara, it's Carter. Michael's talking to dispatch, but I wanted to call you and tell you I want you on this case."

"What is it, sir?"

"It's a residential fire."

She was already up and on her feet, and she could hear Michael prowling around on the other side of the bed. "A fire? That's not our—"

"They found a body."

"Yes, sir. I'm on it. Text me the address. And thank you, sir."

"You're welcome. I'd come too, but Sharla's pulling an all-nighter and I've got the baby, so I can't go."

"Yes, sir. Understandable. I'll be on my way in three. Thank you, sir."

"You're welcome. Thank you." She hung up the call and tossed the phone on the bed.

Michael was trying to dress and talk on the phone at the same time. "Yes. Tell the fire marshal I'll meet him in approximately ten minutes or less. Who?" There was silence, and she watched as he turned and stared at her, still talking on the phone. "Yes. Yes, thank you. Anything else I need to know? Okay. En route in five. Thanks, Renee."

She pulled a pair of jeans on. "Dispatch?"

"Uh, yeah." He'd gone back to dressing, but there was something unspoken in his voice. "We need to drive separately. It's not that I don't want them seeing us together. It's that I'll probably have to leave but you'll still be at the scene."

"Copy that, babe. I was going to suggest it anyway." She'd drawn a tee on, put on her tool belt, and slipped on her shoes. "I'm ready to roll." She watched as he did the same, but he said nothing. "Michael?"

He didn't look up at her. "Hmmm?"

"Michael, what's going on? There's something you're not telling me." He said nothing. "What is it? You have to tell me."

When he'd gotten his shoes on and was completely dressed, tool belt around his waist and badge clipped to it, he strode around the end of the bed and gripped her upper arms in his hands. "Listen to me. This has the potential to throw you, but don't let it. You have a job to do, and I'm pretty sure you're going to have a killer to catch. You can't let this change the way you do your job. Do you hear me? Everybody will be watching, so do everything by the book and don't cut a single corner."

"Oh, yeah. That's fine. But there's something else. What aren't you telling me?"

"The house?" She could feel her brows tipping toward the bridge of her nose, but the words he said almost knocked her feet from under her. "Their last name is Stadler."

CHAPTER 6

"Initial impressions?" she asked the coroner as he stood there, taking pictures of the body or, rather, what was left of it.

"I initially thought maybe something had started the fire. You know, a bad light fixture or something. But the firefighters pointed something out. Hey, could you come talk to the detective?" he yelled at a firefighter, who waved back and ran toward the truck.

In a couple of seconds, the fire chief strode toward her. "I don't think I know you."

"Detective Samara Futrell, Trigg County Sheriff's Department. The coroner was telling me there are some things you noticed."

"Yeah. Take a look at this." He stopped at the back corner of the end of the house in the area that had sustained the most damage. "See these marks?"

"The black striations?"

"Yeah. That indicates that an accelerant was used. We won't know what it was until the fire investigators arrive."

"But it's my job to—"

"Yes. I know. But in the case of a fire where there's a human loss, we have a team that comes in from out of town. The county pays for it. They're fair and impartial in an area where relationships color everything, and they've got skills and methods, equipment and chemicals and testing abilities, that neither you nor I have as professionals."

"Got it. So they'll be open to working with me?"

"Oh, absolutely, detective. They'll want you here. You being here keeps them from having to report multiple times. They can report directly to you, and you have the information at hand."

"Thank you. Sounds good." As the fire chief walked away, she heard footsteps and turned to find Michael coming up beside her. "And?"

"I talked to all of the spectators over there. House next door to the west was the one that called it in. Neighbors said nothing has seemed amiss lately. They came and went like always."

She side-eyed him. "And you confirmed—"

"Yes. It's his house. I called the Post 1 commander and told him. Stadler isn't on duty right now, and rumor had it that he was going fishing this weekend. Was supposed to be back to work on Tuesday."

"And … Glenna?"

"Yeah. She's been in and out just like always. Works at the military hospital at Fort Campbell, and usually not on the weekends."

"Okay. Did you get a contact for her work?"

"They don't have it. We'll just have to call down there and ask for a supervisor, I guess."

She tapped her notepad with her pencil. "Or we could go down there."

"Yeah, we could. At least one of us could." He waited a few seconds, then asked, "You doing okay with this?"

"Yeah. Hoping that was him in the house, but it sounds like it probably wasn't."

"Detective!" a voice called out.

"Yeah. Whatcha got?"

"Nothing." The coroner handed her a clipboard. "Just need you to sign off on moving the body to the state medical examiner's office, if you've got enough photos."

"Yeah, I do." She took the pen, then turned to Michael. "You're the chief deputy. Would you mind—"

"Of course not." He took the clipboard from her, signed it, dated it, and handed it back to the coroner. "Let us know when the body's out so we can get in there with the fire investigators."

"Will do, sir. Thanks."

They watched him walk away, and Samara's hope started to fail. "You do realize that ten to one, that's Glenna in there."

Michael's voice was a low murmur. "Yeah. I know."

"Are *you* okay with that?"

"Oh, yeah. That was over a long time ago. There's nothing left of that for me."

"Good. Anything else you need to do here?"

"Just watch as they load the body. I signed off on it, so I'm supposed to witness that."

"Got it. I'm going to the other end of the house to look around. They told me it's plenty safe enough."

"Good plan. Talk to you in a bit." She watched him walk away, thankful that he was there. There was plenty of experience in her past with those types of situations, but she hadn't been in the department very long. Having someone there on scene with her, someone who'd been with the department for a while, gave her the ability to report back without anyone doubting her.

She opened the door going from the attached garage into the kitchen of the home. The laundry room was directly to the right, but everything there seemed to be in perfect condition. There were a few dishes in the sink, the kind of stuff you'd find for someone who'd been alone for a few days. The kitchen trash can was full, and she pulled out a pair of gloves to go through it, but it yielded nothing important. She did note, however, that there were numerous food containers in it, but only one of each. That told her whatever had been eaten had been a meal for one.

The smell of smoke almost gagged her in the living room. There were a few magazines on the coffee table, just common kinds of things like women's magazines and a couple of men's periodicals, a fishing magazine and one for law enforcement. She had a subscription to that one too. Nothing really seemed out of place in the living room. She would most definitely be combing through it, but the initial view was nothing unusual. The dining room was directly behind the living room, and it didn't look like anyone had eaten in there in months.

The bathroom looked pretty normal, but when she opened the medicine cabinet, she noticed something. There were gaps in a couple of places, like someone had removed a bottle of medication. She took pictures and then noted it. The rest of the bottles had been filled at Pharless Pharmacy, the place where they'd stopped the night before. She made a note to check with them to see what they prescribed for Glenna, and if they'd tell her what they had on file for Alex, she'd take that info too.

Other than that, things looked pretty normal in there as well. She'd be going through and bagging anything she felt was evidence at a later time, but at that moment, all they could really do was secure the scene.

What appeared to be the guest bedroom was across the hallway from the bath, so she looked in. Everything seemed completely in order. Then she opened the closet door.

A wave of panic washed over her as she stared into the opening. Uniforms. All of his KSP uniforms. His heavy winter jacket was in there, an extra lid, a pair of tactical boots, and several handgun cases. One by one she checked them. The empty one was obviously his service weapon. He always carried a Colt M1911, and she knew that had to be its case. Damn thing was really too heavy to be a carry gun, but he felt ten feet tall when he carried it, the arrogant prick.

The rest of the handguns were nestled in their foam cradles inside their boxes until she came to the last one. It was empty. There were no markings on the outside of the case, but under the cutout in the foam she could see some papers, so she pulled the foam cradle out and retrieved them. It was exactly what she thought—a Glock 22 that carried .40 S&W rounds. Another quick look at the foam told her a section had been cut out where the magazine went, and she knew what that was about. Standard issue was a fifteen-round magazine, but the cutout indicated that he'd had two of their twenty-two-round magazines. Between their polymer frames, their Safe Action triggers—no traditional safety that has to be flipped off—and their accuracy, they'd been the standard for law enforcement for years, but she'd heard a lot of departments were moving away from them. Why, she wasn't sure. So was he carrying it as his backup weapon? Or was it somewhere else?

A voice called from somewhere at the back of the house, "Hey. You're gonna want to see this." She was pretty sure it was Michael, so she headed that direction.

She found him standing outside the back door and wearing rubber gloves. "What are you doing?" she asked him, looking at the garbage on the latex.

"Going through the trash. I thought I'd better do that immediately. It's the easiest thing for suspects to get rid of. And I found something." She followed him to the refuse bin, and he held open a bag. "What do you see?"

With her service torch pointed into it, she looked at the contents. There were receipts, empty boxes and bags, a bunch of paper bathroom cups, plus some really nasty-smelling food waste. But when she moved some of the paper, she saw it.

A pregnancy test. And it was positive.

All she could squeeze out was, "Holy shit."

"Yeah. The minute I saw that, dozens of possibilities flew through my head."

"Give 'em to me," she said and pulled her notepad and pencil out again.

"She was pregnant. Or he's been banging somebody else and they're pregnant. Maybe they brought the pregnancy test over to show him and she saw it. Maybe they brought the pregnancy test over to show to her and she confronted him with it. But somebody is, or was, pregnant. The medical examiner might be able to tell us."

Samara shrugged. "If it's in the trash, it's probably recent. That means she wouldn't have been very far along—if that's her."

"True. I guess we're at the mercy of the medical examiner. Hopefully they can find something that will indicate her cause of death. I mean, there's not much left of the body." Michael glanced at his watch. "I've got about an hour before I have to be at the office. I talked to Gray. He's coming over to babysit, and the guys will take turns on watch to keep the place secure until we know more. So before I go, do you want something to eat? I'll go get you something if—"

"After looking at all this? I'm not sure I could."

He frowned. "Maybe some yogurt? Or fruit?"

"I think I could get some yogurt down. That would be good. And a cup of coffee. Thanks. I appreciate it."

"No problem. Be back shortly. You're here, so I'm not concerned about security." Then he stepped up right in front of her and looked down into her face. "I'm so fucking disappointed. I was really hoping to wake up with you in my arms, not to a damn phone ringing."

"Yeah, it is what it is. Won't be your last chance." She stopped and stared at him. "Will it be your last chance?"

"Not unless that's what you want."

"I do not want. Sounds good to me too. It'll happen."

"I certainly hope so. Back in a flash with that yogurt." She watched him walk away, but just before he rounded the corner of the garage, he looked back and winked.

There was really nothing left to do except wait for the ambulance to roll away, so she put the garbage bag back, then tore a piece of crime scene tape from the roll she was wearing on her arm like a bracelet and sealed the bin.

Samara gave Michael's ideas some thought and tried to come up with yet a few more scenarios. She'd admit to herself that if it was someone he'd been screwing around with or someone he'd raped and they'd brought the test to Glenna, that would be hysterically funny. Well, not the murder, if that was her. That wasn't funny at all. But if the body was him, well, good riddance to bad rubbish. She hated to say that about anyone, but she really couldn't think of one redeeming quality the asshole had.

Back inside the house, she took a few more pictures. There was a curio cabinet in the living room and inside it were figurines, small trinket boxes, and a bud vase. She took pictures of all of them sitting there on the shelves together.

Nothing in the house except possibly the medications and the gun case really had much value as evidence, at least on the surface, but she wouldn't know for sure for a little while. One of the things she'd be looking for was a slug, if that was what had killed whoever it was. She was wondering when Michael would get back with the yogurt when she heard a commotion outside and glanced out the window.

A light-colored pickup truck had pulled up, and there was a man yelling at the top of his lungs. It only took her a second to recognize him.

It was Alex Stadler.

She really didn't want to see him. Of course, she knew if they discovered the body was Glenna, she'd love seeing him squirming at the defense table as she testified in a trial. Maybe he'd be smart and plead guilty. But at the moment, what she wanted most was to let him know that there was a great chance his fate would rest in her hands. "Bring it," she muttered under her breath.

Gathering her courage, she stepped out of the house through the back door and rounded the corner of the garage. Instead of going farther, she stopped and folded her arms across her chest, her feet shoulder-width apart. She halfway expected him to attack her. "Who's in charge here?" he screamed at a random firefighter. "Who's in charge? What's going on? What happened to my house?" he bellowed.

"Sir, calm down. If you want to speak to the detective in charge—"

"I do! I'm a fucking Kentucky State Police trooper! I want to see the detective in charge *right now!*" he screamed.

Then the firefighter talking to him turned and pointed toward her.

She wished she'd taken a picture or a video of the expression on his face when he saw her. It was beyond priceless, somewhere between disbelief and knowing he was screwed. It started to look like he might run back to his truck, but that moment passed and he straightened his spine, squared his shoulders, puffed out his chest, and strode right up to her, then leaned in to direct a threatening stare straight into her eyes. "*You're* the detective?"

"Yes, sir. Trigg County Sheriff's Department Detective Samara—"

"I know what your fucking name is, bitch," he hissed through gritted teeth. "You'd better play this by the book or I'll end your career."

Her hand instinctively went to her service weapon, and she wrapped her fingers around the retaining strap on its holster. "Sir, I'm going to have to ask you to go back behind the crime scene tape and—"

"This is *my* house and I'm law enforcement. I can be here if I want to be."

"No, sir, this is *our* crime scene."

"Crime scene? Who said anything about a crime?" There was a smugness in his voice that made her stomach pitch. "What makes you think a crime has been committed?"

"The body we found inside the house. And before you say anything that could incriminate you, just know that I made note of what you said when you got out of your truck. You asked who was in charge, what was going on, and what happened to your house. At no time did you ask about your wife. Not once. So if I were you, I'd tread carefully. Very carefully."

"Do I need an attorney?" he asked, his words full of venom, and he moved just a little closer.

Samara stood her ground. "I don't know. Do you?"

Deep and low, almost in a growl, he said, "Watch out, bitch. I'll bury you."

"Oh, really? Do I look scared of you? Because I'm—"

"Hey, I didn't know what flavor so I got … What the hell is going on here?"

"Oh, Mr. Stadler and I were just talking about the fire."

From the corner of her eye, she saw Michael rest his hand on top of his service weapon and unsnap the retainer strap. "You need to move away from my detective immediately." Alex glared at Michael, but in that moment she was so proud to know the chief deputy. "Now. Do not make me arrest you for threatening a peace officer, because I will."

"I'm a fucking state trooper," Alex hissed.

"I don't give a god damn if you're the fucking Pope, you move away from my detective *now*. I *will not* tell you a third time." He'd lifted his weapon about halfway out of its holster and his trigger finger lay along the side of the trigger guard.

"Your detective and I have a history, and I don't think she can be fair and impartial toward me."

"I'm sorry, but I disagree. I've seen her demonstrate more professionalism in the last three weeks than a lot of officers do in a career that lasts, oh, maybe twelve or thirteen years."

Alex had been staring at Michael. "Hey, don't I know you?"

"Oh, yeah. I used to be engaged to Glenna Thomas."

The man's face paled. "You assholes had better pass this off or I'll get you both fired."

"I'd invite you to go straight to Sheriff Carter Melton and tell him that. He'll tell you to stick it up your ass. Don't believe me?" Michael pointed toward town. "You can drive right on into town and ask him. Even with your limited intelligence, I believe you could find him. It's a building with a whole bunch of cars like mine sitting out front."

"I should just punch you in the face," Alex spat.

Michael never flinched. "Fuck yeah. I wish you would. Nothing would make me happier than to see her put you in cuffs."

Alex pointed his finger into Michael's face, then turned and glared at Samara. "This is not over."

Samara gave him the wickedest smile she could muster. "No, sir. It's not. There'll be a full investigation. You can count on that."

He finally stepped back and turned to storm across the yard to his truck, but halfway across, he turned and looked back at Samara. She hated that fucker.

A voice brought her out of her thoughts. "Babe, you okay?"

She hung her head, then lifted it again. "Yeah, yeah. I'm fine. Asshole. In a way, I hope that *is* her and we can destroy him."

"That makes two of us. Here. You probably need this by now." He handed her the coffee and by the time she'd taken two sips, he was sitting on the front porch, so she sat down beside him. The yogurt he'd brought to her was vanilla, and she knew he'd figured that would be a safe flavor. She took the plastic spoon he gave her and ripped the top off.

After what might very well have been the best evening of her life, it had turned out to be the start of a very, very interesting day.

MICHAEL STOOD IN FRONT OF CARTER'S DESK, TRYING hard not to fidget. "Can you go to lunch with me? Us? We need to talk to you about something."

"If it's employees dating, I think I've already—"

"No. That's not it. It's something far more personal, and I really think you need to hear it."

"Just close the door and—"

He shook his head. "No, sir. We can't take the risk of anyone hearing this. No one. It can't get out. Period."

Carter stared at him for a few seconds before he spoke, and the furrows in his forehead softened. "Oh, what the hell. Might as well. How 'bout ... How 'bout you pick up something and the three of us can meet over at the park. It's quiet over there and I doubt there'll be anybody there."

"Okay. When?"

"Uhh, lunchtime?"

"So noon?"

"That is lunchtime."

"Not for everybody, sir."

"Yeah, noon. I'll see you over there."

"Okay."

"How's it going over at the fire?"

"I'll let Samara bring you up to date on that."

"Okay. Fair enough. Lunch it is. And don't bring me anything that'll give me heartburn."

Michael chuckled. "Sharla says even water does that."

"I swear to god, I'm going to have an ulcer from this job at the rate I'm going."

Michael almost sighed. If that was the case, then what they had to tell him was going to send him right into a hemorrhage. "I hope not."

"I'm eating antacids like they're candy. See you in a bit."

"Yep." God, he dreaded doing what they had to do, but it was necessary. Keeping Carter in the dark simply wasn't an option.

Back at his desk, he sent Samara a quick text.

Lunch with Carter at noon

She texted back:

I'm not done here yet.

No. No, no, no. That didn't matter.

Look, after what happened earlier, we have to tell him today. Now. He deserves that.

She didn't respond.

Samara, if you want me to tell him, I will, but he has to be told.

He waited and waited, but she didn't respond. "Fuck it." Touching her contact, he waited while it rang. As soon as she answered, he asked, "Are you not going to answer me?"

"Babe, there's an awful lot to do here."

"Then you need to tell me it's okay for me to tell him."

It was quiet for longer than he liked. Finally, she said, "Okay. Fine. I'm not happy about it, but I understand."

"Good. Thanks. You know I won't tell him any more than he needs to know."

"Like what?"

"Like that little scar right above your—"

"*Stop*! Stop. Okay. Tell him. I'm fine with it. But no, you'd better not tell him about that."

"Ha. I wouldn't. Talk to you later."

Well, that was that. The bomb had to be dropped, and it looked like he was the bombardier.

"WHAT DID YOU BRING ME?"

Michael opened the bag and handed it over. "Roast beef and potato cake sandwich from Randy's Grill."

"My favorite! If you talk to my wife, you brought me a salad." Michael laughed. "I'm serious! She's on me all the time for eating junk. Did you get a side?"

"Here ya go."

Carter opened the little tub. "Fruit? Are you kidding me?"

"So if she asks, you can say you had fruit."

Carter stared at the cup like it was on fire. "Well, there ya go. So what's this big secret?"

Michael unwrapped his BLT and pulled out his fruit cup. "Okay, so you know I was engaged, right?"

"I don't think you ever told me that."

"Well, I was. Until I wasn't." He told Carter the whole story, but he didn't give him names. When he finished, he said, "At the time, I was still working at the home improvement warehouse in Hopkinsville. I went to community college at the same time."

"Because of that guy?"

"No, because I had a job and I wanted a career. And there's not that much around here. You know that."

"True."

"I graduated from high school when I was sixteen, and when I applied at the store, they didn't think anything of it. Just assumed I was eighteen. I went to community college too, and I decided to go to the academy when I was twenty."

"Do the guys know this?"

"No, but that's why they treat me like I'm a little kid."

"A fucking smart kid."

"Yeah, well, thanks. Then twelve years ago, Samara took the job at McCracken County. She worked there for four years. Then she went to KSP."

"I know that."

"What you don't know is that five years into her time there, she was sexually assaulted on the job."

Carter stopped chewing. "Samara?"

"Yeah. Overpowered her in the back of a cruiser."

"Did they catch the guy?"

"No. He was a coworker. A state trooper."

"Seems like a lot of bad troopers," Carter said and took another bite.

"Yeah. It does. So she finally gets a chance to go elsewhere, and it's here, after dodging and ducking him for three years."

"Wait. She didn't report him?"

"Carter, think for a second what you're saying. A black female state trooper accuses a white male trooper of raping her, one who's been on the job a good while. Who are they going to believe? And she knew if she reported him, he'd probably kill her, even if no one believed her."

"Well, yeah, that's probably true."

"Okay. Fast forward to the present. She picks up all of those rape cases and starts to think about them. All of those young women were afraid to name their attacker. Why? Who would they be that afraid of?"

Carter placed his sandwich on the wrapper and sat there, stunned. "A state trooper." He sat there for a minute before he said, "Why do I get the feeling that this gets worse?"

"Because it does. Guess who showed up at that fire this morning? A state trooper."

Carter seemed frozen. "Are you saying … Because I think you're saying … It can't be …"

"Yep. The guy who cheated with my fiancé, the guy who raped Samara, and the house that burned with a body inside? All the same guy."

Carter finally took a deep breath and huffed it out. "Holy shit. And if he's the same one who's been attacking women in Trigg County …"

Michael nodded. "Yeah. We have to believe it might be

him. So she decided she'd talk to all the victims again and see if she could get them to tell her anything. She's going to carry a picture of him with her to show to them and then watch for a tell."

"Oh, if it's him, she'll get a tell. At least one of them will probably start to cry."

"Exactly. But this is Post 1. She's going to call the other counties in the Post 1 sector. She's also going to call the counties on the border of Post 1 to see if they have any similar cases."

"A guy takes your fiancé, rapes Samara, becomes a serial rapist—if he wasn't one already—and then kills someone and puts them in his house? Did I get all that straight?" Carter asked, still looking a bit stunned.

"Yeah. We don't know who the body is, but I'd be willing to bet it's either his wife or a woman who confronted him. He was supposedly fishing out of town this weekend, but I have a feeling we'll be seeing if we can shoot holes in his alibi."

"Have you had any contact with his commander?"

"Yeah. Called him this morning about the fire, but I made no other comments about Stadler. That was before he showed up at the scene."

"And how did that go?"

"He got up in Samara's face and threatened her."

"Did she stand her ground?"

Michael grinned. "She sure did. Even better, when I got there, he recognized me. I told him if he ever threatened one of my officers again, he'd live to regret it. She basically told him to go fuck himself. But now he knows we're onto him. Funny part is, he asked what was going on and who the detective was, but you know what he didn't ask?" Carter's brow twitched upward. "He didn't ask about his wife."

"Okay, I want you and Samara working on this as much as you can. She can work on it when you're tied up with admin duties, but I'll try to keep those to a minimum so you'll have time. If this is a bad cop, and it sure sounds that way, I want him out of a cruiser and behind bars." Then Carter's shoulders fell. "But I've got to call his commander."

Michael couldn't believe his boss would say that. "Why?"

"Professional courtesy. If I don't and this comes to an arrest, he's gonna be pissed, and no other posts will want to work with us. Ever. We'll be totally on our own with no KSP support. And as small as our force is, I can't take that chance."

"But if you call him, he'll alert Stadler."

"We can hope that he won't. But I have to do it."

And idea zipped through Michael's mind. "What if you didn't have to? Because you went above him?"

"To …"

"The commissioner."

"No, Michael. I can't just cold-call the state police commissioner and tell him all this."

For the first time since it all began, Michael felt a spark of hope. "No, but I can."

"You're just a chief deputy. He won't listen to you."

"Oh, yes, he will. Do you know who he used to play golf with?" Carter shook his head. "My dad."

The sheriff's eyes almost popped out of his head. "Seriously?"

"Yup. Matter of fact, he's my godfather. He and his

wife and Mom and Dad used to play canasta sometimes, or go to movies, or things like that. Matter of fact, he was the one who fast-tracked my admission into the academy. When Dad died, James was the first person at the house, offering to help however he could and telling me that if I ever needed him for anything, he'd be right here. And this time, right now, I really think I need him."

Carter set his lips in a straight line and sat there. After a minute, he stared straight into Michael's eyes. "Do it. Let's roast this bastard."

"Okay. Good as done. I'll call him when I get back to the office. And if I can sense that it would be better for me to meet with him, do you think—"

"You could go to Frankfort and see him? Hell yeah. Do whatever you have to. But listen to me: Keep a close eye on Samara. If this guy really did all of this, he knows if he gets caught, he'll have nothing left to lose, so he'll be very, very dangerous."

"Yes, sir. I'm aware of that. I'd normally say that she can hold her own, but I really do think she needs extra eyes right now. He's a sneaky sumbitch, and he knows all the cop tricks."

"Yeah. By the way, how did last night go?" Carter gave Michael a sly grin.

"Amazing. We're perfect together. We had a great day, peaceful and fun, and then ..."

Carter held up a palm. "No. I don't need to know. I really don't. I guess the call this morning interrupted you."

Michael started laughing. "God no! I'm not eighteen anymore! I'm twenty-six. We got an early start, but we were asleep by eleven."

Carter snorted at him. "Jesus fucking Christ, are you an

old man?"

"No. Just don't mind going to bed at nine for the right reasons."

His boss gave him a lopsided smirk. "I hear ya there. At least Angel's sleeping through the night most of the time now. There for a while, we were both so exhausted that it was a struggle to stay up and watch a movie, much less anything more intimate. Mom watched her a couple of times so we could go out, but I didn't ask often. Pretty soon she'd be telling everybody in town that she was raising our kid because we were too busy."

"Yeah. Sounds like something she'd say."

Carter took the last bite of his sandwich and wadded up the paper. "Do what you have to do. I trust your judgment, Michael, and I'll do whatever you need me to in order to keep her safe."

"Thanks. That's all I needed to know."

"And let me know what the commissioner says. Can't wait to hear that."

"Yeah." Michael tossed his sandwich wrapper in the trash. "Me either."

THE PHONE RANG A COUPLE OF TIMES AND WAS ANSWERED with a bright voice. "Good afternoon. Commissioner Reed's office. May I help you?"

"Yes, ma'am. This is Chief Deputy Michael Edwards of the Trigg County Sheriff's Department. I'd like to speak with Commissioner Reed."

"I'm sorry, who did you say you were?"

Michael chuckled. "Tell him it's his godson on the

phone."

"Oh! Okay. Hold, please."

The hold only lasted about thirty seconds. "Michael! Great to hear from you!"

"Good to talk to you, James. You and Eileen doing okay?"

"Oh, yeah. Hey, Katie and Bruce just had a new baby!"

"Wow! Boy or girl?"

"Boy. That makes three for them, two boys and a girl right in the middle."

"She'll keep 'em busy. How's Ben?"

"Doing well. Still traveling all over the place. We thought he was going to marry a guy he met in Copenhagen, but it didn't happen. I don't know when he'll be back. Sleeping in hostels and monasteries. Craziest thing I've ever seen. You married yet?"

"No, sir, but I've got a girlfriend."

"Good! What's she like?"

"Her name is Samara and she's a detective here in the department."

"Well, that's great. And Marjorie?"

Michael sucked a big breath in and sighed. "I really wish you guys would come to visit soon. She's driving me crazy. I bought a house and it's finally close enough to finished to live in, and she's having a fit because I moved out of their house."

"You think seeing us would help?"

Michael laughed. "Well, it sure couldn't hurt!"

"I'll talk to Eileen and we'll make it a priority to get down there. So, enough catching up. I'm sure there's something on your mind. Whatever you need, I'll try to help."

"I'd really appreciate it. You know a long time ago, I was engaged."

"Yes. I remember."

"Well, so, when we split, she …" Michael launched into the whole thing, exactly as he'd told Carter. James asked him questions along the way, but there was one thing Michael knew for sure. James would never doubt his word. When he finished, he said, "I told the sheriff I'd call you. We wanted to call the Post 1 commander, but we were afraid he might tip our hand, and if this guy is guilty, we need to get him off the streets and behind bars."

James was silent for a few minutes before he finally said, "Michael, I can't believe …" Michael held his breath, terrified James was going to tell him he didn't believe him. "… that his commanding officer doesn't know at least some of this. He's bound to. Damn, son. I hate this kind of thing. It makes all of us look bad. So she's going to start investigating the assaults from the past cases and then check in other counties?"

"Yes, sir. She said she also thinks she needs to check the counties on the other side of the Post 1 boundary."

"Good thinking. So what do you need from me?"

"The only thing I really need is assurance that if we go forward with this, you'll run interference for us with the post commander. We can't afford to be denied KSP assistance if something big happens, and we're afraid we'll be blackballed and left to shrivel in the sun."

"That will *not* happen. Do what you have to do, and keep me posted along the way. I would like to do some damage control, so before you make an arrest, please get in touch. I'll soften the blow."

"Thanks so much, sir. I really appreciate it. I just … I

want Samara to have some justice, and if he's responsible for what happened to the other women, I want them to have some justice too."

"I do too. And please, let me know what the medical examiner says. Do you really think it's his wife? Your ex?"

"Yeah. I do. Almost positive. It's a mess, but we're trying to sort through it a little at a time."

"Take your time, son. Be scrupulous in your methodology. That always pays off."

"Yes, sir. It does."

"We'll come down as soon as we can. Want to do a little fishing?"

"I'd love to. We've got a deputy who has a boat. Might want to see if he wants to go so we can get out on the water."

"Sounds great! Keep me posted and do your best. I know you will. Your dad would be so proud of you, son."

"Thanks, James. Please say hi to Eileen and Katie for me. And Ben when you can find him!" he said with a laugh.

"Will do, Michael. Take care, son."

The phone went dead and Michael sat there, barely able to breathe. Everything was on track. "Sheriff Melton?" he called out from his desk.

"Yes, Chief Deputy Edwards?"

"Green light."

"Got it. Thanks."

It was a go. Their asses were covered and permission had been granted. Now to find a killer before he could hurt anyone else.

CHAPTER 7

By the time Samara came in, she was sooty and smelled to high heaven. She showered and dressed in the department's locker room, then headed out into the office to find a work spot.

To her surprise, a small desk had been set up in the conference room's corner and it was stocked with supplies. "Whose desk is this?" she asked loudly.

She heard Michael's voice call back, "Yours."

"Thanks." A smile spread across her face. It was nice to have somebody watching out for her.

It was almost time to go when the phone rang out front and she heard Gray yell, "Sheriff, line two."

"Thanks." She could hear him talking and clicking around on his keyboard. In a few minutes, she heard him hang up the phone. Before she could think, he stepped into the conference room, then leaned out the door and called out, "Michael, you need to see this too."

He had a piece of paper in his hand. "What is it?" she asked, afraid of the answer.

"Preliminary medical examiner's report. When he was told what kind of case this is, he expedited the preliminary." He handed it to Samara. "Take a look."

She was smiling when she handed it to Michael. "Holy shit. We were right. It's a woman," he whispered in response. "And she was dead before the fire. Having a chunk of bullet-shaped bone missing from your scapula is kind of telling, especially since it could've gone through your heart or lungs first."

Carter nodded. "I also told him we really needed the testing fast, and I made him aware that there was a chance she was pregnant. He said he didn't know how much luck he'd have finding any evidence of that, considering the condition of the remains, but he'll try. Some kind of tests of the bone marrow."

Samara nodded. "Testing for HCG levels. That's about all we can hope for. They've got to run the DNA anyway. Might as well test it for that along with basic toxicology, although that probably won't turn up much."

"He said he's going to try it anyway. But until we have an I.D., there's little we can do. In other news, I think your idea is sound, Samara. Go ahead and work with the assault cases we already have, then move out to other Post 1 counties. Michael, I think you should interview Stadler."

"You know that's never going to happen."

Carter's eyes were steely. "Oh, yeah it is. I *will* call his commander over that if he refuses to talk to us. Since neither of you have ever done this, let me tell you how it works. He can plead the fifth if answering what he's being asked can cause him to be arrested and charged. However, he cannot plead the fifth if answering the questions would result in the loss of his job, like in an internal affairs investigation."

Michael wasn't sure how that was going to work. "Okay, so if he doesn't have to tell us anything that could incriminate him and might cause him to be arrested and charged, how do we proceed?"

"I'd say make this about his job. I'll call his commander and ask him if he really wants a trooper at his post who won't assist another law enforcement agency with a simple question and answer to see if he has any idea who victimized him. His house is gone and a body was in it. Does he think he's being framed? Who could it be? I mean, if he *doesn't* think that's her, has he tried to find her? If not, why not? If he's found her, can we talk to her? There's an expectation of honor within their hierarchy. His commander can put his feet to the fire better than either of you can. And Samara, I want you to stay clear of this guy."

"I will as best I can, but I have a job to do."

"I get that. I just don't want him retaliating against either of you. That's my greatest fear. So check in often and let me or Michael know if you're going to be out of pocket. That's the best we can do."

"Will do," Samara assured him.

"Okay. Hit it. A lot of ground to cover and not much time. Edwards, reach out to Stadler and ask him to come in for a sit-down. If he refuses, let me know and I'll call his commander."

Michael nodded. "Got it. Thanks, sheriff."

"You're both very welcome. Get on it." With that, he walked out and left Michael and Samara sitting there, deep in thought.

"Can I make a suggestion?" Michael asked quietly.

"Sure."

"I'd suggest that you check with the other counties before going to talk to the victims in Trigg first. If you find some, that might be additional impetus for them to talk."

"Good idea. I can start that right now. And thanks."

"For what?"

"For not insisting on babysitting me."

He shook his head. "I can't do that to you. As much as I want to keep you safe, you have a job to do, and some of that is out of my control. But as long as you're *with* me, you'll be safe. I'll see to it. I'm gonna go make this call and see how mad I can make Alex Stadler."

"If he's coming here, please tell me when so I won't be here."

"You can be sure I will. I don't want you anywhere near him." He leaned down and kissed her cheek gently, then whispered in her ear, "Never again."

After he'd gotten a soft drink from the break room refrigerator, Michael sat down at his desk, drank it, and closed his eyes, trying to clear his mind. He wanted to be focused and calm when he talked to Stadler so the guy didn't think he was being looked at. The last thing Michael needed was to be rattled.

When he thought he was ready, he picked up the receiver on the phone, dialed the number, and waited. A male voice answered, "Hello?"

"Alex Stadler?"

"Who wants to know?"

"This is Chief Deputy Edwards at the Trigg County Sheriff's Department. We'd really like to have you come in and talk to us, see if we can find out who burned your house down. Regardless how any of us feel about each other, you're a victim of a crime and you need some answers. It's our job to give them to you."

There was silence for a bit before Stadler finally said, "Can't you come here?"

"I would, but we're shorthanded and I need to stick around here as much as I can. It'll only take a few minutes."

He was quiet again. Michael was about to ask if he was still there when he said, "Okay. When?"

"I'm going to be around here due to the staffing shortage, so anytime you want to come by will be fine. Of course, the sooner we talk to you, the sooner we can find out who was responsible for burning down your home and give you some peace of mind. If you get here and I'm not here for some reason, ask them to find me and I'll come back."

"Okay. I'll try to do it today. But I don't want that bitch in—"

"Sir, please. I'm trying to treat you with courtesy and respect, and talking about our detective that way makes it difficult for either of us to do our jobs. I'm going to have to ask you to tamp that down for the sake of getting you some justice for the arson of your house."

"Okay, okay. But I'd prefer it if she wasn't there though."

"We can make that happen."

"Okay. Um, thanks, I guess. I'll get there as soon as I can."

"Thank you, sir. Have a good afternoon." As soon as he hung up, Michael shook his head. The guy still never mentioned his wife. And he didn't question the idea of arson. Had someone talked to him?

Michael called the fire chief, and he said Stadler hadn't called him. The fire marshal and the arson investigation company both said they hadn't reported to him, just to law enforcement. Michael knew the fire department had gotten a copy of the reports from the fire marshal and the investigation company, because Carter had them too. Every time Stadler opened his mouth, he made himself seem more guilty. Why? He should know better.

And then he understood. It wasn't about not knowing better. It was about thinking he was so fucking untouchable that he'd never be found out. "Well, I've got a little surprise for you, Alex Stadler," Michael mumbled under his breath. "I've got your number and before I get finished with you, you're gonna be singing *my* song."

MICHAEL TOLD SAMARA TO PACK UP HER FILES AND GO home. She could work from there, but he didn't want her in the office if Stadler showed up. Carter told Watson to follow her home and make sure she was inside and locked in before he left.

Two hours later, he heard the front door open and a deputy named Carlin speaking. In a couple of seconds, the deputy appeared in Michael's doorway. "He's here, sir."

"Thanks." Michael pulled out the little mirror he kept in his top desk drawer and checked his hair. He straightened his badge just a little more, straightened his spine and flexed his shoulders to loosen them, tipped his head to either side to free up the muscles in his neck, then strode out to the front. "Mr. Stadler?"

"That's Trooper Stadler to you," the taller man snapped.

"Yes. Sorry. Trooper Stadler. Thank you for coming down to talk to me. I appreciate it."

"Yeah, well, let's just get this over with. It's a huge waste of my time." He was trying so hard to be cool, but Michael could tell he was curious and maybe even a little nervous.

"Sure, sure. I won't keep you long. Want a cup of coffee or a soft drink?"

"No."

"Suit yourself." Michael reached into the refrigerator in the break room, grabbed a soft drink, and rejoined Stadler in the hallway. "Right back here. We've got a nice conference room. You've never been in our office before, have you?"

"Why would I be? It's a sheriff's department," Stadler fairly spat.

"Still, pretty nice. Have a seat. You don't mind if I record this interview, do you?"

"No. Standard procedure."

"Yep." He placed his phone in the middle of the table and spoke into it. "This is Chief Deputy Michael Edwards interviewing *Trooper* Alex Stadler," he said, then gave the date and time, plus the incident of which they'd be speaking and date of its occurrence. "Trooper Stadler, can you confirm your presence, please?"

"Yes. This is Kentucky State Trooper Alex Stadler, Post 1."

"Thanks. Okay. Just have a few questions. First, do you know of anyone who'd want to burn your house down?"

"I'm a state trooper. Probably dozens of people."

"I'm just wondering if you can think of a specific instance."

It was quiet for about fifteen seconds before he said, "Yeah. Maybe one or two. Busted one guy for meth a couple of months ago and he said he'd kill me. One last year, dealer, caught him with a couple of kilos of cocaine. Said the cartel would come after me."

"Did he say which cartel?"

"No. I had to assume he meant the *La Hermandad Viciosa*." Michael wrote that down.

"So you know them to be active in the state?"

"Yes. Very."

With every question Michael asked, he could see Stadler relax a little more. That was his plan, to make the trooper think they were looking in a completely different direction. "So instead of you, do you know of anyone who'd have a grudge against your wife?"

That initial look of suspicion hit Stadler's face. "My wife? Why would anyone want to hurt my wife?"

"I don't know. That's why I was asking. I mean, did she have words with someone, or had anyone threatened her?"

"Not that I'm aware of."

"So you have no idea whose body that could've been in your house?"

"No."

"Could we talk to your wife?"

"She's on a cruise with her sister." And that was it. Stadler had forgotten how well Michael had known Glenna, or maybe he didn't think Michael knew her that well. Maybe he thought Michael had forgotten. Or maybe she'd downplayed their relationship.

Because Glenna didn't have a sister.

"Could you give us her employer's number? They might know of someone who'd been bothering her."

"I don't have it. I'll have to get it."

"You can look it up on your phone, can't you?"

"Ah, phone's battery ran down."

"Oh. Well, I could look it up on mine. It would only take—"

"Look, this didn't have anything to do with my wife. She'll tell you that when she comes back from her cruise."

"How much longer will that be?"

"Three weeks. It's one of those Alaskan things where they stop at every little town along the way."

"Oh, yeah. I've seen brochures for those. They look like a lot of fun. I mean, polar bears, right?"

The man slouched down in the chair and folded his arms across his chest. "I can't imagine why anyone would go on vacation to a place that cold. Makes no sense."

"I know, right? I'd want to go to Cancun or St. Thomas or somewhere like that."

"Exactly." He sat there for a few seconds, and Michael wondered what was going through his mind. "Anything else?"

"Oh, yeah. So you were fishing over the weekend?"

"Yeah. Up in Indiana."

"With friends?"

He shifted a little in his chair. "Was supposed to be with friends, but they cancelled at the last minute. So I just fished alone."

"Gotcha. Which lake in Indiana?"

"Not a lake. Anderson River."

"And did you camp?"

"No. We were supposed to have a camper, but since the guy who owns it didn't come, I had to get a motel room."

"And the motel?"

"The Ramada Inn in Tell City. There really isn't much around there."

"Isn't that close to Santa Claus, Indiana?"

"Yeah. Kinda."

"I remember my parents taking me there when I was a kid. So, when did you get there and when did you leave?"

"I got there on Friday night. Supposed to come back Tuesday, but then I got the call about the house."

"So you just fished and ate and stayed at the hotel?"

"Yeah. That's about it."

Michael wanted so badly to say, *Yeah. I fish. With the KSP commissioner.* But he didn't. He couldn't. "I think that's about all I need. If you'll just have your wife give us a call when she gets back into town, that would be great."

"So you have no idea who was in the house?"

"Probably the person who set the fire. That's what we're thinking."

"And you don't know who it is?"

"No. And the body was so badly burned that we may never find out."

"Wow. That's a shame. Well, let me know if you figure it out. I've got to talk to the insurance company about it."

Stadler stood, so Michael did too. "Thanks for coming in."

"Yeah. No problem." With that, Stadler stalked off up the hallway and out the door.

When Michael stepped into the front lobby, Carlin handed him a piece of paper. "Here ya go."

"Thanks. Good work." In his hand was a slip of paper with the make and model of Stadler's truck, as well as the VIN and the license plate number. Running a plate would leave a record of their inquiry, but having Carlin get the info had left no trace. Stadler would never realize they had the information.

Now to acquire some video footage and look for a truck at the Ramada Inn in Tell City, Indiana.

THE DAY WAS WINDING DOWN WHEN CARTER STOPPED AT Michael's door. "How's it going?"

Michael looked up from his desk at Carter's question. "I'm going in so many different directions that I really don't know which way to go next."

The sheriff sat down in the chair beside Michael's desk and leaned in. "I may have a little help for you."

"Oh?"

"Yeah. You remember Cruz Livingston, right?"

"Of course! How could I forget Cruz?"

"I started thinking about our DNA and some of the other forensic aspects of the case, so I gave him a call. Turns out that he was about to call me. He's working on a case that has some ties to St. Louis, so he was thinking about trying to get together while he's already headed this direction, since we aren't that far away. I told him what's going on, and he said he'd be glad to look at some of the information and maybe even see if their lab could do some work. I mean, he's no forensics guy, but he's seen a lot of evidence from all kinds of cases, so any help he could give us would be great."

Michael threw his head back and sighed. "Damn, that would be such a big help, Carter. This is going in so many different directions and I'm feeling a little overwhelmed."

"Then I'll make it happen. Learn anything from Stadler?"

"I'll let you be the judge of that. Listen to this." Michael laid his phone on the desk and motioned to the chair beside it, so Carter sat and Michael hit "Play." The sheriff listened intently. When the recording was over, he grinned. "Whoa. You're slick."

"I dunno about—"

"No, really. That was slick. He thought you wanted him in here to *help* him. And I noticed something."

Michael smirked. "No mention of his wife?"

"Exactly. Not until you asked. I'm almost positive that's her body at the medical examiner's office."

"I am too. But there's something else. Saying she's on a cruise with her sister?"

"Yeah?"

"Carter, she doesn't *have* a sister."

Carter grinned. "Well, look at that. Alex Stadler lies. What a big shock. By the way, Samara's at home working so she's not in his sights?"

"Yeah. Watson said he stood on the porch until he heard her lock the door, and the guys will be driving by there from time to time."

"Good. Does she have a panic button?"

"No, but I've got one ordered. Of course, she'll need internet before it'll work, and they haven't come to install it yet. And by the way, I want to be there when they do. I wouldn't put it past Stadler to try to pay someone to come in and hurt her."

"You're probably right. Lying bastard. But good work on your part. I made the right decision when I promoted you."

"Thanks, but I wish I knew a little more about detective work," Michael said, thinking about Samara.

"That's why we hired Futrell, to do that stuff so you don't have to. Don't worry. You work with her long enough, you'll pick up a lot of it."

"I'm hoping so. Thanks, Carter."

"Thank you. I know you think you're falling behind, but you're doing a great job. Let me know if you need anything, and I'll let you know when Cruz will be here."

"Thanks." His boss disappeared out the door, closing it behind him, and Michael sat there, trying to quiet his mind. What a hideously fucked-up situation.

Maybe he'd get some help from the tall Texan. Then he snickered. He wouldn't mind getting help straight from Hell as long as it didn't set everything it touched on fire.

"I'M LEAVING THE OFFICE. WHAT DO YOU WANT ME to do?"

The smile that split her face was so big that it hurt. "Come here. Please."

His voice was molten sex through the phone, so hot that it made everything between her legs tingle. "Be glad to."

"Thanks, babe. See you when you get here."

"Hey, what about dinner?"

She sighed. "I hadn't even thought about it."

"I'll pick something up. Anything you hate?"

"Ummm, if it comes on a crust with a lot of pizza sauce, I'll eat it."

He laughed loudly. "I think that's your way of telling me you want pizza!"

"If not, you need to go back to the academy, 'cause you don't know shit about info harvesting!"

"I'll be there in a few. Hey, call it in over at Bolivar's Pizza and I won't have to wait as long."

"Okay. See you in a few. Bye."

"Bye, baby." And the phone went quiet.

It took her less than thirty seconds to find the phone number, and the pizzas were ordered in under a minute. She went ahead and paid for them with her card. He'd fed her. She could damn well feed him.

"Oh, god, this is good," she said with a full mouth as she ate. It was her third slice, and she wasn't even embarrassed about it. What she had in her hand was easily the best pizza she'd had in years.

"Yeah, they use really fresh stuff." He put down a pizza bone and wiped his mouth. "Okay, so what did you get done this afternoon?"

"I took a map and mapped out the locations where the women reported the assaults."

"Any pattern?"

She shook her head. "None that I can tell. So I set up interviews with two of them tomorrow, and I'll try to get in touch with two more before I go out. I might be able to get a third one that way."

"Good plan."

"You gonna eat that?" she asked and pointed at the last slice of pizza.

Michael threw his hands up in surrender. "Nooo. You go right ahead. Damn, girl, that's what, four pieces?"

"Some gentleman. Everyone knows you shouldn't criticize a lady's consumption of pizza."

"Oh, is that right? Nobody ever told me that. Thanks for informing me."

"You're welcome."

There was something on his mind, she could tell, and she wondered if he'd finally spill it. "Listen, I don't want you to think I don't trust you to take care of yourself. I do. But I'd be lying if I said I was comfortable with you being alone right now."

Well, there it is, she thought. "I can handle myself."

"I know you can, but he managed to overpower you once before. He's a slippery bastard. He could do it again."

"I'm keeping my guard up. Plus I'll only be out during the daytime. I don't want to be out at night."

"I'd prefer if you weren't."

"Then fine. It's fine."

He stood and started picking up their mess from the pizza. "I should tell you, we're getting a little help from another agency."

"Who?"

"Carter has a friend who's an FBI agent in Texas."

"Wow. Okay, so what do you think a Texas FBI agent is going to be able to bring to the table?"

"Some expertise we don't have. A long, solid history of seeing stuff like this and being able to analyze it. And he may be able to expedite our DNA and tox screens."

He picked up his drink and her drink, so she followed

him to the sofa and sat down. "Now that *would* be helpful."

"Yeah. Problem is, if the victim is Glenna, we can't match the DNA unless we have familial DNA. The best way would be at the time of family notification. But I don't know of a way to get that done. You can't notify a family about the death of a person you can't confirm is deceased, and I'm afraid if we tell them what we suspect, they'll tell him, which is what we need to avoid. I really don't know which direction to go from here."

She nodded. "Yeah. I see the problem. But maybe this Texas guy can help you in some other way. I dunno. It's worth a shot. Nice guy?"

"Extremely nice guy. Cruz Livingston. Works at the field office out of San Antonio. Came here to investigate after Trooper Palmer's murder. He helped us a lot. Carter wouldn't still be here if it wasn't for Cruz."

Her smile was gentle. "That's what he says about you."

"I didn't do anything, really. I just—"

"Michael, stop it." She was surprised at the pinkness that spread across his cheeks. "You're an amazing guy. Amazing. Your mother doesn't appreciate you. Your old fiancée didn't appreciate you. But Carter does. I'm pretty sure Gray does. And I do. You're finally around people who know what kind of man you are, and they all highly respect you."

It broke her heart to watch him as his head dipped and he stared at his hands. "And what kind of man am I?"

Samara slipped her hand under his chin and lifted his head until she could look in those gorgeous eyes. "The most amazing man I've ever met. Someone who is as smart and resourceful as he is gentle and kind. The man who makes me feel like a queen."

"Because you are," he whispered.

"And you … You are my king." There was no point in holding back. If she didn't get the words out, she was pretty sure she would explode, so she stared into the depths of those hazel orbs, took a deep breath, and sighed it out. "Michael, I love you. I know we've only known each other a few weeks, but I've never met anybody else like you. I can't wait to see you every time my eyes open, and your smile takes my breath away." She felt a tear as it rolled down her cheek, but she didn't care. Her heart was full. If he didn't feel the same way about her, she thought she'd probably die, but she needed to know for sure. "I love my family. I love my job. But you're the most important person in my world, and I never want to live a single day without you."

One hand rose to wipe the tear from her face and he tried to smile, but she could tell he was slowly losing his composure. "There are no words to tell you how much I love you, Samara. You're everything to me." The hand that had captured the tear cupped her cheek, and the warmth from it gave her a peace and calmness she'd never known. "I'm not going to lie to you. I'm terrified. Until I took this job, nothing I ever did came out the way I wanted. It's been the first real success of my life. And it'll be my best, unless I can win your heart."

"It's too late. You already have." She leaned out and pressed her lips to his, and he deepened the kiss, breathing into her and making her his. There was no stopping the tears that slicked her face, and when she wrapped her arms around his neck, he pulled her in closer and kissed her a little deeper.

That made her cry even harder. He pulled back and their eyes locked. "Why are you crying?"

"Because I was so scared when I said that to you."

He seemed surprised. "Scared of what?"

"That you wouldn't feel the same way."

"Why wouldn't I? Baby, I fell for you the first second I saw you in the office, but I told myself that a woman like you would never pay any attention to a man like me."

"Why would you think that?"

"Because you're beautiful and smart, accomplished, confident, strong. Why would I think you'd want to be around me?"

"You're all those things and more. I've watched you, Michael. You may be a little hesitant in a social setting, but when you're at work, you have a confidence that instills more confidence in everyone who works under you. And I can tell you this. I have never—*never*—felt safer around anyone than I do with you. When you're around, I know nothing can hurt me because you're watching. And if you told me to do something …" She chuckled a little. "I don't take well to being told what to do, at least not in my personal life, but if you told me to do something, I know it would be because you were looking out for me, not trying to control me or manipulate me. I trust you, Michael. I really do trust you."

The eyes that looked back into hers were clear and bright. "And I will never, never do anything to betray that trust, babe. I'm all yours for as long as you want me."

"I want you forever. A very, very long forever."

"Good." Michael's hands followed her arms to her

hands clasped behind his neck, then separated her hands, brought them down, and held them in his own. "I'm gonna take this trash out and then we're going over your map so I can see your game plan. After that, we're going to bed and I'm going to show you that everything I just said to you is true."

She stroked a finger down his cheek. "And I'm going to do the same for you."

"Okay. Spread all that stuff out while I take out the trash."

Thirty minutes later, he nodded as he looked through the paperwork. She'd covered every detail he could've thought of and some that he never would've. The map was folded up and put away, and the papers slipped into a folder. "So are you going to try to start the interviews tomorrow?"

"Yeah. Thought I would." He was trying to say something, but she didn't know what it could be. After watching him for a full minute, she finally said, "Okay. What's going on in your head?"

"Would you please let me assign somebody to ride with you? I'm worried that—"

"No, Michael. No. I have to do this. Besides, I'm the only female deputy. If you assign one of the guys, the women won't want to talk to me. I'll be fine, I promise. Situational awareness is now my middle name," she said and patted his hand.

"I just … Nothing can happen to you." The brokenness in his voice surprised her. He really was worried.

"It won't. If I see anything that looks wrong or out of place, I'll call it in. I promise. Can we just forget about this for a few minutes and get ready for bed?"

"Of course. I'll lock up and be there in just a minute or two." When he stood from the table, she did too, and gave him a little kiss on the cheek before she wandered to the bedroom.

Cleaned up and ready for bed, she gave him her sexiest smile as he strode through the bedroom and into the bathroom. Damn, she loved to watch him walk past! He had no clue how sexy he really was, and the way the front of those jeans tented just a little didn't hurt anything.

The bathroom door opened and when he stepped out in nothing but his boxer briefs, there was no doubt what was on his mind. But when he turned with his back to the bed and slipped off the cotton garment, she reached out and put a hand on each of his hips. "Turn around," she ordered as she gave him a twist.

Cocks had never been something she'd thought of as beautiful, but his was. It was perfectly proportioned, plenty big enough, and hard as a rock, its crown purple with the blood coursing through his flesh. His smile was wicked. "And what do you think you're doing?"

Samara reached out and fondled his balls. "Making you the happiest man in town tonight."

The laugh he let out was throaty and deep. "And you're going to do that how?"

"I think you know." Before he had a chance to say anything else, she opened her mouth and took him right down.

A hiss erupted from his lips, and he pressed a hand to either side of her head. "Fuck, baby, that's so fucking good." She hummed around him. "Oh, fuck yeah. That's … Hey, hey, hey, babe? Hey, can you turn loose for a second?"

Her lips made a *pop* sound when she released him. "What?"

"Can I just sit down on the bed? I don't want my knees to buckle."

"I'm that good?"

He laughed again. "Oh, hell yeah!"

By the time they were situated, she was on her elbows between his legs, sucking away, her ass in the air. At least twice he leaned out and slapped it, and it made her giggle around him. That just made him groan. After about five minutes, she started to add a twisting motion around the base of his dick and he flexed upward toward her face. "Damn, Samara, you know how to suck cock, girl. Oh, god. God, god, god. Damn, babe." She could taste the little dollop of precum he'd released, and that just drove her on. "Babe, I'm getting close. You don't really want to swallow, do you?" She nodded, her mouth full of his hardness. "What? No. You don't want to … I know you don't." Nodding again, she doubled down on her sucking and bobbing. "Babe, really, I'm gonna turn loose. I'm trying to hold out, but I don't think I … I don't think I can. I think … Baby, if you don't want to swallow, you should … Samara, you … You'd better … Fuck. Oh, fuck, fuck, fuck. I, I, I … Fuuuuuuuuuuuuck," he moaned as his hot cum filled her mouth. It was salty, bitter, and something only he could give her. That thrilled her more than he could ever know.

It only took her a couple of swipes with her tongue to clean him up. When she had, she crawled out from between his knees, pressed his legs together, and straddled them. Working his softness with both hands, she smiled into his eyes. "Good, huh?"

His hands pulled her head toward him and he kissed her. "Damn, that's so fucking hot, tasting me on you."

"Yeah? Kiss me again, babe." He kissed her again, and she ran her tongue into his mouth only to find his sliding against it, curling and dancing. One touch of her hand told her he was hard and ready again, so she rose up and let herself down on his hardness, never releasing his lips. His fingers dug into her hips as he pulled her forward until she was seated firmly on his shaft, and she could feel his crown push against the end of her channel. "Damn, boy, you feel good."

"So do you. I told you that you're my queen. And this is your throne, beautiful." She felt his hands slide from her hips, up her ribcage, and cup her breasts, his thumbs stroking her nipples until he brought his fingers to them and pinched.

Her belly contracted and her whole body folded forward. "Oh, fuck, baby. I need you."

"I need you too. Ride me for a bit and then I'll roll you." Rising up just a little, she fell back down, and his hands left her tits to grip her ass, helping her rise and fall on him. She rested her forearms on his shoulders and pressed down to help lift herself. Their lips were less than an inch apart, and he stared straight into her eyes. "Damn, I love you, girl."

She had to have it. She just couldn't wait. God, he felt good slamming inside her as she dropped each time. It surprised her when he pressed his hands onto the tops of her hips and stopped her. "What are you doing?"

"Lean back. Go on. Lean all the way back. Keep going. I won't let you fall." As her forearms slid back and her hands reached his shoulders, he gripped them and held her hands as she leaned back until she was lying on top of his legs, hers bent under her. "Look at you. Damn, you're hot." Before she had a chance to ask what he was doing, she felt it.

Along the length of her body, she could feel nerves lighting up, gooseflesh popping up here and there, and her nipples hardened as he stroked her clit. "Play with your nips, babe. I wanna watch." As soon as she pinched and pulled them, she heard him groan. "Oh, god, yeah. Just like that. Fuck, I want you so bad, girl. Come for me, babe. Just turn loose. Come on. I know you can. You want it. I know you want it. You want this red-hot cock pounding up in you, don't you? Say it."

"I do. God, I want you to fuck me, Michael. Please?"

"Not until you come. You've gotta—"

"Damn!" she screamed, her back arching and head thrown back, lifting her torso toward the ceiling. Fisting the sheets above her head, she rocked against him as he drove her on. "Please, Michael, stop. Babe, stop! No more! No more!"

"Yes, more. Another two minutes more."

"God, Michael, please!"

"Come on, one more time, Samara. I know you can do it."

"I can't! I can't! Oh, please, please, please ... Gaaaaaaaahhh!" The second orgasm hit and she shook uncontrollably, still clutching the sheets in her fists. "Michael, please! Oh, god, no more! No more!" And he stopped.

There was no time to catch her breath before he pulled her up to sitting, then scooted down and rolled them until she was on her back. Lips pressed against her neck, he murmured, "God, I wanna fuck you so hard."

"I want you to! Please, baby? Please?"

He drew back slowly, then slammed into her. "Ohhhh, damn. I'm gonna take care of you, baby. My cock is gonna make you the happiest woman in five counties." His hands closed around her ankles as he leaned back, and he drew her legs up, pressed them together, and pushed them up toward the headboard. Her back bowed and her ass lifted up off the bed a good two inches. "You okay?"

"Yeah, but what—"

"Just hang on." Then he drew back and rammed her again.

The head of his shaft rubbed across the little ridged spot inside her and she thought she'd come undone. All she could growl out was, "Fuuuuuuck. Oh, god. Oh, god. What are ... Oh, god. Fuck, fuck, fuck, *fuck*!" Everything inside her clenched and her belly spasmed. "Fu-u-u-u-uck, baby. Oh, fuck." Reaching for him was pointless, and she gripped the headboard as he powered into her over and over.

Two more orgasms and he finally emptied into her. That was the moment she realized something. "Fuck, Michael, you forgot to wear a condom."

"You're on the pill, right?"

"Yeah, but nothing is—"

"Samara." She stopped babbling and watched his face. "I told you that I love you. If you were to get pregnant, do you have any idea how happy I'd be?"

"Well, I wouldn't be very happy. It would probably cost me my job."

"No. It would not. Carter would work with you. And it's not like you'd be alone."

"Yeah, but I'm not ready to—"

"I get it. I'm really not either, but if it happens, I'm not going to be unhappy about it. I'll just be more careful from now on, okay? And I'm sorry. I just kinda got lost in the, well, you know." He dropped to the mattress beside her and lay there, panting. "I think you almost killed me."

"*I* almost killed *you*? I thought you were going to send my head through the headboard!"

"But you gotta admit," he said with a tweak to her nipple, "that it was pretty great."

"No. It was very great. And you do make me feel like a queen." Then she laughed. "Even if my throne is your dick."

"Especially if your throne is my dick." He reached for her, and that was all she wanted, to be wrapped in his arms.

"I love you, baby."

"I love you too. So here comes the hard part."

She drew her head back and stared into his eyes. "What's the hard part?"

"We're gonna have to go see my mother."

The sound of her eyes rolling could've been heard five miles away. "Oh, damn. I was hoping that day would *never* come."

"Well, I really do think we've got to do it. She's going to get wind of us and if I haven't told her, that's going to make everything ten times worse."

"Do you think she'll like me?"

Michael lay there, and his silence made her nervous. When he did speak, it was every bit as bad as she'd been afraid it would be. "Actually, I think it's going to go something like this. I take you over there. She's going to have a little trouble talking for the first two minutes because she'll be so shocked. Then she'll seem to get over it, but it'll just be because she's found the little slot she needs to put her personality in to make us both feel like everything's okay. She'll probably hug you when we leave."

"Don't tell me. And then you'll get the phone call."

"Exactly. And I'll have to hear about how I could certainly find a white girl who'd have me, and why am I with a black woman anyway, and am I sure I want to do this, and how she hopes you understand how lucky you are to have me, a white man who'll take care of you."

"Please tell me you're joking."

"Nope. I can hear it now. Oh, and then she'll ask me if I realize how much trouble our children might have because they're mixed race, as the people around here say."

"Not that."

"Yeah. Don't take it personally. Every white mother of a son in this town would have the same damn reaction. I'm just warning you in advance so you know what to expect."

"Great. I get to defend myself against—"

"Oh, no. You won't. Because she'll never say anything to your face. She'll just say it all to me behind your back. To your face, she'll be sweet as pie."

"Great."

"But I'm also telling you this so you know that nothing she says will sway me. I don't give a damn what she thinks. I love you, and that's all that really matters."

"I love you too. As long as I know you love me, I can handle it."

"I'll always have your back, babe, when it comes to my mother or anybody else in this town who gives you trouble. If they do it once and I find out, they'll never do it again."

He really meant it. She could tell. "I believe you," she whispered into his skin, then pinched his nipple.

"That's gonna get you in trouble," he warned and pinched hers.

"I want it to get me some more cock."

"Not tonight. Go to the bathroom. Don't want any honeymoon cystitis going on here."

She couldn't believe what he'd said. "How do you know about that?"

"Quit asking questions and just go to the bathroom so I can have a turn."

"Gah. Okay. Bossy."

"That's me. The boss." That made her laugh. He might be her boss at work, but he made her feel like an equal everywhere else, and that was surely because he thought of her as one.

She crawled to the edge of the bed and stood, but before she left the room, she leaned over and kissed him. "I love you, boss man."

"I love you too, beautiful girl. Go. Get finished. I'm tired and tomorrow's going to be a long day."

When she was finished, he went in, and she lay there while he was gone, thinking about what had just taken place. Michael looked meek and shy most of the time, but he was one helluva fuck, and she'd hit the motherlode with him. If a guy could be the whole enchilada, he was definitely a whole plateful of them.

His arms felt good around her as they snuggled there in

her bed, and she smiled. It was hard to believe she could possibly be happier anywhere than she was in his arms. "Michael?"

"Yeah, babe?"

"I love you."

"Oh, baby, I love you too. I can't wait to see what morning brings because I know it'll be another day that I can spend with you."

Samara felt the same way. The man holding her was the one she wanted holding her when she was eighty. A lifetime with Michael wouldn't be long enough. But it was what she wanted more than anything.

CHAPTER 8

Samara was planning to work from home again, so he told her that the guys would be driving by from time to time, and he made her promise that if she went anywhere, she'd let him know. She said her plan was to visit at least two of the rape victims, and she told him which two, so he felt good about that.

His desk was fairly clear, so he worked on the few things he had lying there and wondered where Carter was. He was usually there bright and early, but he hadn't been in as far as Michael knew, unless he'd been there even earlier.

Anand had been out at the front desk all morning, answering the phones and filling out some reports from activity he'd had the day before, when Michael's desk phone came to life. He hit the speaker and said, "Yeah."

"It's Sheriff Melton on line one for you."

"Thanks, Chadha." He left the speaker on and pushed the button. "Hey, sheriff!"

"You got me on speaker?"

"Yeah."

"Pick up the receiver."

Michael did as he was told. "Okay."

"Listen, Cruz will be here this afternoon. I don't know what he's up to, but he wants to talk to us before he does whatever it is."

"Okay. So what are we—"

"I told him to let me know when he passes Exit 40 and we'll meet him at Coach House for drinks. We need to be plainclothes. Whatever it is, I think he doesn't want us to draw attention to ourselves, and he doesn't want to be at the office."

"Got it. When he calls, ask if he's eaten and if he hasn't, we can get some appetizers or dinner or something."

"Sounds good. You got clothes with you?" Carter asked.

"Yeah."

"Okay. I do too. I'll be there in a bit, but don't say anything about what we're doing. The less the other guys know, the better off we all are."

"Agreed. Thanks."

"You bet. See you shortly."

Michael sat there, trying to figure out what was going on. It wasn't that he didn't trust Carter, because he did, implicitly. He was just curious to see what an FBI agent came up with that they hadn't.

A feminine voice cut into his thoughts and in seconds, he was at the front desk. "What are you doing here? I thought you were going to do interviews."

"I was supposed to get a picture for them to look at and I forgot."

"Oh, yeah. Come on back and I'll get that for you." As soon as they stepped through his doorway, he closed the door. "I'm so sorry. I totally forgot to print that for you."

"That's okay. Gives me an excuse to see you." She leaned across his desk and gave him a little kiss as he typed away on the keyboard.

"Okay. Here's one … Wait! This is perfect!" He spun the screen and pointed. It was Stadler in his KSP uniform, and he saw Samara recoil. "I'm sorry, baby, but really, don't you think it would help for them to see him in his uniform?"

"Not if they didn't know he was a cop."

"So you think he wasn't in uniform when—"

"I think it's entirely possible that he wasn't, but he showed them his credentials and told them he was a cop. They wouldn't have had enough presence of mind to notice where he served, just that the credentials looked legit and it made them afraid."

"True. You may very well be right. Okay, how about this one?" It was a picture from his driver's license.

"Yeah. That's good." Michael printed it off, but before he handed it to her, he pulled a manila envelope from his desk drawer and slipped it inside. "Thanks. I really don't want to have to look at him all afternoon."

"Don't blame you one bit. So you be careful. We're meeting with Cruz tonight, and we're doing it at Coach House. I'm not sure what's going on, but he wants to talk to us about something privately and plainclothes, so I don't know when I'll be finished."

"I'll text you when I'm home so you'll know."

"Okay, and I'll try to let you know by then what's

going on and when you can expect me. And I'll bring you dinner if you want."

"Sounds good! Okay. Before you say it, I'll be careful." She leaned across the desk again, but that wasn't good enough for Michael.

He stood, walked around the desk, and wrapped his arms around her, then planted a solid kiss on her lips. "I know you'll be careful. Just be extra careful for me."

"Will do." She opened the door. "Thanks, sir."

"You're welcome, Futrell. Be safe out there."

"Always, sir," she called back as she headed up the hallway, and he heard the front door close behind her.

Anand was in his doorway almost instantly. "This came for you. He said to make sure you got it immediately."

"Thanks, Chadha." In the upper left-hand corner of the envelope was a printed address, the one for the medical examiner. It briefly passed through his mind to wait until Carter got there, but he couldn't. He had to know.

The report was pretty thorough. There had been enough DNA to use for a comparison, but they had nothing to compare it to, although it did confirm that it was a female. The remains were so damaged that dental records weren't even of any use. They'd also managed to run some testing on the marrow, so he went down the list.

There were no illicit drugs of any kind in the victim's system. No prescription medications either. He'd never realized how much they could tell about a person by testing their marrow, but there were a lot of things. Finally, he got to the bottom where all of the testing levels were explained, and he shook his head.

Most values indicate this individual was not under the

influence of any type of mind-altering drug at the time of death. Note the HCG levels, which indicate a high probability that the victim was pregnant.

Michael sat down hard in his chair and closed his eyes. Whoever she was, she was indeed pregnant. He'd been afraid of that ever since he found the test in the trash, and that made for a motive if Stadler wasn't pleased. Then he flipped to the very last page where he knew he'd find what he was looking for.

There was a drawing of a person there, the outline with minimal details in both front and back views. Numerous lines pointed to various things on the skeleton, such as a previously broken ankle and a plate in the woman's arm, probably from a car accident, based on the area of the break. But several were truly of interest. One was labeled *GSW1* and another was *GSW2*. He dropped his eyes straight to the bottom of the report.

GSW1 nick on rib #4, left side of ribcage body in intercostal space between 4th and 5th levels consistent with .45 caliber projectile. Trajectory indicates it passed from that position through the left scapula, most likely passing through the heart muscle.

GSW2 through the left scapula consistent with a .45 caliber projectile, secondary to GSW1.

FINDING:

PRIMARY COD: GSW causing cardiac failure, with fire damage to body postmortem.

Just as they'd thought. Whoever she was, she'd been shot.

It was time. Michael did a little digging and found out where she worked on the army base. When he finally found the right department, a voice answered, "Pre-op, Annette speaking."

"Annette, this is Trigg County Chief Deputy Michael Edwards. I understand that you have an employee there by the name of Glenna Stadler."

"Yes, sir."

"Could I speak with her, please?"

"Could you hold just a moment, sir?"

"Sure."

Cheesy hold music played, and then a voice said, "This is Janice Moore. I'm the nursing supervisor on this unit. May I help you?"

"Yes, ma'am, I'm Trigg County Chief Deputy Michael Edwards. I understand that you have an employee there named Glenna Stadler?"

"Is there something wrong?"

"This is just a welfare check, ma'am."

There was silence for a few seconds, and he was sure he heard a door close. The other end of the phone was much quieter when the woman said, "I'm so glad you called. I'm a little worried."

There was no doubt in his mind what she was going to say next. "About Mrs. Stadler?"

"Yes, sir. She hasn't been to work since Saturday night. We've called, but we haven't gotten an answer."

"Did you try reaching her family?"

"The only emergency number we have is for her husband, and he hasn't returned our calls."

"Are you calling her cell?"

"Yes, sir."

"Can you give me that number, please?"

"Sure." The woman read it off and then asked, "Is everything okay?"

"Ma'am, I don't know if you know this, but their house burned on Sunday night."

"What? No! Was there anyone in it?"

"I'm sorry, ma'am. I'm not at liberty to say. It's an ongoing investigation. Has she said anything to anyone at work about any problems or issues at home or with anyone else?"

The woman let out a little huff. "Nobody except that asshole husband of hers. She came in several times with her wrists bruised. I don't know what that guy's problem is, and to think he's a state trooper. I'm sorry, sir, but that kind of individual does absolutely nothing to inspire confidence in the public regarding your positions."

"Yes, ma'am, and I'm sorry for that. But thank you for speaking with me. Is there a better number to reach you at, in case I have more questions or have news for you?"

"Yes, sir." Janice gave him another number. "That's my personal cell."

"Thank you very much."

"And your name again?"

"Michael Edwards. I'm the chief deputy at Trigg County Sheriff's Department. My number is …" He recited it slowly so she could write it down. "If you think of anything else, please give me a call."

"I will. Thank you for calling. We're all wondering what's going on."

"So are we, ma'am. Thanks again." No surprise there. It was exactly as he thought. Then another thought crossed his mind, and he punched some numbers into his phone.

"Hey!"

"Hey yourself. I've got a question for you."

"Okay."

"We got the medical examiner's report."

"Oh? And what did it say?" Carter asked.

"It was definitely a woman. Definitely pregnant. And definitely dead before the fire."

"Cause of death?"

"Gunshot wound."

"Just as we thought."

"Exactly. So I've been trying to think of a way to get some DNA from one of Glenna's relatives, but I have no idea how we're going to do that without spilling the beans."

"Then spill the beans. Maybe they'll pressure Stadler and he'll crack."

"Okay. Just wanted to run it by you before I went."

"You know I'll back whatever you want to do, Michael. I've got your six."

"And I've always got yours. Thanks, Carter. I'm on it."

"Let me know." And the call ended.

He gathered up the things he thought he needed, then headed out. "Going to talk to the family of a suspected victim. I'll be back as soon as I can get back."

"Gotcha. Anything you need me to do while you're gone?"

"Yeah. Call the cleaning service and ask them why our bathrooms look like they haven't been touched in three weeks. If you ask them the right questions, they'll fold and come clean them this afternoon. Their number is on the board outside Sheriff Melton's office."

"Will do."

"Thanks, Chadha. Be back as soon as I can."

By the time he reached the SUV's door, he'd already hit the remote start and it was ready to roll. Glenna's family owned a small vineyard out near the old winery, and he'd loved it there when they were dating. He'd loved her parents too. They'd been devastated when Glenna dumped him, and he couldn't wait to see them.

The house looked exactly the same from the outside, so he parked on the circular drive and climbed the big stone front steps. It was an old farmhouse that dated back to the late eighteen hundreds, with a high porch and tall columns. As soon as he pushed the doorbell button, a voice came through. "Hello. Who is it?"

"Is this Mrs. Thomas?"

"Yes it is. Can I help you?"

"Norma, it's Michael Edwards. Could we talk for a minute, please?"

She didn't answer, and he didn't know whether to stand there or leave when the door opened. "Oh, Michael! It's so good to see you, honey!" There was no opportunity to so much as move before she launched herself at him and hugged him tightly. That was when he noticed.

She was wearing a turban. And he knew what that meant.

"Hi, Norma! Good to see you too."

"Oh, Michael, we've missed you! Come in, come in! Would you like something to drink?"

"You know, that would be nice, but how 'bout if I get it so you can sit down?"

"You always were such a gentleman. I think I'd like a lemon-lime soda."

"Coming right up." Michael headed through the house he'd spent so many hours in and walked into a kitchen he almost didn't recognize. "Wow! You've completely redone the kitchen. It looks great." That wasn't an exaggeration. A renovation like that had cost them at least his entire year's pay.

"It needed it. It was definitely time." By the time he returned, she'd scooted back into the sofa and drawn her legs up on it. "I'm so glad to see you. Tell me, how are you doing? You're a deputy now?"

"Chief deputy. Carter Melton is my boss."

"I've met Carter. Such a nice man, and that sweet little baby they adopted. What's her name? Angela?"

"It's actually Angel. They got her right before Christmas year before last."

"Oh! Well, she's adorable, and his wife is very pretty. Shame about her niece."

"Yes, it was. So how are you?"

"Pretty good, I suppose. It was in remission, and now it's back. Damn breast cancer. You'd think by now they could cure it."

"You'd think. And how's Glen?" Glenna's dad had always liked him.

"He's doing pretty good. Fell a few months ago and twisted his ankle. He's still nursing it, but I think it's okay."

"Good. Is he here by any chance? I'd love to see him."

"I wish he was. He'd love to see you too. He's at the garden center, getting topsoil. Flower bed out back keeps washing out."

"Oh, I'm sure he can figure out how to stop that. He's a pretty handy guy."

"You always were too! And always so kind and caring. Sure nothing like that no-good son-in-law of ours. What a piece of shit." It took everything he had not to laugh out loud. Norma never said anything like that, so she had to really hate Stadler. If he was right, she was going to hate him a whole lot more very soon.

"So you know about their house?" She gave him a curious stare. "Sunday night?"

"I have no idea what you're talking about."

"You haven't talked to Glenna?"

"No. We don't talk much anymore," she huffed.

Boy, there's gonna be a whole lot of regret in this house very soon, he thought. "Their house burned Sunday night."

"What? Are you serious? And she didn't call me? I can't believe it! I mean, I know she's mad that we don't like Alex, but that's no excuse for not at least calling us and telling us that! Where are they staying?"

"I have no idea. When was the last time you talked to her?"

"Ummm, let me think … Maybe last month? She called to tell me that she got a promotion at work to the surgical team."

Michael made a mental note of that. *So she hadn't worked in that position very long. Good information to have.* "So you haven't heard from her lately?"

"No. Is something wrong?" She stopped for a few seconds, then asked, "Has that asshole done something?" He knew she wasn't talking about Glenna; it was Alex she was referring to.

"We don't know for sure, Norma. I talked to Alex and he said she was on an Alaskan cruise."

"An Alaskan cruise? Seriously?"

"Yes. With her sister." And he waited for the response he knew he was going to get.

Norma's face clouded over immediately. "That lying son of a bitch."

"Yeah. That's what we thought too. I called her work. She hasn't been there since Saturday night."

The look of anger on Norma's face instantly turned to fear. "Oh, no. What has he done?"

Michael stopped before he spoke. Maybe he should wait for Glen to get back. "I have some information for you, but I'd really like to wait until Glen gets here."

Somewhere outside, he heard a car door close. "Oh, I bet that's him now." Michael checked out the back window and sure enough, Glen was coming up the back porch stairs.

"Whose cruiser is that … Michael!" Hand outstretched, the man made a beeline for Michael, so the younger man stood and shook his hand. "It's so good to see you, son!" Glen's free hand grasped their clasped ones, and Michael thought about how good it was to see them both, even if it was for a shitty reason. "What brings you here?"

Before Michael could answer, Norma blurted out, "Oh, Glen, I think that asshole son-in-law of ours has done something horrible. Michael said their house burned down Sunday night, and Glenna hasn't been at work since Saturday."

Glen sat down heavily next to his wife and rested a hand on her knee. "I was afraid something like this would happen. Do you know where she is?"

Before he could answer, Norma piped up again. "Alex told Michael she's on an Alaskan cruise." When Glen stared at her, she added, "With her *sister*."

"What the hell? What's wrong with him?"

Michael looked straight at the two of them. "Far more

than you could ever imagine. Have you talked to Glenna lately?" Glen said nothing, but his eyes gave him away. "Glen, if you know something, I really need to know."

"She called me a couple of weeks ago. Said he'd roughed her up and bruised her wrists." That was information Michael had been given by the nursing supervisor, so it was confirmed by Glen. "I told her she needed to leave that sumbitch, but she loved him. Why I'll never know. I wish she'd stayed with you. We've missed you so much."

"I've missed you guys too. So there's something I need to tell you, and I don't want to, but I feel I have to."

Glen's voice was barely more than a whisper. "We already know what you're going to say. You're going to say he's killed Glenna, aren't you?"

"We don't know that for sure. But what we do know is that there was a body found in the burned portion of the house. The medical examiner's report says it was female. Dental records were of no use. The fire burned really hot because there was some kind of accelerant used."

"So somebody set the fire," Norma whispered.

"Yes, ma'am. But the person in the fire was already dead. The coroner's report said it was due to a gunshot wound." Norma gasped, and he felt sorry for both of them. "They did get enough DNA from the bone marrow to know a couple of things." He steeled himself for what he knew was about to happen. "The first is that there were no drugs in the person's system, so they were probably shot outright, and if the medical examiner is correct, it was instantaneous. There was no suffering."

"Oh, thank god. Was there anything else?" Glen asked.

"Yes, one other thing. Based on hormone levels, the person was most likely pregnant."

Norma dissolved into tears and Michael felt horrible. There was nothing he could say or do that would make things better for them. Their only daughter was dead. They'd already sensed it, from what he could tell, and yet they'd hoped against hope that she was fine. Glen was doing a good job of being strong for her, but Michael could tell he was crumbling too. "Is there anything we can do?" Glenna's father asked.

"Yes. Please. We need a DNA sample from both of you so the medical examiner can compare it to the DNA they extracted from the bone marrow. We'd like to be able to positively identify the person. Would you be willing to give us a sample?"

Norma nodded. "Absolutely. Even if it's not Glenna, someone's family needs closure, and that's our duty as Christians."

"Yes, ma'am. I've got a couple of kits in my cruiser. I can go get them and we can do it right now."

"Is there a needle?" Norma asked.

"No. It's a swab on the inside of your cheek. It'll only take a second. We do them all the time. I'll be right back." As quickly as he could, he headed to the SUV, pulled out his go bag, got two of the test kits, and turned to go back. Just as he did, a text came in on his phone, so he checked.

Real interesting stuff.

He shot a quick one back to her.

Yeah. I'm at Glenna's parents' house. Real, real interesting stuff.

She sent one back immediately.

I'm finished with first interview. I won't do second until I hear from you. Call me plz.

He smiled.

Will do. Love you.

He got a smiley face and a heart back, and that made him smile even wider. But he wiped it off his face before he stepped back inside. Glen and Norma were speaking in soft, quiet tones, his comforting and hers grief-stricken. "Okay, this is all they are. I can do them, or I can tell you how to do them and you can—"

"I'd rather you did them. I'm afraid I wouldn't do it right," Norma said, sniffling.

"Sure. It'll only take a second. Let me put your names on the little packets so we know whose is whose." He wrote her name on the first one, then broke it open and pulled out a swab. "Okay, open your mouth. I'll take it from inside your cheek. We'll do two each in case one of them doesn't work correctly." It only took him a few seconds to swab hers, then he turned to Glen. "Okay, here we go." Once he'd swabbed Glen's cheeks, he put the swabs in the little vials, broke the sticks off, and slipped them into the appropriate packets. "There we go. I'll take these to the medical examiner and they'll have the results in a day or two, hopefully."

"Is there anything else you can think of that we can do?"

"No, sir, except to let me know if Stadler contacts you and what he says. I'd be most interested to know. But for your own safety, I wouldn't contact him. Leave him alone. There's a lot going on that you don't know about, and you could be in danger if he thinks you know something that would incriminate him."

"Okay. We won't. And if he calls, we'll give you a call immediately," Glen said.

Michael nodded. "Day or night. Doesn't matter. I'm always glad to talk to you."

Norma's eyes were glittering with tears. "Michael, thank you so much for coming to talk to us. I really appreciate it. But I think I need to go lie down. I'm not feeling very well."

"Of course, of course. And I'm sorry that we had to see each other again under these kinds of circumstances, but seriously, I love you guys and if I can do anything to help you in any way, please let me know. I'll let myself out. Glen, good to see you again."

"You too, son. Take care of yourself and tell Marjorie we said hello, please."

"Will do. Thanks again." It was hard to leave, seeing them in that much pain and wanting so badly to do something to help, but there was nothing left for him to do.

When he got out on the highway, he pressed his phone into the dash-mounted holder and used his hands-free system to call Samara. She answered with a bright, "Hey, babe!"

"Hey."

"What's wrong? You sound, I dunno, upset or something."

"We got the medical examiner's report back. I'm about ninety-nine point nine percent sure it's Glenna. Gunshot wound. And she was pregnant."

"Damn. You got it just now?"

"No. I just left her parents' house. Babe, it was horrible. Her mother's cancer is back and she looks terrible. And her dad … He was so sad. They hadn't had much contact with her because they despise Stadler."

"Well, that's certainly one thing everyone who knows him seems to have in common."

"Did you find out anything?"

"I went to talk to one of the victims. Kandy Sykes out on Pine Cone Trail. She was very tight-lipped, said she couldn't remember much, never really saw his face. And then I took out the pic."

"And?"

"The look on her face totally gave her away. She knows it was him, but she's not going to talk. Still, I have the satisfaction of knowing that I'm on the right track."

"You definitely are. Going to another one?"

"In just a few minutes. Almost there now. Where are you next?"

"I'm going back to the office. I left Chadha there alone, so I think I probably should be there."

"Probably. Okay, I'm gonna get going. Let me know if you know anything else."

"Will do. Love you, babe."

"Love you too. Bye."

Michael hit the END button on the steering wheel and thought about her smile and those beautiful, dark eyes. He'd much rather be sitting beside her right that minute, but he had a job to do, and so did she.

But he'd be glad when that particular case was over.

"Hi. I'm Detective Futrell. We spoke on the phone?"

The young woman seemed to fold in on herself. "Yes, ma'am, but I don't know what to tell you."

"Could I come in for just a few minutes? I promise I

won't take up much of your time. I just want to go over your statement and see if everything is correct. That's all."

"Sure. I guess. Come on in." She held the door open and Samara walked into a house that looked like it was trapped in the nineteen sixties. Worn floral linoleum covered the floors, and the avocado green and harvest gold plaid sofa had seen better days.

The girl motioned for her to sit in a chair adjacent to the sofa, so she took a seat and pulled the folder from her bag. Then she took out a sheet of paper. "Your name is Diedra Bradley, correct?"

"Yes, ma'am."

"And the assault took place here on Crooked Creek Drive?"

"Yes, ma'am. I was coming in from work and he came up behind me. I never saw his face."

"Says here that it was eleven fifteen at night."

"Yes, ma'am."

"So what do you remember?"

"I remember him slapping me around and holding me down. I remember that it hurt, and I screamed but nobody could hear me. I remember when he finished, he told me if I ever told anybody, he'd kill me."

"And your mother was the one who reported the assault, correct?"

"Yes, ma'am."

"Could I talk to her?"

"She passed last year."

"Oh, I'm so sorry for your loss."

"Thanks."

"This says you were … twenty-three at the time."

"Yes, ma'am."

"And you never saw his face?"

"No, ma'am."

"So it couldn't have been this man." She whipped out the pic of Stadler and placed it on the coffee table.

The girl visibly flinched. "Uh, no. No, that couldn't be him."

"But you said you couldn't see him."

"No, ma'am."

"So how do you know that's not him?"

"I don't. I guess … That's not him," she repeated.

"I see. Did you know the same man who assaulted you seems to have assaulted six other young women in the area?"

Her eyes went wide. "Before or after?"

"Actually, you were only the second of seven we had reported."

"So one before me and some after me?"

"Yes."

"That means I couldn't have helped the one before me."

Yep. She knows it was him. "No. Not the one before you. But you could help all of them now."

"I can't. I didn't really see him." Diedra was trying to be cool, but her hands were visibly shaking.

"Okay, well, that's all the questions I've got for you. If you think of anything else that might help us catch him, here's my card." She handed the girl one of her business cards and then stood. "And thanks again. I appreciate it."

"You're welcome."

"You take care."

"Yes, ma'am. Thank you."

Samara turned when she got to her car and looked. The

girl had closed and locked the door instantly as she'd walked out of it. She almost felt like there was no point in talking to the other five women, but every one of them that she interviewed might get her closer to some kind of evidence that would put him away.

With another look at her watch, she decided to go to a third victim's home to interview her. It was still early in the afternoon and Michael was going with Carter and the guy from Texas later. She shot Michael a quick text.

Two down, five to go.

Three little dots wiggled, and then her phone pinged.

How'd it go?

Samara rolled her eyes.

Same old same old.

More wiggling dots and another ping.

Sorry, babe. Love you.

It was so good to see that.

Love you too.

With a look at her mapping program, she set out to the third interview. All she needed was one piece of evidence that she could use to bring him in. Would she ever get it?

It didn't hurt to hope.

CHAPTER 9

CARTER HAD CALLED to say he'd be there in twenty minutes when Michael's phone rang again, and he smiled when he saw her name. "Hey, babe."

"Hi. Get anything else done?"

"Not really. Made a copy of the report to give to Cruz and Carter and highlighted the information I thought was important. Figured they could look at it while we talked."

"That's a good idea."

There was a sound in her voice that he hadn't heard before. "You okay?"

"Yes. No. I dunno. This is exhausting. Why is this so exhausting?"

"Because there's a personal emotional component to it that you haven't had on other cases."

"Yeah, I guess that's true."

"That's why I sounded the way I did earlier when I was at the Thomas' house."

"Were they angry?"

"No. Matter of fact, they were really glad to see me. I

loved them and they loved me. We thought we were going to be family until Stadler inserted himself into the picture. And boy, let me tell you, they have *nothing* good to say about him. Nothing. They hated him before, and they really hate him now."

"I bet. I just stepped inside, so I'm going to take a quick shower and lie down. Maybe take a nap. I dunno. I'm just wrung out."

"I think that's a good idea. Make sure to lock everything up and keep your phone close by."

"I will. I love you."

Hearing those words made his heart skip a couple of beats. "I love you too, and I miss you."

"Miss you too. Call me and I'll tell you what to bring to me."

"I will. Talk to you in a bit. Bye, babe."

"Bye."

Ten minutes later, Carter came in wearing street clothes. "Just heard from Cruz. He's about fifteen minutes out. Go change."

"Yep. Going." He headed to their small locker room, changed into jeans and a tee with a sport coat over it, and put on his athletic shoes. As soon as he checked his backup weapon at his ankle, he clipped his badge to the inside breast pocket of the jacket and straightened himself up. He looked like a guy going to have drinks with his buddies, and that was the look he was going for.

They drove separately, and he pulled his dark green Ram pickup in beside Carter's Ford F150. The copies of the ME's report were folded and slipped into an inside jacket pocket, so anyone watching them walk in thought they were just buddies out for a pleasant evening.

Tasha was doing hostess duty that evening, so Carter asked her for a booth in the back and told her there would be a tall man with a Texas drawl looking for them. They'd been shooting the shit for about five minutes when Cruz walked in, and he spotted Carter almost immediately.

"Hey, good to see you!" Carter said as soon as the man stepped up to the table, and they shook hands with a one-armed hug.

The Texan grinned. "Good to see you too."

Michael had slid out of the booth and was standing as Cruz turned to him and smiled. "Michael! Good to see you!"

"And you too." Cruz greeted him the exact same way he had Carter, and Michael felt like he was finally a member of whatever club he'd been missing out on.

"Congrats on the promotion!"

"Thanks. Have a seat." He turned to find Lindsey at the next table. "Hey, Linds, can you get our friend here a drink?"

The girl looked positively starstruck as she made her way to the table. "I sure can! So what'll it be, darlin'?"

Cruz seemed a little taken aback, and Michael almost laughed. "Uhhh, you got Miller on draft?"

"Yes, sweetie, sure do. Tall one?"

"Sure. Why not. Thanks."

"You're very, very welcome," she said and wiggled her ass just a little as she headed toward the bar.

One of Cruz's eyebrows shot up. "What the hell was that?"

Michael rolled his eyes. "We call it desperation."

The Texan shook his head. "Are things that tough for the women around here? Because I'm pretty sure if I asked that girl to go back to my hotel room with me, she'd ride me piggyback all the way there."

Carter snorted. "There's little doubt in my mind."

"That should be a good thing for you, though, right?" Cruz asked Michael.

"Nope. I have somebody."

"No! Who is it?"

The proud sheriff papa was grinning. "I hired him a girlfriend!"

"That sounds so wrong," Michael said with a frown.

"Sounds like something KDCI needs to investigate," Cruz answered, laughing.

The three men chatted for a while until their food came. "Okay, brought you guys something." Michael pulled the papers out of his jacket pocket and handed a packet to each of them. "I highlighted everything very important. And I've got some new information as of this afternoon."

"Do tell," Carter said as he cut his steak.

Michael filled them in on the call to Glenna's work and to the things he'd learned from her parents. "I know none of this is enough to do anything with him, but we've got to find something. There's got to be some way to take him down."

"Okay, so what am I missing here?" Cruz sat back in his chair. "There's more here than I'm hearing."

"Tell him," Carter said as he glared at Michael.

"I didn't get her permission and I really think—"

"Okay, look." Carter leaned in, his forearms on the table. "Cruz isn't going to betray your trust or hers, but he wants to help us, and he needs all the information. This is serious, Michael. You know that. If he hurts her, you're going to wish you'd told him—"

"If who hurts whom?" Cruz asked, stopping the conversation cold.

It was put up or shut up time, and Michael knew he had to do it. He didn't want to. "Hang on just a second, okay?" In a flash, he sent a text to Samara.

Babe, I'm with Cruz. I have to tell him. If he's going to help us, he needs all the details. But I won't tell him if you say no. It's up to you.

He waited, and in a couple of seconds, he got his answer.

I trust you. And I trust Carter. I haven't even met Cruz, but if you guys trust him, I trust him too. Just make sure he knows that this isn't something I'd want many people to know.

That hurt his heart, so he shot another one back to her.

I would never tell anybody anything if I thought they'd hurt you with it. I love you and I wouldn't do that to you. And trust me, Cruz doesn't want to hurt you either.

All he got back was a thumbs-up emoji. He sighed out a long breath, then launched into the story of Stadler and all the shit he'd been up to for years.

When he finished, Cruz sat there, dumbstruck. "I know it's a lot to take in, but it's all very true," Carter said, glancing at Michael. The younger man nodded in agreement.

Cruz sucked in a heavy breath, blew it out from between pursed lips, and handed Michael a sliver of hope. "I'm not sure how much I can help you, but I know a couple of people who can. Are you open to bringing them into this?"

Michael barely let him get the sentence out before he barked, "Do you trust them?" He knew he sounded cross, but he didn't care. It was Samara's life they were talking about, and he had to be sure.

Cruz didn't seem the least bit offended. "I wouldn't suggest them if I didn't. One of them I know personally, and I know he's straight as an arrow. The other is someone my friend Conor knows, and I've heard him talk about the guy, how great he is, how trustworthy he is, and better yet, how dog on a bone he is when he's trying to do or find something or someone. The guy never gives up. And both of these men are in unique positions to help you all. Are you willing to take that leap?"

Michael sat there, thinking. They were up against a wall and time was running out. When Stadler found out Samara had been checking up on the old cases, he'd be furious, and there was no telling what he might do. Matter of fact, Michael was pretty sure it would be an almost-fatal attempt at best. A voice pierced his thoughts as Carter whispered, "Michael? Michael, I know this is hard, and I know you care about her—"

"No, Carter. I don't just care about her. I love her and she loves me. I can't do anything that will put her at more risk."

"Honestly, son, I think you've run out of options. This may be our best chance to get this guy gone."

"He's right, Michael." Cruz leveled his gaze with Michael's. "You want to give her the absolute best possible chance? This is your opportunity. Say the word and I'll make it happen."

For the first time, he knew how a cornered animal felt. His heart was pounding and his palms were sweating. He was terrified. What if he made the wrong decision? What would Samara do if it was him instead of her?

He knew exactly what she'd do. "Set it in motion. The sooner, the better. And when can we meet these guys?"

Cruz's smile was gentle. "I had a feeling we'd need them, so I already asked them to be on standby. I can get them in here tomorrow morning if that's what you want."

Michael nodded. "Let's do this thing." In twenty-four hours, he'd have a very good idea if he'd done what he needed to do or if he'd signed her death warrant. And if anything happened to her, they might as well kill him too.

He didn't want to live without her.

———

THE ALARM CLOCK HAD BARELY BEEN SHUT OFF WHEN Michael's phone pinged. He opened his social media messaging app to find a message from Cruz in a group chat that included Carter.

Can you guys meet in Hopkinsville?

Michael waited, but when Carter didn't answer, he did.

Don't know about Carter, but I can.

Another one came in immediately.

We need her there too.

Michael didn't hesitate.

I'll have to ask her.

There was no doubt in his mind that she'd balk, but he knew why they needed to talk to her. They considered him reliable, and yet it would be hearsay until she spoke up. The water had been turned off in the shower, so he called out, "Samara?"

"Yeah, babe?"

Here we go, he told himself. "Uh, Cruz wants us to meet him in Hopkinsville."

"So you gonna go? Can Carter go?" She didn't understand.

"He wants you to come."

The towel was barely wrapped around her when she stepped out of the bathroom. "Uh, no. I really don't want to."

"Babe, they're talking to me and getting it secondhand. You know how that is. They need to hear it from you, and you've been working on these other assaults, so that will help. I haven't been there for the interviews, but you have. There could be some little something that you heard or could pass on that would answer a question you didn't even realize needed asking. Please. If we don't get some help, I'm …" And he stopped.

She tipped her head. "You're what?"

Michael dipped his head and stood there, his chin resting on the depression in his clavicle. It took him a few seconds to quiet the screaming in his head so that he could finally give it voice. "I'm scared."

His phone pinged again, and that time, it was Carter.

I'm all in. Tell us when and where. Michael, is Samara coming?

"Carter wants to know if you're coming."

She stood there, and he could see the war going on in her head. She finally let out a deep sigh. "Yeah, okay. Will I have time to do one more interview before we go?"

"I have no idea, but let me tell them you want to do that." He messaged Carter and Cruz, and they both gave him a thumbs-up. "They're good with it."

"Okay. I need to get moving then." As she dressed, he

pulled out what he'd need after his shower and headed that direction.

The water was still running when he heard her say, "I'm going."

"Come kiss me goodbye," he called out.

Her eyes smiled up at him when she pulled the shower curtain open just enough for her face to show. "Okay. Wish I could get in there with you."

"You could."

"Nope. Duty calls." Leaning in ever so slightly, she gave him a sweet kiss on the lips. "And before you say it, I will."

"Say what?"

She let out a laugh like wind chimes. "Be careful."

"Okay. So be careful."

"I said I will! Gosh, bossy butt!" She was laughing as she left the bathroom, and by the time he'd rinsed his hair, he heard the front door close.

Just a few more hours and he'd get to meet this dream team Cruz was putting together. He hoped they were some kind of miracle workers, because that was what it was going to take.

He and Carter met at the office and left together in Michael's pickup. Samara met them at the interstate and left her car behind to ride with them. Michael had made a suggestion, and Carter thought it was a good one—they could go to the country club. His parents still owned a membership, even though his mother wouldn't go anymore without his dad, and she called to make them a reservation.

It would guarantee that anyone else who was a non-member probably wouldn't be there.

They waited in the parking lot until they saw Cruz pull up. He hadn't even reached them before two more cars pulled in and Cruz wheeled. "There they are." Two men got out. One was older, probably late forties or early fifties, and the other was most likely early forties or late thirties. "Hey, guys. We'll make our introductions inside, if that's okay." Everyone voiced their agreement, and the six of them stepped into the opulence of the restaurant.

"I'm Michael Edwards. My mother called and ..."

"Yes, sir. If you'll all follow me." The hostess hustled away and they almost jogged to keep up with her. To Michael's relief, she took them straight to a small, private dining room. "Will this be agreeable?"

Michael nodded. "More than. Thank you so much."

"You're quite welcome. Savannah will be your server and she'll be with you in just a minute."

"Thanks." After they'd all gotten seated, Michael looked around the table. "Thank you all for coming."

Cruz smiled. "You're very welcome. Michael, Samara, and Carter, this is KSP Detective Albert Griffin," Cruz said as an introduction to the older of the two men.

"You can call me Bud. Everybody else does," he said with a soft, slow smile. It made Michael nervous that a KSP officer would be there, and the way Samara gripped his hand under the table told him she was a little afraid.

"And this is Agent Amos Fletcher. I thought of Amos because I'd worked with his brother, Jack, on a case. He was actually on the case for Trooper Palmer's murder, but we never really got to meet. I helped him with another case too. But this is the first time we've really done a face-to-face."

"And you are …" Michael asked.

"Oh, sorry. I'm KDCI. Jack, my younger brother, is a state trooper out of Post 4."

"Thanks for coming. Both of you. We appreciate it," Carter said, and Michael nodded in agreement. Samara was being extremely quiet, and it worried him a little.

"So let's eat and drink and then we can dive in, if that's okay," Cruz said.

Michael smiled. "It's all on me."

"You don't have to—" Bud started.

"Oh, yes. I do. Not a problem. Just my way of saying thanks."

"Well, thank you," Amos told him. "So what's good here?"

Lunch was nice, but Samara was still very quiet. Bud and Amos asked her a couple of questions and she answered them, but they were really general, like how she was liking the new job and where she was originally from. That seemed to help relax her a little. When there was a lull in the conversation, Michael asked Bud, "So you're out of Post 1?"

"Oh, lord, no. That would be a bad idea. I'm not sure who you could trust over there. No, I'm Post 16."

Carter squinted in concentration. "So that's …"

Bud wiped his mouth with his napkin. "Ohio County. Muhlenberg County. Union County. That area right around Owensboro."

"Oh. Got it. Amos, where are you from?" Michael asked.

"I work in our small field office in Louisville, but I

spend some time at our headquarters in Frankfort. We live out in Shepherdsville. She owned the house before we met, and it has some property, so we kept it and sold mine. She's got this menagerie of weird animals she's rescued, and we wouldn't have had a place for them at my house."

Samara seemed to perk up. "Weird animals?"

"Yeah, weird as in something's wrong with every one of them. She's got a horse, Ivory, who's totally blind and kept falling in the pond. We finally had to fence it to keep her out. There's a goat named Azalea that some kid set on fire, and a donkey named Felix who's had a broken back leg repaired and some idiot cut his ears off."

Her eyes went wide in shock. "Cut his ears off?"

"Yeah. Stuff kept falling into them after they were cut off, so he got several ear infections that affected his balance and he kept falling down. That made the idiots mad, so they intentionally broke his leg. He wears these funny little tea strainer things Daesha made for him to keep debris out of his ears. And the goat had skin grafts for its burns. Its hair grew back, sort of, and it looks strange but it's fine."

"Is that all she has, animals with weird handicaps?" Samara asked.

"Yeah. She's a physical therapist, but she was also military. Lost a leg in the war. So she has a real soft spot for broken things. She may be mine, but she's the kindest person I've ever met."

"That's such a sweet thing to say," the lovely woman sitting beside Michael said.

"Bud, what about you? Married?" Michael asked.

"Yep. Pretty little thing. I met her while I was investigating her daughter's disappearance."

Carter looked up from his plate. "Find her?"

"Yeah. Postmortem."

Samara frowned. "Oh, that's sad."

"Yeah, it really was. Her husband had died, and her other daughter had died years earlier. Renita was her last immediate family member, so it was really difficult for her. And then she was shot as everything was coming apart."

Samara's jaw dropped. "Oh my god! That's horrible!"

"She's okay now. Has a little bit of a deficit, but otherwise fine. Oh, and she's partially blind in one eye, but her vision's actually getting better. Her name's Martina."

"That's a pretty name," Michael said with a smile.

"She's a pretty lady." Bud practically glowed as he talked about his wife. Michael wondered if he looked the same way, because he felt the same with Samara.

As soon as the dishes were cleared and they'd all gotten fresh drinks, Cruz glanced at the men on either side of him, then gave Samara an apologetic smile. "I'm sorry. I know this is going to be hard, but you've got to tell all of us everything that happened and everything that you know. I understand you've started reinterviewing the victims of the assaults, and we need to know what came from those too."

Her face turned toward Michael and the light seemed to go out in those big brown eyes. Instead of saying anything, he dropped his hand to the table, palm up, and waited. In a couple of seconds, she pressed her palm to his and he wrapped his fingers through hers. He could feel her strength even through her fear. "Okay. I'll just start at the beginning."

From time to time as she talked, one of the men would ask a question, and it was obvious to Michael how careful they were being with their words. They made sure they didn't say anything that would be disrespectful or hurtful to Samara. At one point, Amos stopped her. "I have to ask, you seem like someone who can definitely take care of herself. How did he manage to overpower you? I mean, did he hit you from behind, or restrain you, or what? I'm sure you fought—"

"I didn't realize he was behind me, and he hit me full force between the shoulder blades and knocked me to the ground. As soon as I hit, he was on me, and he zip-tied my hands behind my back. From that point on, he was in control. I was too off-balance to do much else. And I was on the back seat of the cruiser with my legs out the door and bent toward the ground. There really wasn't much of a way to get enough power to land a kick hard enough to fend him off."

Bud sat there, arms folded across his chest, and looked down at the table before looking back up at Samara. "Did you get the impression that he'd done it before to someone else?"

"Yes. Absolutely. I don't know who or when, but I felt that was a distinct possibility. Then when I started talking to the victims, it was confirmed. He did practically the same thing to them."

"So he found a formula that worked and used it repeatedly. Okay. Just wanted to clarify. Sorry I interrupted you."

"No, that's fine." She kept going, and Michael noticed something. The longer she talked, the stronger she seemed. Those men were treating her with respect, handing her dignity back to her, and she was responding. They'd never know how much he appreciated that, watching her reclaim her power as she spoke.

She outlined what she knew about each of the assaults, and then began to tell them about the house fire and the things they'd discovered there. At one point, she turned to him and said, "Michael, do you want to fill in the details on that?"

"Sure. So when we got there …" He outlined everything they'd done, then talked about going to Glenna's parents' house, and the interview he'd done with Stadler at the station. "Oh, and I'm going to call him when I get back and ask if she's ever gotten back from that Alaskan cruise," he said, rolling his eyes.

"Wow, he's an arrogant bastard, telling you stuff that he knows full well you can check out for validity," Amos growled. "I want this guy taken off the streets."

"Me too," Bud agreed. "He's a menace and an embarrassment to the badge. And that's *my* badge. I'm part of KSP, and I'm not happy about this."

Carter leaned back in his chair. "I'm sure you aren't. I'm not either, and I'm not KSP. He's been pulling this shit in my area, and I want it stopped."

"And that's what we're here for. So let's do this. We'll go home and Amos and I will talk back and forth, call you guys, just talk this out and work on it until we come up with something that will take care of this arrogant asshole." Bud glanced around the table. "Does that sound like a plan?"

"Sounds good to me," Carter agreed.

Michael nodded. "Me too."

Amos turned his attention to Samara. "Does that sound okay to you?"

She nodded and quietly said, "I trust you."

Cruz sat back in his chair. "Good. I think I've got the

right people together here, so I'll probably be going back to San Antonio in a day or two, but I'm confident that you guys are in the best possible hands. Bud and Amos will work with you, and you'll get it taken care of. And I'm always available to help or offer ideas if you need me. I'll get on a plane and be here in a few hours if I'm needed. I'm not abandoning you. This is just outside the scope of my jurisdictional limits, but I'll still do what I can and offer support."

"Listen, you guys …" Michael could feel himself losing his composure and he was trying hard to regain it before he spoke. "I, we, appreciate it. Anything you can do. Any way you can help. You just can't know …"

"Yeah. We do. We all do. Wherever we are, whatever we're doing, we're going to be thinking about all three of you and trying to come up with something that will knock this bastard down. In the meantime, keep doing those interviews, Samara. You may eventually find a woman who'll crack, and when you do, it won't just be your word against his. There will be two of you, and then maybe three. And maybe four. And check the other counties around. You guys have a good handle on this, but we're going to do everything we can to give it all a boost." Amos stopped, then smiled. "Because we know all of you would do it for us."

Carter smiled. "We absolutely would."

"Okay. We've all got our assignments. Let's touch base in a couple of days and we'll see what we come up with. You guys, please—be careful. This man is dangerous," Bud said, his voice firm. "That's one call I do *not* want to get."

"I promise, we will be." Michael hoped he was telling

the truth, but it was hard to know for sure. How could you possibly keep yourself safe from a madman?

That was the question of the century.

––––––

THERE WAS TIME FOR ANOTHER INTERVIEW BEFORE SHE WAS done for the day. She'd just assumed it would only take her a few minutes, but she was wrong.

The Burgess woman seemed to have some kind of medical problem, and it was hard to understand her speech. Her mother was there, and the older woman basically translated for her daughter. It was slow going.

"So, in the initial report you said that you didn't recognize the man." The woman nodded. "But would you know him if you saw him again?" The woman nodded again.

I wonder if she really understands what I'm asking her? She tried again. "If you saw a picture of him, do you think you'd recognize him?" Another nod. Samara pulled a picture from the file, one she'd printed as a control. It was of Gray Lewis. "Is this him?" The woman shook her head furiously. "How about this one?" she asked as she pulled Stadler's picture out and placed it on the table.

"Da him," the woman mumbled.

"You're sure?"

She nodded vehemently. "Yah."

The mother was still sitting there, so Samara turned to her. "Could I speak with you in the other room for just a minute."

"Sure." The mother's name was Amy, and her daughter was Brooke.

Once they'd cleared the doorway, Samara turned to Amy. "Can you tell me what happened to her?"

"She had a stroke about a year ago. They think she had a blood clot that was caused by birth control pills."

"And it affected her speech?"

"Yes."

"What about her cognition?"

"Her what?"

"Understanding. Does she understand what's going on around her?"

Amy's eyebrows shot up. "Oh, yes. She knows everything going on around her. She reads four or five novels a week. There's nothing wrong with her mind. She just can't talk."

"Okay. That makes her very helpful to me. Can you understand most of what she says?"

"Yes. I'm here with her all the time, so I can tell pretty well."

Samara returned to her chair beside Brooke and picked up her pencil. "Brooke, can you tell us why you didn't identify the man before?"

She mumbled something garbled and Samara couldn't understand, but Amy seemed to. "She says she didn't have a picture to look at. And she was afraid."

"And why aren't you afraid now?" That got another string of stuff that was foreign to Samara. When Brooke finished, Samara looked at Amy. "What did she say?"

"She said she's not afraid because if he saw her, he'd think she was an idiot and couldn't talk, so she'd be no threat to him." Amy laughed. "Joke's on him. She can type very well, and the program translates into spoken word, so she can type something and actually talk to you."

"Could I see?" She'd never seen anyone do that, and Samara was very curious.

"Sure. The battery on her laptop was drained, so it's been charging. Maybe it's got enough of a charge to use. Hang on." Amy left the room and came back with a small laptop. "Yeah, looks like it's usable. Here you go, honey," she said as she opened the lid and set the laptop in front of Brooke.

The young woman started to type furiously, then hit a key. A computerized voice said, "I know this seems weird, but it works for me. I can talk to you this way just like I would if I used my mouth."

"Wow. That's impressive, Brooke. So what can you tell me about him?"

Brooke typed like a maniac, then hit the key. "Not much. He was behind me, but I did get a look at him when he put me in the back seat. His face, I mean."

"And you're sure that's him?"

More typing. "Yes. He was a Kentucky State Trooper."

"And would you be willing to testify against him?"

"As long as he's arrested before he knows I'm going to. I'm scared of him," the voice said when she'd finished typing.

"I understand that completely. Listen, Brooke, thank you so much. I may have some questions for you later on, if that's okay."

She nodded, then typed something out. When she hit the key, Samara almost fell out of her chair. "He did it to you too, didn't he?"

She closed her eyes, then opened them again. "Yes. He did."

"I thought so," the laptop said.

"Why? What was it that told you he'd done it to me too?"

She typed away, then gave Samara a crooked smile. "You knew the right questions to ask."

When she'd told them goodbye and closed her car door, Samara sat there for a minute, totally overwhelmed. Her head had started to hurt, and she felt completely drained. But she had someone who'd testify. Maybe if Brooke would and she told the other victims that, they'd finally come clean and decide to do the right thing as well.

By the time she got back to the office, almost everyone was gone, even Michael. Anand was at the front desk. "You the only one here?"

"Nah. Sheriff Melton's back there."

"Thanks." Making her way down the hallway, she knocked on Carter's door jamb. "Hey."

"Hey. Any luck?"

"Yes, actually. One of the victims has had a stroke, but she was willing to talk and she identified him."

Carter's face lit up. "That's awesome! Oh, Michael told me to tell you he'll call you. I think he's got a surprise planned."

"A surprise?"

"Yeah, and I think you're going to kill him."

"Wha ... Why?"

"You're not going to like it."

That was the moment her phone rang and she looked at the screen: Michael. "Yeah. Here he is."

"Oh, god, I wanna see this," Carter whispered as she answered the phone.

Samara answered hesitantly, "Hey, babe."

"Hi, baby. So I've got a question for you. How do you feel about casseroles?"

Why did that scare her a little? "Did your mom make us one?"

"Yeah."

"Why is this making me nervous?"

"Because I told her we'd come there to eat it so she can meet you." Samara could feel her eyes bugging, and Carter was staring at the desk as he tried hard not to laugh.

"After the day I've had, you … Michael, what were you thinking?"

"It wasn't me! She called me and told me she had food and I should come over to eat. I asked her if I could bring a friend."

"A *friend*? Is that what you just called me?" she barked into the phone, and Carter's face was beet red from trying hard not to laugh loudly.

"Look, I really didn't know how to tell her no. I haven't seen her since Sunday, and she's alone, and—"

"Fine, fine. Do I come there in my car, or are you coming to get me?"

"I'll come and get you."

"Where are you right now?"

"At my house."

"Oh. Okay. Yeah. You come get me. I'll call you when I leave here."

"Sounds good. I love you," Michael crooned.

"Of course you do. Bye." She hit END on the phone's screen and Carter howled with laughter. "What's so fucking funny?"

"Oh, god, you haven't met Marjorie. I can't wait until

tomorrow morning to hear what happens! This is gonna be epic!" Carter was belly laughing.

"I'll remember you sitting there, laughing at my pain," she snapped, but she was grinning.

"Yeah, yeah. Go have fun. This should be great," Carter said, still laughing as he crammed stuff into his desk drawers.

As soon as she got in the car, she sent Michael a text.

I'm leaving, but I'm going to drive around a bit to calm down.

She got one back almost immediately.

I love you.

Her fingers tapped the screen furiously.

Carter wants to hear all about it in the morning.

That didn't get a reply. "Well, I guess you've figured out that you've screwed up," she said aloud. Home wasn't nearly far enough away. And town wasn't nearly big enough to drive around for long. It had been a hard day.

And it was only going to get harder.

CHAPTER 10

"YOU LOOK AMAZING."

Samara glared at him. "Oh yeah? Think she'll think I look amazing?"

Michael snorted. "I really don't care what she thinks."

"You say that, but—"

"Babe, I don't. If she doesn't like you, she'll at least be polite. Then the one who'll catch hell is me. But we need to go. If we're late, she *will* have something snarky to say."

"Okay, okay. Let's go."

The drive was quiet for a minute or two, and he couldn't stand it. "Did you get another interview done?"

"Yeah. I interviewed that lady out on Goat Path Lane. Monica Hunter."

"And?"

"Same thing. Insisted she didn't know who it was. No reaction when I showed her the picture of Gray. But when I dropped Stadler's picture onto the coffee table, you could practically hear the air crackling around her. She didn't have to tell me. I could see it instantly. Getting her to testify … That's another thing altogether. But I think if we had him in custody, she'd talk."

"Unfortunately, that's backwards. We need her to testify so we can take him into custody."

Samara sighed. "Yeah. And there's the problem. We can't hold him unless she's willing to file a report, and she won't file a report unless we have him. Chicken and egg thing."

"Yeah. We'll figure it out."

"But I managed to interview Brooke, and she identified him. She doesn't want him to know until he's in custody though. She's terrified of him."

"From where I sit, she should be." He pulled into the long drive and powered up to the door. "Well, here we are."

As soon as the truck's door opened, Samara slid out and looked up at the house. "Wow. This is where you grew up?"

"Yeah. Lived here for as long as I can remember."

"No wonder you took your time moving out. This is a damn castle," she whispered.

"Nah. Just a different kind of house. Come on." With her hand in his, they climbed the four steps up to the big brick porch and he opened the door. "Mom? Mom, we're here."

There was some kind of rustling around from deep in the house and then a woman appeared. "Oh! Hello. I'm Marjorie. And you're …" she said, waiting expectantly.

"Mom, this is Samara Futrell. Samara, my mom, Marjorie Edwards."

The young woman extended her hand. "Pleasure to meet you, Mrs. Edwards."

"And you as well, my dear." Michael watched carefully and saw his mother take the hand Samara had extended, but she didn't grip it very hard. That was a bad sign. "Come on in, both of you. I made a casserole." She turned and smiled warmly at Samara. "I hope you like poppy seed chicken casserole."

"Oh, yes, ma'am. I do. Very much."

"Good, good. Michael, could you get the tea glasses while I grab the bread? Just have a seat wherever you like," Marjorie instructed Samara, and the younger woman looked around.

Sit in this one, Michael mouthed without a sound as he pointed to a chair, so Samara took it. Then he hustled off to get the glasses. The one thing he didn't want to do was to leave Samara and Marjorie alone. There was no telling what his mother would say, and monitoring it would at least help deflect some of the problems, he hoped.

When they'd all gotten seated, Marjorie asked Michael to "return thanks," as they called it, and he said a simple prayer. When he finished, he dipped casserole out onto Samara's plate, then his mother's, before taking some for himself. Once the bread was passed around, Marjorie was settled securely on the launch pad. "So how do you two know each other?"

"Samara is one of the new deputies Carter hired," Michael answered.

"Oh! So you're coworkers."

Samara nodded as she looked down at the table. "Yes, ma'am."

"Actually, we're dating," Michael announced and waited to see what kind of ignition would take place.

Marjorie stopped and stared first at Michael and then at Samara before she returned her gaze to Michael. "Oh. I see."

"Samara's field of study was criminal justice. She worked as a deputy for McCracken County for four years and then as a trooper for KSP for eight."

He could see the gears turning in his mother's head, and she directed her comment to Samara. "Oh, so you're older than Michael."

"Yes, ma'am."

"So this is just a fun thing then," Marjorie chirped and turned to Michael.

Michael wasn't feeling desperate. Not yet anyway. But he could definitely see things weren't going the way he'd hoped. "No. It's not just a fun thing, Mom. We're together."

"So where are you from, Samantha?"

"Mom, that's Samara," Michael corrected.

"Oh, right, right. So where are you from, Samara?"

"Lived all my life in Ballard County."

"And what do your people do?"

"My mom is a nurse's aide. She works at the big long-term care facility outside Cairo."

"Oh, how awful," Marjorie said, her voice taking on a pitying quality.

"Actually, not really. It's a very nice place. For some of their residents, it's the nicest place they've ever lived in their lives."

"I see. And your dad? Is he in the picture?" Michael wanted to scream.

"Yes, ma'am. My dad's an engineer."

"You mean like an engineer who runs a train?"

Michael wanted to tell his mother what a ridiculous question that was when Samara spoke up. "No, ma'am. He's an electrical engineer. Has a master's degree. He works for TVA Shawnee Steam Plant. Has for years. He's in the top five of their engineers across their operation."

Marjorie's eyes went wide. "Oh, my. That's … impressive."

"Yes, ma'am. My dad's a great guy. I can't wait for him and my mom to meet Michael." Samara took the hand Michael had resting on the table, and he squeezed hers back.

"Well, that should be interesting," Marjorie murmured. It took everything Michael had to keep his eyes from rolling until they unscrewed, fell out, and wobbled across the floor.

"I think it'll be fun," Michael said, smiling.

His mother was nowhere near finished, he could tell. "Are you an only child too?"

"No, ma'am. I've got three sisters and a brother. I'm the middle kid."

"My, a big family. How old is the oldest child?"

"My oldest sister is forty-two." Almost like she was anticipating the next question, she added, "My parents just celebrated their forty-sixth anniversary."

"Oh, how lovely! That's amazing. Wilson and I had been married for almost forty years. We tried for years to have a child before Michael finally came along. He's been the biggest blessing of my life."

"He's a big blessing in mine too," Samara said and

gave him a wink. That made Michael smile in spite of his mother.

"So you're a new deputy here?"

"Yes, ma'am, but Sheriff Melton also hired me to do the bulk of the detective work, since I have experience with that through KSP."

"I would think you would've preferred to stay there. Bigger organization, more funding, more troopers, more advancement possibilities and all that."

Samara shook her head. "No. More gender discrimination. There were only two other female troopers at my post, and all three of us were relegated to little more than housekeeping duties. I tried to go back to McCracken, but they didn't have any openings. And with Gray leaving here—"

"Gray's leaving? You didn't tell me that!" Marjorie very nearly shouted at Michael.

"Yeah. I just found out three weeks back."

"Where is he going? What is he doing?"

Oh, boy. Here it comes, Michael thought. "He's leaving to go to Little Rock and get married. Has a job waiting for him down there too."

"Oh, wow! Have you met his girlfriend?"

"No, ma'am," Michael answered, delighted that he was going to get to drop that bomb. "He actually has a boyfriend."

Marjorie was pie-eyed and her brow wrinkled down until Michael thought it would take a crane to pull it back up. "A *boyfriend*? And they're getting *married*? I never would've thought Gray would do something like that. I've known that boy his whole life."

Poke the bear, he told himself. "Do something like

what? Like fall in love and want to spend the rest of his life with that person? Why is that so unusual?" Samara gave his foot a tap under the table, and he knew what that meant, but it frosted him to hear his mother say things like that about Gray. The man was happy, and it didn't matter if that happiness was a result of something she could understand or not.

"Well, why couldn't he find a nice girl? I just don't get some people."

"No, and you never will." Michael took another bite of casserole. Poppy seed chicken. If he and Samara got married and someone gave her casserole dishes, he was going to chuck them into the dumpster behind the station.

If he and Samara got married. Michael stopped chewing. It was the first time that had occurred to him, even though he wanted to spend the rest of his life with her. Was that what he wanted, marriage and kids and all that went with that commitment? Yes. He absolutely did. One glance at the beautiful woman sitting there beside him and he was overwhelmed by the feelings he had for her. If she didn't feel the same way, he was going to get his heart torn out of his chest and stomped on, because he'd already given it away to her and he knew it.

A voice cut into his thoughts. "Michael? Did you hear me?"

"Uh, no. What?"

Samara gave him a funny look. "You were a million miles away."

"Yeah. Sorry. Kinda zoned out there." If she had any idea what he'd been thinking about, she'd freak out.

"It's okay. Mrs. Edwards, this casserole is delicious. Could you give me the recipe? I'd love to try it."

"I can just make it for you and Michael can pick it up. Right, son?"

"Yeah. I guess so." *Oh, shit. I won't be living here and I'll still be eating her casseroles. That's depressing as hell.*

"That would be very nice. Thank you."

Michael just sat there and let the two of them chat. The evening had been his idea, and he regretted it, even though everything seemed fine.

They'd been gone for about five minutes when his phone rang. Without thinking, he just hit the button on his steering column and said, "Hello?"

"Michael, we need to talk."

He could feel Samara watching him. "About what?"

"About that woman you brought here."

"What about her?"

"She's black."

"Seriously? I hadn't noticed," he said as calmly as he could.

"Michael Wilson Edwards! Don't be a smart aleck with me!"

He was trying to keep his composure, but it was hard. "Mom, what is your point?"

"I mean, if you had kids with her, what would become of them?"

"I'm hoping one would become a doctor and the other a lawyer so they could buy me a vacation home," he said and didn't dare turn to Samara. He was sure she was laughing.

"I don't mean that, Michael. You know what happens to half-breed kids. They're not accepted by either their white or—"

"Uh-uh. No You're not going there. I'm saying good-night. Thank you for dinner, but this conversation is over."

"But Michael—"

"No. Over. Bye." And he pressed the disconnect button. "I swear to god, I can't believe she said all of that."

"Why not? That's how a lot of white people feel. And she trotted out all the conventional stereotypes. No surprise there."

"Do you think your parents will like me?"

She shrugged. "I have no idea. They'll probably corner me and say the same kinds of things."

"And what are you going to tell them?"

"I'm going to tell them that when I fell in love with you, I didn't fall in love with your color. I just fell in love with the person you are."

All of his anger dissipated, and Michael smiled. "And I feel the same way about you."

BY THE TIME THEY GOT BACK TO HER PLACE, THE WIND had kicked up and it had started to sprinkle rain. Michael took one look at the radar and said, "Pack a bag. Bathroom door or no bathroom door, you're coming to my house. We are *not* staying in this trailer."

They lay there on their sides, arms and legs entwined as he rocked into her, and she met him with her own thrusts. He wasn't sure their lips had parted a single time. All he wanted was to kiss her, hold her, and be the man inside her, holding her heart in his hands. The thunder and lightning outside only heightened the experience, and at least twice when the sky lit up, he could've sworn the air was filled with electricity. The pounding rain seemed to balance the fury of the storm, its steady roar soothing and calming.

The storm raged on when they were finished, and he pulled her close to him, their arms around each other. He didn't care that he was going soft inside her. All he cared about was that she was there with him and they were safe. He dozed a little, but she roused him when she unwrapped herself from him and made a trip to the bathroom. She was back in under two minutes, and they cuddled up again, the deluge outside filling the air with white noise.

He had no idea what time it was when the phone rang, and it took him a few seconds to even figure out what was happening. He grabbed it and groaned: Carter. "Yeah, boss."

"Is Samara with you?"

"Yep."

"Can you put me on speaker?"

"Sure." She'd sat up and was rubbing her eyes. "Okay. You're on speaker."

"We've got a situation here, and I'm more than a little worried. Samara, is Mallory Bledsoe one of the women you just reinterviewed? Out on Valdemont Circle?"

"Yes, sir. She is."

"She's dead."

He could feel Samara tense beside him. "What? Dead?"

"Yeah. Husband came home from his shift in the guardhouse at the HVAC factory in Clarksville and found her."

"COD?" Samara asked, and Michael's heart started to slam against his ribs.

"Shot through the back of the head execution-style, wrists and ankles bound, face down on the floor. I have a feeling if the slug made a through-and-through, it'll be embedded in the floor."

"Has she been moved?" Samara asked.

"No. I haven't let anybody touch anything. They've been making pictures, and I called the coroner. He's going to want you here before he moves her."

"I would hope so."

"And we need to talk about this. I don't see this as random, although it might be."

Michael shook his head even though Carter couldn't see him. "I don't see it as random either."

"Okay. We're on the same page. Hustle up and get here. We've already sent the husband to the hospital because he was having chest pains. You'll want to talk to him too."

Samara was already up and rummaging around for her clothes. "Roger that, sir. I'll be in the car and on the road as fast as I can get dressed."

"Okay. And Michael?"

"Yes, sir?"

"I don't want her alone."

"My thinking exactly. Thanks. Be right there." Michael already had his jeans on, and he'd pulled on a tee and was working on his socks. "I guess you heard that."

"Yeah. I did. And I don't need a babysitter."

Michael stopped and stared at her. "You do know what we're thinking, right?"

"Yeah, and I'm not afraid of him."

"Well, I am. If he'd do this to somebody, I'm very afraid of him, and you should be too."

She stopped and glared at him, hands on her hips. "I'm ready to go. You?"

"Right behind you." He grabbed his service weapon, his backup weapon, and his badge, along with his keys and wallet. There was little doubt in his mind that it was going to be a long night.

And he dreaded what they were about to walk into.

MICHAEL DUSTED FOR FINGERPRINTS AS SAMARA LOOKED everything over. There was no chaos in the house, so even though she hadn't really looked around when she'd talked to Mallory, there didn't appear to be anything gone. There was no sign of forced entry, and that meant he'd either followed her home and gone in behind her, or he'd broken into the house before or after she came back.

"What are you thinking?" Michael asked as he sidled up to Samara.

"You know exactly what I'm thinking. So is he watching me, or is he tracking me?"

"He doesn't have your phone number, so if he's tracking you, he's doing it some other way."

Before he could get another sentence out, Carter stepped into Michael's field of vision. "Hey. Got anything interesting yet?"

Michael shook his head. "Nothing that anyone else couldn't get. Where have you been?"

"At the hospital with the husband."

"Did he say anything about anyone following her or harassing her or anything like that?" Samara asked.

"No. I asked and he said this is completely out of left

field. Poor guy's just bewildered." He stopped for a second, then trained his gaze on Samara. "How many of these interviews have you done so far?"

"Five."

"I need the names and addresses of the victims and indicate on the list which ones you've talked to. I think this asshole is following you somehow, and if so, they're all in danger."

"Yes, sir. I'll jot down a list quickly so you'll have it."

"Good." Both men watched as she headed toward her car. As soon as she was out of ear shot, Carter side-eyed Michael. "He's got a tracking device on her car."

"That's what I'm afraid of. And if that's the case, he now also has her home location and mine as well. She's not safe anywhere."

"Oh, there's one place she'd be safe." Michael couldn't imagine where that could be. "Marjorie's."

"Oh, no. I can't do that to Samara. My mother—"

"Would do the right thing, Michael. You know she would. Personal feelings aside, your mom has the same code of ethics that your dad did, the same one you operate under, and you know it. As long as Samara went there via a transportation mode that he couldn't track, she'd be perfectly safe."

Carter had a point, but could he talk Samara into it? And his mother … What would she say?

He didn't know, and he didn't care. Those two women were going to stay in the same house, and there would be no discussion.

By the time morning came, they were all exhausted. Everyone had been up all night, and there was no time to stop. They'd had a murder in their backyard, and they had to keep going.

And then the world exploded.

At a little after eight, the phone rang at the office and Anand answered it. A second later, he called out, "Chief deputy, there's a call on line two for you. Someone named Fletcher."

"Thank you." Michael picked up the receiver, hit the button, and answered, "Hey, good morning."

"Good morning to you. How's it going down there?"

Michael rubbed his left eye. "Not good. Not good at all."

"What happened?"

Even though he was the one detailing what had happened, talking about the events of that early morning frightened him just hearing the words. Things were escalating quickly. "So I've got to find a safe place for her, and I think I'm going to take her to my mom's."

"Are Samara and Carter there?"

"Yeah. Let me put you on hold. I'll get them, and we'll pick up in the conference room."

Less than a minute later, he'd shaken Samara awake from her sleeping spot on the sofa in his office, and he'd retrieved Carter from across the hallway. They all sat down at the conference room table, and Michael hit the button. "Okay, Amos. You're on speaker."

"Michael filled me in on what's happened."

Carter rubbed his eyes too. "Yeah. It's a clusterfuck of enormous proportion."

Amos quietly said, "Yeah. Sounds like it."

"Not gonna say it couldn't be worse. Nothing good ever happens from me asking how it could possibly be worse," Carter grumbled.

Michael nodded. "Yeah. We usually find out immediately."

It took Carter two breaths to ask, "So what's our next move?"

"I've asked Bud to contact Post 1 and tell them what's going on, ask for their cooperation. He'll get farther with them than I would. Then we wait to see what happens. I told him that if he can get a sit-down with Stadler and his post commander, I'd like to be there too, and he agreed that would be best. If the post commander sees a KDCI agent sitting there, he's less likely to try to cover for someone and more likely to tell the truth, because we have the ability to place him under arrest and deem his entire post under suspicion. No KSP post commander wants that on his record. Do you have any idea where Stadler's staying?"

Carter let out a deep sigh. "No. Not a clue."

"We need that piece of information. We now have probable cause, so if we could find him, we'd be a step ahead. Can you guys work on that?"

"Sure. And let us know what the next move should be. Until then, we'll be doing what we can do to keep everyone involved safe." Carter had started jotting things down as they'd talked, and Michael wondered what was on his notepad.

"Do that and I'll be back with you as soon as possible. You guys take care. Samara?"

"Yes, sir?"

"It's just Amos. And you be careful out there. This guy is as dangerous as they come."

It hurt Michael's heart to see her looking so defeated. "Will do. Thanks."

"Later, guys."

Michael listened as Amos hung up and sat there, tired and stressed. "So now what?"

"We've got to get people on every house where Samara has done an interview. I've got your list and we'll get them covered in the next hour. I'm calling people in. Something's gotta give, and the three people in this room are exhausted. You know what happens when exhausted people are working a case."

Michael nodded. "They miss things."

"Exactly. Futrell?"

"Yes, sir?"

"We've got to have a safe place for you to stay. I'm going to suggest that you go to Marjorie's and—"

The minute Marjorie's name slipped from Carter's lips, Samara started to shake her head. "Sir, with all due respect, I don't think she likes me very much."

"I don't care if she thinks you're Beelzebub, he wouldn't know to look for you there."

"But, sir, you need everybody pulling their weight and this puts me out of commission."

Carter leaned back in the chair. "Know what puts you out of commission? Death. That will permanently put you out of commission. And I don't want that happening. So go to Marjorie's. Maybe she'll get to know you and it'll change her opinion of you."

Samara's shoulders fell. "I doubt it, sir."

"Guess we'll find out. I'll have Justin take you."

"I can drive there."

"No. We think he's got a tracking tile on your car," Carter said, his voice stern.

"Yeah," Samara said in agreement. "I've about come to that conclusion too."

"So I'm going to have the guys go over the vehicles—yours, your cruiser, and both of Michael's vehicles—and see if we can find them. But I really doubt he managed to slap a tile on all of the cruisers, so Justin can take you."

"What about my things? Clothes and shampoo and toothpaste and all that stuff?"

"Make a list. Michael can pack it up and bring it here, and we'll have Chadha or Carlin or somebody take it to you. The more we can mix it up, the safer you'll be. And Michael?"

"Yes, sir." He was terrified to hear what Carter was about to say.

"I'll take care of calling your mother and breaking the news. I think it'll be better coming from me than from you."

I'm finally catching a break, Michael thought. "Thank you. I was dreading that conversation."

"You're welcome. Oh, and call the insurance company that covered Stadler's house. Maybe they can tell you where he's staying, because they should be issuing the checks."

Michael gave Carter a small nod. "Good thinking, sir. I'll get right on it. I'm going to call the commissioner too and let him know what's going on as a courtesy."

"Yes. Please." Carter didn't say another word, just rose and went back to his office.

The sad face Samara was wearing made Michael want to hold her, but he couldn't, not in the office. "Talk to me, babe. I know you're unhappy."

"I feel just like I did at the KSP post when I was given nothing but secretarial duties."

"No. This is *not* the same. You weren't in danger there. This is different."

"I *was* in danger there."

"Yes, but your superior officer didn't know that, at least not that we know of. He was just being a dick."

She sat down in the chair in front of his desk and sighed. "So what now?"

"I think my mother's place is the safest."

"Michael—"

"I know, I know, but this is serious. We have to do something. Doing nothing isn't an option. I think I can safely take you there because I can't believe he'd track my car. I'll use one of the other guys' cruisers and it'll be fine."

"Fine. I'll go, but I don't like it. Not—" The radio out front squawked and Michael threw up his hand to silence her. "What?"

"Did you hear that transmission?" He was already on the move, and he could hear her right behind him. Anand was out of his chair and heading to his cruiser. "What's going on?"

"Shooting. Nineteen forty-three Byford's Ridge Road. Dispatch called for us and an ambo," Anand yelled as he ran out the door.

"I've gotta … What?" He'd turned to find the color draining from Samara's face.

"That's Amy and Brooke Burgess' house."

He could feel a tremor of fear run through his body. "A woman you interviewed?"

Her voice was nothing but a whisper. "Yes."

"Okay, that's it. You stay here. Lock the doors and do not go out." Michael grabbed an extra go bag just as Carter appeared in the hallway. "You coming?" Michael asked his boss.

"Yeah." Then he pointed at Samara. "But not you. You stay here."

"That's what I told her."

Samara shook her head. "But I'm partially responsible for this and—"

"You absolutely are *not!*" Carter bellowed, and Samara jumped. "You're in no way responsible for this. You were doing exactly what you were told to do. You were doing your job. Stay here. Keep the door locked. As soon as I find somebody I can spare, I'll have them drive you to Marjorie's house. Do not disobey this command. I mean it."

"Yes, sir." It hurt Michael to see the defeated look on her face as she backed down.

He couldn't just leave. Before he ran out the door, he took her chin in his hand and held her face so he could look into her eyes. "I love you. I do not want something to happen to you. Do as we said and it'll be okay. Take the extra cruiser out there and go to my mother's house. Promise me, angel. Promise?"

"I promise. I love you too. Go on. I'll be fine."

As he ran out the door, he took one glance back to where she stood, wearing a look on her face that he never wanted to see again, an anguish he couldn't even name.

And he blamed himself.

THE SCENE WAS CHAOS. THERE WAS A FILLED BODY BAG and a gurney with a woman on it. Carter was trying to talk to her, but he couldn't make any sense out of the odd sounds she was making, and Michael knew who she was. She was a stroke victim whose only caregiver was dead.

After ten minutes of trying to make sense of things, Carter grabbed Michael by the arm and dragged him aside. "I want you here with me for this." After he'd gone into his contacts and hit one, he put his phone on speaker. It rang three times before a voice said, "Lyon County Sheriff's Office. This is Deputy Hester. Can I help you?"

"Yes, this is Trigg County Sheriff Carter Melton. Could I speak with Sheriff Thomasson, please?"

"Sure. Hold on just a second."

They waited and finally a voice said, "Carter! How the hell are you?"

"Bad. Really bad, Phillip."

"What's wrong?"

Carter spent five minutes telling the Lyon County sheriff what was happening, and he finished with, "And I really need some help. I don't have the manpower to cover something like this. I just don't. And I sure can't call Post 1."

"I've got four off-duty deputies I can call in for you. Will that help?"

"More than you could possibly know. I'm calling Calloway County too. I've got locations scattered out all over the county and not enough people to cover them."

"They'll be there as fast as I can get them there. Have their duties ready and they'll do whatever you ask."

"Phillip, thank you so much. You have no idea how much I appreciate this."

"You're very welcome. Don't mind at all. And stay safe."

"We're trying. Thanks again." Carter sighed after he'd hung up. "Well, at least reinforcements are coming." The sheriff's phone rang and he groaned. "Oh, shit. Amos." He hit ACCEPT and said, "Hey, Amos. What's up?"

"Got some bad news. Bud and I called the Post 1 commander and told him we needed to talk to him about Stadler. And he informed us the trooper hadn't been at work in three days. Nobody's seen him or knows where he is."

"We've got another dead body here and an attempted. One of the women Futrell reinterviewed. He's picking them off one by one, Amos. I've got reinforcements coming in from Lyon County, but this is quickly getting out of hand."

Before Amos could say anything, the radio in Carter's cruiser bellowed, "TCSD, this is central dispatch. Have a five-oh-three at the Budget Inn behind Broadmore Gifts. Repeat, five-oh-three behind Broadmore Gifts. Copy?"

"Hang on, Amos. Roger that, dispatch. TCSD is ten seventy-six to that location. And ten seventy-nine to the location on Byford's Ridge Road. Copy?"

"Roger that, TCSD. Notifying the coroner now."

"Show us ten six at that location. Out." Carter looked up at Michael. "You take the five-oh-three at the motel. Let me know what you find."

"But I need to—"

"Go do that. I have this feeling it's related." Without another word, Carter turned back to his conversation with

Amos, so Michael headed to his SUV and tore out of the scene.

When he got to the motel, he didn't even make it to the office before a man came running out of a room. "Hey! Hey, it was me. Somebody took my car."

"Yes, sir. Where was it?"

"It was sitting right there." The man pointed to a parking space.

"And when did you notice it missing?"

"Right before I called. I was going to load up my stuff and it was gone."

Michael glanced around. There was no sign that anyone had broken into the vehicle—no glass, no tool of any kind. He took one more look around, and that was when he homed in on it.

The pale gold pickup truck sitting down the way in the parking lot. "Have you seen the person who drives that truck?"

The man shook his head. "No. Nobody."

"Stay here." Michael ran to the office and threw open the door. "That truck down there. Do you know who it belongs to?"

"One of the guys staying here," the clerk said, a look of confusion on his face.

"Is his name Stadler?"

"Yeah. How'd you know—"

When he reached the man in the parking lot, he barked, "What kind of car do you have?"

"Two thousand seven Chrysler 300, gold."

Michael grabbed the radio from his tool belt. "All units, all units, this is TCSD unit one forty-eight. Looking for a gold-colored Chrysler 300, two thousand seven model. Suspect in the incident on Byford's Ridge Road." He stared at the man. "Do you know the license plate number?"

"No, sir. I don't."

"Central dispatch, I need a plate number on a gold Chrysler 300, two thousand seven model, registered under the name ..." He pointed at the man.

"Kenny Hart."

"Registered under the name Kenny Hart." Ten seconds later, dispatch had relayed it. "All units, gold Chrysler 300, Kentucky plate number ..." He read it off, then finished the transmission before he turned back to the theft victim. "Sir, I'm sorry. I've got to go. Here's my card. Give me until tomorrow and call me back, and I'll make a report on it, but we've got an emergency right now and I have to get going."

"Okay. Um, just call you?"

"Yes, sir," Michael called back as he ran to his cruiser.

As soon as he was on the road, he called Carter, and the sheriff answered, "Please, god, tell me you know something."

"Yeah. That broadcast I just made? Stadler stole that car. His truck is sitting at the motel."

"Shit. Shit, shit, shit. Where's Futrell?"

"I told her to take the extra cruiser in the parking lot and go to my mother's."

"Michael, you shouldn't have done that. I told her to stay put and I'd send somebody."

"We don't have anybody to send!" Michael all but yelled.

"You need to check on her in a little while and make sure she's okay." It got quiet for a few seconds before

Carter said, "I don't understand it. How did he find them that fast? Has he been tracking her all this time? He didn't know those women's names or where they lived, from what we could tell. It's like he's been one step ahead of us all along. I don't get it."

That was the moment when it all came crashing down around Michael's ears. "Oh, fuck."

"What?"

"I interviewed him in the conference room." The tires on the SUV squalled as Michael spun it and headed back to the office. "He's been listening to everything we've said."

"You think he—"

"Oh, I'm almost positive. I'm headed to the office right now to look."

"Michael, if you're right—"

"I'm pretty sure she hasn't left the office yet. I'm headed back that way. I'll give you a call when I know more."

"Roger. I've about done all I can do here. Keep me updated."

"Will do." Michael's cruiser was screaming down the highway, and he whipped onto the main thoroughfare that ran through town, traveling at about sixty miles an hour, siren blaring and lights flashing. His heart sank when he pulled up to the office.

The extra cruiser was gone.

He was running as fast as he could go when he unlocked the front door and threw it open, then ran straight to the conference room. There was a logical place for it, so he dropped to his hands and knees and looked under the table. He checked every crevice in the underside, but he didn't find anything. Still on his knees and looking around the room, he remembered which chair Stadler had sat in that day, and he rolled to his back and pulled it to him.

And there, held by a magnet, was a tiny microphone. Michael's heart dropped into his shoes. She wasn't safe at his mother's. He was about to call Marjorie when his phone rang. "Mom, is Samara there?" he asked, not even saying hello.

"That's what I was calling you about, honey. There's a cruiser sitting at the end of the driveway. I thought maybe it was you, but nobody came to the house, and I saw a little gold car drive away. I don't know what …"

Michael didn't hear anything else she said. He didn't have to. He knew exactly what had happened to Samara. And he had no idea what to do about it.

CHAPTER 11

THAT'S what I get for trying to be helpful, she grumbled in her head. She'd stopped at the end of the driveway to pick up Marjorie's newspaper, but before she could get back in the car, the prongs of the TASER had hit her right at kidney level and she'd dropped to the ground. She was trying to pull herself together when he zip-tied her hands behind her back, then picked her up and tossed her in the unfamiliar car's trunk.

Samara pondered the predicament she was in. How had he found her? She had no idea, but she had been certain it was going to happen. Of course, he wasn't interested in a fair fight. He wanted to ambush the people he hurt and take advantage of them. The original coward. What a tool. But there was no time to waste on hating him. She had to figure out how to get herself out of the trunk and away from that lunatic.

It was impossible to see much, but if she was correct, her back was turned toward the front end of the car. If that car was like every other car she'd ever seen, the back seat would push out into the passenger compartment. She felt around as best she could. There was all kinds of junk in that compartment, and she had to believe she could find something in there that she could use to cut the zip tie and free her hands. One sharp thing. That was all she needed.

And where was he taking her? Somewhere to rape her? Somewhere to kill her? If he wanted to kill her, he could've shot her and driven away. He wanted to torture her. That had to be the answer. Or maybe … Maybe he wanted to use her as a way to get away, a hostage he could bargain with, or as a human shield. The possibilities were endless, but that idea made the most sense.

They bumped along, and she wasn't sure where they were going. When the car stopped, she heard the door open and then close—he was out of the car. Frantic and scrounging in the dark, she rummaged around until she felt something famil-iar—a hacksaw. *Perfect*, she told herself as she tried to find a way to brace it against something so she could rake the zip tie along it. Twice she felt it cut her arm, but she couldn't worry about that. Hacking through that zip tie was all that mattered.

Sure enough, in under a minute, the zip tie fell away, but she grabbed it with her hand. If he opened the trunk, she needed to be able to hold it and keep her hands behind her back so he'd think she was still restrained. With her hands free, she grabbed the duct tape at her ankles and started to unwind it, then ripped it in half and wrapped each piece around one ankle. With a quick glance, it would look like her ankles were still bound, but they were sepa-rated, only held together by one flap of tape that would come free in an instant. She was ready to roll over and kick the back seat when she heard it.

A distinctive pop.

Her heart fell. She didn't know which one, but they were stopped at the home of one of the women she'd reinterviewed. The sound she'd heard was his weapon discharging. Her chest filled with guilt and grief. If she'd left those cases alone and never spoken to those women, they'd still be alive. They were dying, one by one, because she'd tried to get to the bottom of their stories so she could arrest the person responsible and close the cases. Rationally, she knew she could've never imagined the hell he'd rain down on each of them, but on the surface, the fear and sadness she felt was overwhelming. They were dead because of her. Carter had said it wasn't her fault, but it was, and she knew it.

Less than a minute later, the car door opened and slammed shut, and the car started. It backed down, turned, and took off. Were they going to another house to kill another woman? How had he known about all of that? They suspected he'd been following her, but this was too efficient. It would've been hard for him to keep up with more than two of her stops, but so far, he'd gone to three of them, and she was betting they were headed for the fourth one.

And what about Amy and Brooke? How were they? Were they seriously hurt? She feared the worst, knowing what he'd done to Mallory.

The car rolled along for a good distance, and then it stopped. She heard the door open and footsteps outside of the car, something that sounded like gravel under boots. Taking a piss, no doubt. Then she heard the footsteps again, and they stopped at the trunk of the car.

The lid opened and the bright sunshine blinded her for a few seconds. "Nothing to say, bitch?"

"Oh, I've got plenty to say, you rotting piece of possum shit," she spat. *Get him to lean down over you somehow,* her brain whispered as she felt around for the screwdriver she'd found a little earlier. Once it was in her hand, she stared up at him. "But you're not man enough to hear it."

"I was man enough when I was giving it to you up that hot, tight little pussy of yours, wasn't I, slut? Didn't you get enough? Or do you want more?"

Piss him off, she told herself. "I don't want any more of your microdick, you asshole."

"Oh, is that right? How 'bout I drag you out of this car and show you what you're missing, since your memory is faulty?" He grabbed her by the hair, pulled her upright, and dragged her out of the car until she was on her feet. "How's that?"

In one fluid move, she whipped out her right hand and drove the screwdriver into the back of his neck. Stadler screamed out and reached for it, and that was all she needed.

Samara ran. She didn't know where she was going, but she headed straight for a tree line and kept running. She could hear him cursing behind her, and then a shot rang out, but it was nowhere near her, so her feet kept pumping and she kept up the sprint, running faster than she'd ever run in her life. She crashed through the tree line and looked up to find dense woods straight ahead, barely fifty yards away, so she ran to her left, back to the tree line, and kept running along its edge until she reached the woods. Somewhere behind her she could hear him cursing and yelling, and his weapon discharged a couple more times, but it was far behind her.

Once she was a hundred feet into the woods, she stopped and listened. There wasn't a sound. Was he right on top of her, watching her? Or had she run far enough? That thought flew right out of her head. There was no way she could have run far enough. She could never run far enough. So she took off again, letting the sun guide her away from the car.

When she came to an old wire fence, she managed to climb over it and keep going. The second one was harder to climb over, but she made it. She was tiring, and between that and the lack of water, she was slowing down. Something had to happen. There was no way she could keep it up. Her options seemed few, and she was about to tell herself that there was nothing else she could do. Then she heard a sound.

Through the trees, she could see half a dozen cows. As soon as she got to the edge of the woods, she looked again. There had to be twenty head of cattle there, big black cattle. Angus. She didn't know a lot about cattle, but she did know that Angus cattle tended to be friendly to people, so she wasn't afraid of them. Matter of fact, as she ran through the pasture, they didn't seem to even notice her, and she decided they had to have come from somewhere nearby, so she headed directly to the ridge that cut off her line of sight from the land in front of her.

She crested the ridge and below it she could see a barn and a farmhouse. Help. She could get help there. A man stepped out of the barn, and just as he did, another *pop* sounded from behind her.

A burning sensation bloomed in the back of her right

thigh, and she fell forward onto her stomach. One glance told her the farmer had headed toward the house, and her hopes shriveled up and blew away. He was afraid, and he was running away, leaving her there to die. Another *pop* sounded from behind her, but it didn't make contact with her body, and she rolled to see where he was, hoping he was far enough away that she could gather whatever strength she had and still make an escape.

Across the wide field, Alex Stadler staggered and stumbled, blood pouring down his right side from where the screwdriver had been. He seemed to more or less be in a stupor, and she was surprised he was still standing. As soon as she rolled back to her stomach, she heard the weapon discharge once again, but nothing hit her, so she decided it was do-or-die time.

Summoning every ounce of strength she could muster, Samara struggled to her feet and took off. It was more of a lope, but at least she was moving. The sound of a shot rang out again, and she felt the same burning sensation in her upper left arm, but she kept going. She was too far from the barn, and she knew without a doubt that when he reached the ridge, she'd still be out in the open. He'd have a clear shot at her, and he'd get her. As determined as he was, he wouldn't miss that time.

But she ran anyway. There was no other choice. As she ran, she could feel the tears pouring down her face, knowing that she'd never see Michael again, that he'd live with all kinds of regret for what had happened to her. She hadn't even had a chance to tell her family about him, or have them meet him. In her mind, she could see the house after it was finished, how proud he was to have such a beautiful home, and how proud she was to live there with him. She wanted a little vegetable garden, and a cat sitting on the porch. Maybe a dog, a little dog, some little wad of fur that she could cuddle and talk to when he was working and she was home, one that would keep him company when she was out working, and she smiled through her tears as she thought about how he'd probably arrange their schedules so they'd be off together. He could do that. He was, after all, the chief deputy. Carter would let him do anything he felt he needed to do. She had a wonderful man. She had a great boss and a job she loved. And she was losing it all, even as her legs kept moving while she was almost blind with fear, pain, and weariness.

No matter. She just kept going. She knew he was probably at the ridge, and it was only going to be another few seconds before he'd end her. There were sounds all around her—were they cows?—and lights and movement, and she couldn't make sense of any of them as she fell. Was she hurt? She wasn't sure. She only knew she couldn't go another step farther, and it was probably her time to die.

———

MICHAEL WAS IN A COMPLETE STATE OF PANIC. HE WASN'T sure what was happening. How would he ever find her? He was driving toward Amy and Brooke's house when the radio crackled. "Central dispatch calling TCSD, report of shooting at eighty-nine twelve Martinsburg Road. Repeat, report of shooting at eighty-nine twelve Martinsburg Road. Requesting police, emergency medical, and all support personnel at that address. Over."

Eighty-nine twelve Martinsburg Road. Michael thought about it for a minute. He'd started out at the Bledsoe home. That was the closest to town. Then he'd gone to the Burgess house. That was a bit farther away, but on the same side of town. Suddenly, things started to make sense. He'd left the Burgess house, and he was probably sitting there waiting when Samara drove into Marjorie's driveway, because the Edwards' house was farther out than the Burgess house, but in the same direction. Then he'd stopped at the house on Martinsburg Road, which followed his pattern. He couldn't remember that woman's name but at the rate they were going it was sure to come across the radio at some point in the near future. He wracked his brain. Where was the fourth house, one whose occupant hadn't been reinterviewed? The one farthest from town on that side? He hit the button on his radio's mic. "This is TCSD unit one forty-eight. Desk at the office, please respond. Over." It was quiet for a few seconds, then he repeated his call. "TCSD unit one forty-eight calling sheriff's department main office. Any officer in the office, please respond. Over."

"TCSD unit one forty-eight, this is main office," he heard Carlin's voice call through the radio.

"Call my phone, please, main office," he instructed.

"Roger that." In an instant, his phone rang. "Yeah?"

"Carlin, I need you to go to the conference room. There are two stacks of folders on the conference room table. Find the stack that has Brooke Burgess' name on it."

"Roger. Hang on." It was quiet, too quiet, and Michael's thoughts ran away with him. Then Carlin's voice came back. "Okay. I've got two stacks here. The stack on the left has the Burgess woman's name in it."

"Who else is in that stack?"

"There's a Bledsoe."

"Yeah. That's the right stack. Who else?"

"Um, there's one here, a Fleming, on Martinsburg Road."

"And where's the other one?"

"Clover Lane. That's Monica Hunter."

His hunch had been right. Clover Lane was the farthest from town. He was picking them off, one by one, and the Hunter woman was next. "Thanks, Carlin. Owe you a beer."

"I'm gonna take you up on that, chief deputy."

For that moment, he hated his title. He had no business being chief deputy. This was his girlfriend, a woman he loved and wanted to spend the rest of his life with, and he'd let the unthinkable happen to her. From the Martinsburg Road house to the Clover Lane location, there were only two possible routes, so he chose the shortest one. When he rounded the second curve on the lane, there it was.

The gold Chrysler sat on the side of the road, the driver's door and the trunk both open, but there wasn't a soul to be seen. Michael slammed his cruiser in park and leaped out, looking all around. There was a broken zip tie and a piece of duct tape lying on the ground, and near it, a small puddle of blood. Watching the drops of blood, he saw that they progressed toward the tree line, and he knew what was happening, so Michael checked his handgun in its holster, then grabbed his long gun and took off.

It was easy to follow them, the brush and vines torn through and pressed aside, and he knew he was headed toward the other side of the tree line. When he came out, he asked himself, *What would Samara do?* The woods directly in front of him made the most sense, and it was also the direction leading away from the car. That's where she would've gone.

Sure enough, there was a lot of vegetation disturbed, and he had no trouble following it. When he reached the other side and burst out of the woods, there was a screw-driver lying on the ground in another puddle of blood, and his heart almost stopped. Somewhere out there was Samara, and he hoped that blood wasn't hers. Michael saw the cattle, then saw footprints in the dirt here and there, so he kept running away from the car and toward whatever was out there. Another twenty yards past, he shouldered his long gun.

Alex Stadler was standing on the rim of the ridge, and he fired a shot down toward whatever was there. There was zero doubt in Michael's mind who he was shooting at, so he ran straight toward Stadler. When he was within ten yards, he yelled, "Stadler!"

The rogue cop spun to face Michael, his right side soaked with blood and his weapon in his hand. Even though he wobbled, he lifted the gun toward Michael.

One pull of the trigger. Chief Deputy Michael Edwards dropped the asshole like a stone with one rifle shot straight to center mass. The taller man fell and Michael ran at him, kicked the gun away from his hand, but didn't even bother to check his pulse. He didn't care. He crested the ridge and his heart broke.

Below him, almost to the barn, was a figure dragging along, and the movements reminded him of one of those terrible zombie shows, an undead body reanimated to less than perfection and struggling to move. He didn't yell her name. He didn't stop. He just ran. He ran down the ridge so fast that he was afraid he'd lose his footing and tumble boots over butt cheeks, but he didn't care. Blood had drenched the back side of her right leg, and she was barely standing, but he didn't slow. That zombie was his, and he had to protect her.

When he reached her, his hand touched her arm and she fought against him, slapping at him. She was mumbling something, and it only took him a second to understand: "Get away. Get away. I don't want to die. I don't want to die. Leave me alone. Get away."

Michael stepped in front of her and took in the sight. Her left arm was bleeding and she was squeezing it with her right hand, blood seeping out between her fingers. "Baby! Samara, it's me. It's Michael. Baby, stop. It's me." Reaching for his radio, he squeezed the mic trigger. "Central dispatch, this is TCSD unit one forty-eight requesting all personnel to Riggins farm on Wyattsville Road. Suspect down, officer shot. Repeat, suspect down, officer shot. Requesting backup and emergency medical to Riggins farm on Wyattsville Road. Over."

"TCSD unit one forty-eight, this is TCSD unit one. All emergency services en route. Stand by. ETA three minutes. Over," Carter said as he ended the transmission.

"Copy, TCSD unit one. TCSD unit one forty-eight, standing by." By the time he holstered the radio, she'd stopped. "Baby, we need to get you some help."

"He's gonna kill me. He's gonna kill me, and he won't stop."

"Samara, honey, look at me." He slapped a palm to either side of her face and held it still so she could look into his eyes. "Samara, it's me. It's Michael. Look at me."

Those big brown eyes went wide and she started to shake and sob. "Michael? Michael? Am I alive? Michael?

Michael!" Her arms flew around his neck and she gripped him so tightly that she was almost choking him. "Michael! Oh, god, he's gonna kill me!"

"No, baby. He's not. I got him. He won't hurt you again. He won't hurt anybody again, you hear me? Let's get you up here in the shade and get some water in you." When he turned around, the old farmer was standing on his back porch, his shotgun hanging from his right hand. "Sir, you won't need that. The threat is gone. I need some towels and some water, please."

"Yes, sir! Got it. Be right back."

As he disappeared into the house, Michael lifted Samara and carried her to the porch, laying her out on its edge so he could stand beside her. The man handed a glass of water out to Michael, then disappeared back into the house, so the chief deputy helped her to sitting. "Here, babe. You need to drink this. You're dehydrated." As soon as the glass touched her lips, she drank greedily. "Just sip it, baby. That's it. Just a little at a time."

"Here ya go," the old man said as he rolled a towel up. "You can use that for a pillow. She got some injuries?"

"Yes, sir. Looks like right leg and left arm."

"I was a field medic in the military. Let me take a look." As Michael rolled her gently to her side, the old fellow poked and prodded. "Yep, she's probably got a slug in there. Let's see that arm. This one looks like a through-and-through. That should be okay. Not a lot of blood loss. I'd say she's going to be fine. Honey, drink that water and then lie down and rest. You've really been through it." He leaned toward Michael and whispered, "I'd done run into the house to get my shotgun. I seen her running, and I seen that guy up on the ridge with that rifle, and I knowed what was going on. If you hadn't got here, I would've shot him myself."

"Thank you, sir. I appreciate it. I might need you to give a statement, if you'd be so kind."

"Not a problem at all, deputy. Don't mind one bit. She a police officer?" he asked Michael.

"Yes, sir. A detective. Works for Sheriff Melton."

"That's a good man there. Good man. You got help coming?"

Michael smiled. "Yes, sir." In the distance, he could hear a siren. "There they are. They'll be here in just a few seconds."

Then he heard a soft voice. "Michael?"

He looked down into her face and smiled. "Hey, baby. I'm right here."

"Is he gone?"

"Yeah, honey. He's gone and he won't be bothering you again."

"I need to sleep," she whispered again.

He swept her hair away from her face and kissed her cheek. "Yes, angel. You do."

THE PLACE WAS CRAWLING WITH LAW ENFORCEMENT. Carter was the first one to show up, with the ambulance right on his heels. Watson and Chadha took over the investigation of Stadler's death. Even though he didn't want to, Carter took Michael's badge and service weapon, as well as the rifle he'd used. As a sheriff's department, they'd be carrying out their own death investigation with the assistance of KDCI. The coroner's office would be doing the same, and the body would go to the medical examiner. He also contacted the district attorney to inform him of the shooting. There was no question in Carter's mind that Michael would be exonerated from any possible fault.

Once they'd loaded Samara up in the ambulance, Carter drove Michael to pick up his cruiser, and they both headed to the hospital. They were evaluating her in the emergency department when they both arrived, and Michael thought he'd have a stroke. He wanted, needed, to be with her, to reassure her and comfort her. She was injured and in pain, and he wanted to hold her hand and tell her it would be fine.

They'd been waiting for almost an hour when the doors slid open and a black couple in their early sixties walked in. "Do not lose your shit," Carter whispered to Michael.

"What are you—"

"They're her parents. I had to call them." Carter rose to greet them, and Michael sat there, dread filling his core. In a minute, Carter led them toward Michael. "This is Chief Deputy Michael Edwards. He's the deputy who shot the assailant and saved Samara. Chief Deputy Edwards, this is Bruce and Debra Futrell."

They both shook his hand, but there was something in their eyes that bothered him. Finally, her father said, "Are you the officer she's been seeing?"

"Yes, sir. I am."

"Thank you for saving her. We appreciate it. But we'll take it from here."

"Sir, I understand your—"

"No, son. You don't. We need to be here with our

daughter. The two of you already let her walk right into danger and—"

Carter immediately interrupted him. "Sir, that's very unfair. Samara applied for the job and, based on her credentials and work experience, she was hired to do a job that she loves. She's been a good employee, and she's been instrumental in solving ten cases that we now know are connected. If it hadn't been for her, some—"

"If it hadn't been for her, you wouldn't be here. We wouldn't be here. We'd be at home, and she'd be working at the home improvement warehouse or a grocery store or somewhere that's safe."

"Sir, as you should know by now from the shooting in Buffalo, New York, even a grocery store isn't safe. And that's not what Samara wanted to do. She studied criminal justice and she worked with two different departments to get where she is right now, and we're damn proud to have her."

"She shouldn't have been mixed up in this!" her mother wailed.

"Ma'am, I can't go into details. Some of that is part of the investigation, and some is personal to Samara, so I'm not free to divulge. But the fact is, she came to us already mixed up in this." Her parents stared at him. "I'm sure she'll fill in all the blanks as soon as she's able, but for right now, she's one of the best officers I've ever had, and if she wants to come back after she's healed up, she's very welcome. Matter of fact, I'll be disappointed if she doesn't."

Bruce wheeled on Michael. "Just what role did you play in getting her shot?"

"I didn't, sir. I'm the one who got her out of it. She got

herself into it, but that's part of her job, and she did it willingly."

"You shouldn't have—"

"Sir," Michael began, "that's not up to me. That's up to her. It's not up to anyone but her. She's here because the KSP commander didn't like women troopers and turned her and two other women into glorified secretaries. That's not what Samara wants. It'll never be what Samara wants."

"She doesn't know what's best for her, but we do," her mother interjected.

"Ma'am, with all due respect, she's thirty-five years old. She can make her own decisions."

"We see how that worked out," her dad groused.

A voice cut through their conversation. "Futrell?"

"That's us," Michael called out.

"No. That's us," her dad said as he stepped up to the nurse who'd called their name.

"She'll want me in there," Michael insisted.

"You don't have any rights. We're her parents," her mother barked.

"Officer, are you her husband?" the nurse asked.

"Well, no, but—"

"Sir, without her express written permission, I can't talk to you about her condition. Just her family. HIPAA laws and all. I'm sure you understand." With that, the nurse whisked the Futrells away and Michael was left standing there, Carter right behind him.

It was quiet for a few seconds before Michael turned slowly to face Carter. "What just happened here?" he whispered.

"You've been cancelled. Come on. I need to get some coffee into you and—"

"I can't leave here."

"You don't have a reason to stay. They won't tell you anything. But I'm the sheriff, and I can get some information. Let's go get some coffee. You can go home, clean up, get dressed in fresh clothes, and we'll come back down here. Maybe by then they'll have a change of heart and you can see her."

Michael let Carter lead him out of the hospital and to the sheriff's car. They went to the diner, got some coffee, and then back to the hospital to get his truck so he could go home. As soon as the door closed behind him, he fell onto the sofa face down, fighting the urge to cry. His arms ached to hold her, but he had no idea when that would happen. Hell, he didn't even know how badly she was hurt.

All he knew was that he loved her, and he wanted to see that beautiful face.

CARTER DROVE STRAIGHT BACK TO THE HOSPITAL AND marched in. "I need to see a staff member who's treating Deputy Samara Futrell."

"Sir, I—"

"This is an active murder investigation, and the deputy was involved. I need to talk to someone responsible for her care. Now. Right now. I don't have time for this silly shit."

"Yes, sir. Hold on." The woman punched a few buttons on the phone and then rested the receiver on the cradle. "They'll be out here in just a minute."

In two minutes, the door flew open and a man in scrubs stormed up to him. "Sheriff, what is the problem here?"

Carter rose and straightened himself to his full height.

"I have an active murder investigation. Not only was her assailant murdered, but she was injured, and she was present when he murdered another individual. Kentucky Department of Criminal Investigation will be investigating, the medical examiner's office and the coroner's office will be investigating, and I'm expecting the Kentucky State Police to want into this investigation too. My own office will be doing its own investigation. We're going to need to talk to her and—"

"I'm sorry, sir, but she's not here."

"What do you mean, she's not here?" Carter was growing more frustrated by the minute. What the hell was going on?

"I mean they took her by ambulance to one of the hospitals in Paducah."

"Which one?"

"I think Baptist, but I'm not sure."

"Who authorized this move?"

"Her doctors. She'll be having surgery there."

Carter was quickly growing frustrated. "And I suppose her parents authorized this?"

"Sir, they're her next of kin. They have every right to—"

"Obstruction of justice. That's the charge. Thanks. I know who to have the district attorney list as the defendants."

"Sir, you—"

Carter didn't give him a chance to finish, just threw up a hand and walked out. They had some nerve! They were acting like their daughter was twelve. His first call was to Amos, and then he called Bud. After they'd finished talking, he called the Post 1 commander and told him what was happening. That was the best he could do.

Four hours later, jingling from the alarm on the door got Carter up on his feet and out into the hallway, and he smiled when he saw the tall shadow thrown by the light from the glass door. "Hey! What are you doing here? I figured you'd go to the hospital."

"I came to get you. I was going to go by myself, and then I decided I'd take you with me. You have every right to be there. Can you leave the office?" Amos asked as he shook Carter's hand.

"I can get somebody in here in just a few minutes, if that's okay."

Amos nodded. "Sure. I could use a cup of coffee anyway."

As soon as Carlin was settled behind the front counter, Carter climbed into Amos' car and away they went. It took them an hour to get to the hospital in Paducah, and they strode into the front lobby. They'd only taken a few steps when another man greeted them. "Carter, how are you?"

"I'm doing great. You?"

"Very well, thanks."

"Brian, this is Agent Amos Fletcher of the KDCI. He's been involved in this investigation since the first minute, and he wants to speak to her too. Amos, McCracken County Sheriff Brian Wertz.

"Good to meet you, sheriff," Amos said, extending a hand.

"And you as well." Brian folded his arms across his chest. "So I've been up to talk to her parents, and they're being really hard-assed about this whole thing. Don't want us talking to her, don't want her talking to us. And they're very adamant that they don't want her talking to the chief deputy."

"Yeah, I got that. But we need to talk to her," Carter reiterated.

"You're going to. I told them they can't impede an ongoing investigation, and I think they understand. They think they're protecting her, but they're really hurting her in the long run. What do they have against the chief deputy?"

Carter sighed. "They've been dating."

"Ah. That makes sense. I assume he's white?" Carter nodded. "Yeah. That's what I thought."

Five minutes later, they stepped off the elevator on the third floor and made their way down the hallway. Brian stopped them at the doorway. "I'll go in first, and then I'll bring you guys in."

Amos gave him a nod. "Got it."

It was less than a minute later when Brian opened the door and stepped out with Samara's parents. "Mr. and Mrs. Futrell, I know you've met Sheriff Melton. This is Agent Amos Fletcher of the Kentucky Department of Criminal Investigation."

To Carter's delight, Amos didn't reach to shake hands with either of them. "We're sorry to have to do this, but it can't wait. We need to talk to Samara about what happened and get her statement."

"Can't you do it without him?" Bruce asked Amos while pointing at Carter.

"No, sir. This is his investigation too. One of his officers was wounded, and another's been suspended pending closure of the investigation. Standard procedure. As far as we can tell, Chief Deputy Edwards did nothing wrong."

"Except let our daughter throw herself into danger," Debra mumbled.

Carter had just about enough. "Ma'am, that's not fair. He—"

"We're not here to lay blame," Amos said as he interrupted. "We're here to find out in Samara's words what happened." Bruce started to say something when Amos added, "Any attempt to stop this process will be considered obstruction of justice, and that's a felony charge in this state."

"Fine," Bruce fairly spat. "Go on in."

Amos opened the door and let Carter step in, then closed it behind him, leaving Brian in the hallway. Carter knew what was happening. Brian would keep the Futrells from interrupting their interview, and he was grateful for his friend's presence.

When Amos swept his hand toward the bed, Carter stepped up to it and rested his hands on the rail. "Samara? Samara, it's Carter. Honey, can you hear me?"

Her eyes opened and she seemed to have trouble focusing before she finally locked eyes with Carter. "Sheriff. Hi. How are you?"

"I'm more concerned with how you are, hon. You feel okay?"

"Hurts, but I'm okay. Where's Michael?"

"We'll get to that in a minute. But right now, you remember Amos, and we're here to ask you some questions and try to piece everything together, okay?" She nodded. "So let's start at the beginning. Michael and I left and I told you to stay at the office with the door locked, but Michael told you that you could take the extra cruiser and go to his mom's, right?" She nodded. "What happened after that?"

The next few minutes were nothing but Samara recalling everything she could. At one point, Carter asked, "Wait. You heard him shoot someone?"

"Yes, sir. I heard it."

Amos glanced at him. "Where were you?"

"I don't know. I was in the trunk."

Amos gave Carter a knowing look, and he understood. She'd heard Stadler kill Jessica Fleming, the woman on Martinsburg Road. They'd been on the way to the intended fourth victim when he stopped on the side of the road and everything went to hell. "So can you tell us what you remember after he shot you?"

"Not a lot. I remember seeing the barn and the house. I remember trying to get to the house and hearing him shoot toward me. I remember lying on the porch and Michael looking down into my face, and the farmer being there. But it's all disjointed and fuzzy, and it's hard to know what order things happened in. And the next thing I remember was waking up here after surgery and trying to figure out what was …" She stopped abruptly. "Where's Michael? Why isn't he here?"

Amos couldn't have stopped Carter if he'd wanted to. "Because your parents have kept him from coming to see you. They don't want him here."

"That's not their call. That's mine," she answered.

"As long as you're on pain medication, they're allowed to make decisions for you by law."

"I want to see Michael. I want to know that he's okay."

"He's okay." Carter patted her hand. "He's perfectly

fine, except he's a mess because he's worried about you and they've blocked him from seeing you."

"No. I need to talk to them. I want to … Where are they? They have to … Carter, please." She was getting worked up and that wasn't what they wanted.

"We're going to let you get some rest, okay? Sheriff Wertz is talking to them now. Maybe he's made some headway. But you've got to rest so you can get back to being yourself. Just rest, honey. We'll talk again soon." Carter patted her hand again and watched as she relaxed a bit.

They stepped out the door and into the hallway to find Brian arguing with Samara's parents. "I realize that's your right under law, but is that really what's best? If she wants to see him, don't you think it could help her heal by seeing him?"

"No. Just no. Did you get what you need?" Bruce spat in Amos' direction.

"Yes, sir. I did. And we'll leave you folks now. Thank you for your time."

"Thank you? You forced us to let you see her!" Debra bellowed.

Carter started to say something, but the look Amos gave him stopped him cold. Without another word, they made their way with Brian to the elevator, and when the doors closed, Brian was the first to speak. "I'm sorry. I did everything I could to get them to let you bring Deputy Edwards to see her, but they wouldn't bend. Can't she call him?"

"Her phone was on the front seat of the cruiser with her tool belt and bag. She doesn't have her phone, and I doubt she's got his number memorized." Carter rubbed a hand across his forehead. "This is maddening. I can't believe in this day and age—"

"I know what you're going to say, but if that were your daughter, you don't know what you'd do," Amos pointed out.

They rode the rest of the way down in silence. Carter was frustrated beyond belief. And worse yet, he had to tell Michael what had been said.

That was one task he wasn't looking forward to. But he had one more ace in the hole. And it was time to play it.

CHAPTER 12

"Did you find it?"

"Yes, ma'am, sure did." Carter read the telephone number aloud. "It says that's her mother's number. Debra Futrell."

"Thank you, son. I appreciate it. I'll see what I can do." She hung up and sighed. *Get yourself in the right headspace, Marjorie*, she told herself before she picked up her phone again and punched in the numbers.

It rang once and a voice said, "Hello?"

"Hello. Is this Debra Futrell?"

"It is. I don't need a car warranty, and I don't—"

"No, ma'am. I know. I'm not calling about anything like that. I'm calling about your daughter, Samara."

The woman's voice was acerbic when she asked, "What about her?"

"My name is Marjorie Edwards. My son—"

"That deputy. *Chief* deputy. I don't want my daughter having anything to do with him, or him with her."

"Mrs. Futrell, they're grownups, and if you—"

"No. I'm responsible for her care right now, and that's my prerogative."

"Michael could easily take care of—" And the phone went dead.

Marjorie sat there for a second, stunned. Then she said aloud there in the room alone, "She hung up on me." In a second or two, she yelled, "She hung up on me! Oh, no. Nobody treats Marjorie Edwards that way. Nuh-uh. I won't put up with that kind of rudeness or disrespect. Not in this lifetime." She punched in a number and waited.

"Hey, Marjorie! Did you call?"

"I sure did, and she hung up on me!"

She heard a chuckle on the other end of the line. "I thought you sounded pretty worked up!" Carter said.

"Darn tootin'! Nobody hangs up on me! How rude! I'm not taking that lying down. I wanted to appeal to her as one mother to another, but she's done gone and pissed this mother off."

"Why, Marjorie, I don't think I've ever heard you talk like that!" Carter said, laughing.

"Yeah, well, when somebody hurts my boy, I'm a mama bear, and this mama bear is gonna fix this mess once and for all. I'm going to that hospital."

He stopped laughing. "Uh, Marjorie, I'm not sure you should—"

"Carter Melton, I've known you all your life. Known your mama all of mine. Now tell me, what do you think she would say if this happened to her?"

Carter let out another sour chuckle. "She'd sound pretty much like you do now."

"Then watch my smoke, son, 'cause they done lit my fuse."

"I'll be sure to stay out of the way then. Please don't do anything you'll get arrested for."

Marjorie snorted. "Yeah, well, maybe I will."

"I hope not."

"You'll bail me out."

Carter sighed. "Yeah, if Michael won't, I will."

"You're a good man, Carter Melton. If you weren't, I wouldn't let my son work for you."

That set Carter laughing again. "You know, anybody else and I'd tell them it wasn't your say, but I really think you could make Michael just sad enough that he was born to get him to do most anything you wanted."

"See? You know me pretty well! Okay, then. Thank you. I'll let you know how it goes down."

"Please do. And be careful."

"Always. Thanks again. Bye." In three minutes, Marjorie had made yet another call. Carter Melton wasn't the only one in town who had a few tricks up their sleeve. They'd never come up against a foe as formidable as the widow of Wilson Edwards.

They won't know what hit 'em, she thought and chuckled to herself. The Futrells were about to meet their match.

THE HALLWAY WAS QUIET WHEN THE THREE OF THEM stepped off the elevator. Carter had given her the room number, so when they found it, she asked the other two to step back and knocked on the door.

It opened and a face peered out. The woman looked to

be slightly older than Marjorie. "Can I help you with something?"

"Yes. We spoke on the phone. My name is Marjorie Edwards and—" The woman tried to close the door, but Marjorie stuck her foot in and held it. "As I was saying, I'm Marjorie Edwards, and I have a couple of people here who'd like to talk to you." Without asking, she pushed the door the rest of the way open and forced Debra Futrell back into the room, then motioned for her two companions. As soon as she saw them, Debra cast a glance over her shoulder at Samara, then stepped out into the hallway, leaving the door barely open.

"You're Mrs. Futrell, correct? I'm Father Ignatius from St. Martin's Catholic Church, and this is Sister Rebecca. We'd like to talk to you for just a moment, if we may."

Samara's mother looked a bit flustered. "Uh, yes, father. Of course."

"We understand that your daughter has been seeing Chief Deputy Edwards romantically."

There was a hesitation before Debra answered, "Yes."

"You should know that pretty much anyone who lives in Trigg County knows Michael and his family, and they're extremely well thought of around the area. I'd love to hear your reasoning behind not allowing your daughter's choice of companion to visit her here in the hospital. She obviously wants to see him, and I know he wants to see her."

"I really don't have to give you my reasoning, father. My reasons are personal."

"You mean your reasons are racially-motivated?" Sister Rebecca asked.

"Uh, no. It's just that—"

"That what? They're unsuitable for each other? In what way?" Father Ignatius asked.

"It's just that ... I really don't know the Edwards, and I'd hoped that Samara could find a nice fellow who's of ... um, I mean, that he would be ..." She fell silent.

"You were hoping he'd be black," the priest said, poking the elephant in the room. "Now, how would Jesus feel about that? You do realize he wasn't a white man, right?"

"It's just that ... I know that doesn't bother a lot of people, but it ..."

"Why *does* it bother you, Mrs. Futrell?" Marjorie asked. "I'm standing here in front of you. You can see that I'm not some backwoods hick, but I don't mind telling you that my initial reaction was similar to yours until I had to ask myself what my problem was. My husband, Michael's father, was the county judge executive here, and he spent years serving the people of this county and making sure everyone was treated fairly and justly. His memory would not be served by his wife acting like a racist bigot. I'm better than that, and I can do better than that. And I'm not going to stand here and say my son is the best person in the whole wide world, but I *will* say I did my best to raise him right and from what I can tell, I did more than okay. He has a heart for helping people and he highly values truth and honesty. I'm sure Samara could do better, but she could do a whole lot worse."

From somewhere inside the room, a voice called out, "Mom? Who's out there?"

"Honey, it's nobody, just some people—" Debra stopped cold when Marjorie's eyes narrowed. "Um, it's—"

The chief deputy's mother wasn't about to let that moment slip past. "Hi, Samara, honey. It's just Marjorie."

"Marjorie! You came to see me! Open the door, Mom." Debra's pursed lips never moved, but she stepped aside and let the door swing fully open.

It took Marjorie three steps to reach the bed. "Hi, honey! How are you feeling?"

"Better now that you're here. Is Michael coming? I need to see him."

"Your parents haven't allowed him into the room to see you. Otherwise, he'd be here."

"We'll fix that." To Marjorie's surprise, Samara picked up the call button and hit it.

"Nurse's desk. Can I help you?"

"Yes, ma'am. I need security up here, please."

"Is there a problem?"

"Yes, ma'am, there is."

"No, there's not," Debra barked.

"There is," Marjorie said, echoing Samara's statement.

The voice answered, "Yes, ma'am. I'll have someone come right up." And the call box went dead.

"I'll just go out here and talk to them at the nurse's station." Debra stormed out and the four people in the room watched her leave.

Samara's eyes were practically begging. "Can you please call Michael and ask him to come up here?"

"Yes, honey. I will." Marjorie whipped out her cell phone and found her recent calls. It only rang twice.

"Hi, Mom."

"Hi, honey. I'm at the hospital with Samara, and she wants you to come up here. Right now. This minute. Get on the road."

"Yes, ma'am! I'll be right there. Tell her I love her. Please."

Marjorie smiled. "I will." Her free hand patted Samara's as the call ended. "He'll be here as fast as he can get here."

"Thank you."

"Miss Futrell, could we pray with you before we leave?" Father Ignatius asked.

Samara smiled up at the priest. "I'd like that very much."

They only stayed in Samara's room for a few minutes, and when they were finished praying with her, Marjorie thanked the priest and the nun and followed them to the door. They almost ran straight into a member of hospital security. "You folks call for us?"

"I did." Samara's voice was strong. "My parents have been here with me, but I want them kept out of my room. Please."

"Samara, honey, are you sure—" Marjorie began.

But Samara stopped her instantly. "Yes. I'm sure. They've been keeping all of you from me, but I'm well enough to make my own decisions, and I'm finished with that. I'll say who comes and goes from my room."

"What is going on here?" Bruce Futrell boomed from the doorway behind all of them.

"Dad, you and Mom will have to stay outside the room. I can't have you in here if you're going to try to control who sees me and who I see. I won't have it, not now, not ever."

Debra appeared beside Bruce. "But all we're trying to do is—"

"Control my life. You've always tried that. You did it

for all four of the rest of the kids, and not a one of them is doing what they *really* want to do. They're doing what *you* wanted them to do, and that's not fair. I'm not going down that road. This is who I am, this is what I do, this is where I want to be, and these are the people I want to be with. And right now, I need Marjorie to help me a little, because Michael will be here any minute, and I don't want to look like death warmed over when he gets here."

"Sweetie, you look fine," Marjorie assured her.

"No. I don't. But I will. Go on, both of you. You'll just have to sit out in the hallway or down in the waiting room. Sir, could you—"

The security guard nodded. "Yes, ma'am. Come on, folks. The patient doesn't want you in here, and I have to make sure you leave. Please don't give me any trouble."

Marjorie couldn't help taking a bit of delight in the distress on the Futrells' faces. *They had no idea who they were dealing with, but they won't make that mistake again*, she told herself, grinning inwardly. As soon as they were gone, she set about to help Samara get her hair straightened up a bit, brush her teeth, and freshen up as best she could. Then she smiled at the younger woman. "Michael will be here just any time. I'm going to go, but if you need me, ask Michael to put my number in your phone. I'm sure he's bringing the phone with him for you."

A tear rolled down Samara's cheek, and Marjorie felt horrible for all the things that had happened to the detective over the previous few days. "Thank you so much. I really appreciate it."

"You're welcome, honey. You make my son happy, and that's all any mother wants. I'll see you later. Rest." She'd no more than stepped out of the room and closed the door behind her when the elevator doors opened and Michael stepped out. "Son!"

"Mom, is she okay?"

"She will be in just a minute when you walk through that door. Did you bring her phone?"

"Yeah."

"Be sure to put my number in it so she can call me if she needs me."

"I will. And Mom?"

"Yes, sweetheart?"

"I don't know what you did, but thank you."

"I didn't do anything. You should really thank Father Ignatius and Sister Rebecca."

Michael's brow furrowed downward. "We're not Catholic. What did they have to do with it?"

"Did I ever tell you that your Aunt Belinda dated a young Catholic guy when she was in high school?" Marjorie asked with a grin.

"No. But I want to hear that story. Just not now. Right now—"

Marjorie stood up on her tiptoes and planted a kiss on Michael's cheek. "Right now, your girlfriend is waiting for you. Go on. I'll talk to you later. And Michael?"

"Yeah?"

"I love you, son."

Her boy's eyes were bright and his smile was huge. "I love you too, Mom."

Marjorie turned and headed to the elevator, walked right past the Futrells, and said nothing. She didn't even look at them when she stepped onto the elevator and turned to watch the doors close. But there were two words running through her mind.

Mission accomplished.

THOSE BIG BRIGHT EYES LOCKED WITH HIS, AND Michael's heart beat a little quicker. His voice was nothing more than a whisper when he stepped up to the side of the bed and said, "Hey, babe."

"Hi. I missed you."

"I missed you too. You feeling okay?"

She nodded. "Yeah. And I'm sorry my parents treated you the way they did. I made them leave. Called for security and they're not allowed back in here if they're going to treat the people I love that way."

"Babe, they were only doing what they thought was best for—"

"I get to make those decisions, not them."

Michael nodded. "That's absolutely true. But right now, I don't care about any of that. I just care about you getting better so you can get out of here." He couldn't hide the emotion in his voice. "I thought I'd die without you."

"You'll be fine. I'll be fine. I'll get out of here and go back to work, and we'll all be fine."

His knees went weak with the relief he felt flooding through his body. She was going to be okay. Everything was going to be okay. In under a week, he'd have her back in his arms. They'd be together.

That was the only thing that mattered.

"Okay. We all have jobs. Everybody knows what theirs is. We've at best got seventy-two hours, but probably more like forty-eight. Are we all set?"

The group of men, including Amos and Bud, all nodded. Then the door opened and Carter couldn't help the grin that stretched across his face. "Heard you could use an extra pair of hands."

"Holy shit, buddy, I never dreamed you'd get to come! Thank you so much!" Every man in the room shook hands with Cruz and greeted him. "What are you most comfortable with?"

"You just tell me what I need to do and I'll do it," the tall Texan replied.

"Okay. We've got it all planned out. And Marjorie, you know what your job is, right?"

"Yes, Sheriff Melton," she singsonged as the guys all chuckled. "I can do my part if the rest of you will do yours."

"Then let's get 'er done," Carter said, and they all split up in teams to get started. They had a lot of work to do.

And they wanted it to be perfect.

On the fourth day, the doctor told Michael he could take Samara home, and Marjorie insisted they come to her house. "It'll just be easier." Michael wasn't sure about it, but he did it anyway. His mother had gathered up all of his things and brought them there, plus Samara's things too, so they were comfortable.

Carter had told him to get his uniform on and come to the station. As soon as he got there, he was handed his badge, his duty weapon, and the keys to his SUV cruiser. "You've been cleared, Michael. It's business as usual."

"Thank you, sir. Can I—"

"Take a couple more days? Sure. No big deal. Everybody's been pitching in to fill in, so you're covered."

"Thank you. And listen, Carter, I—"

"No, you listen. If I hadn't been sure I made the right decision in making you chief deputy, I am now. I can't tell you how proud I am of you, Michael. I'm thankful to have you in our department."

"Thank you. I really … Thank you. I …"

It seemed Carter sensed his emotions, because the sheriff grinned. "By the way, remind me to never get on your mother's bad side. That woman is a bear cat."

The younger man felt the swell of emotions subside as he nodded. "She is. She really is. I owe her a lot."

"You owe her more than you know," Carter said, then stopped.

What? What's he talking about? Michael wondered. "Is there something I—"

"No, no. Nothing. Just that you have a great mom, that's all."

"Uh, thank you. She's pretty great." *That's weird*, Michael told himself.

"So when do you think you're going to go back to your house?"

"Um, probably this weekend. She's feeling much better, and you know Mom. She'll keep us in casseroles, so we won't starve."

"That's true. Well, okay then, go help that young lady feel better and we'll all be waiting for you."

"Thanks. I really appreciate it. Talk to you soon."

Michael strode out of the office and headed to his truck. That had certainly been an odd conversation. He wasn't exactly sure how it was odd. It was just ... odd.

But it didn't matter. He was going back to the woman he loved, and he'd stop and pick up a bouquet of flowers for her on the way. Every time he stepped into a room and saw her smiling face, he was surer that they belonged together. They had a bright future ahead of them, and he could hardly wait to get it started.

***

"CAREFUL. HERE, LET ME TAKE THAT." MICHAEL took the duffel from Samara and helped her get out of the truck. "You okay?"

"Yeah. I'm fine. Whew. That's the most exercise I've had in days."

"Well, we're almost there. Home sweet home. At least I hope you see it that way," he said as he walked with her, his arm around her waist.

"I do. If you live here, then it's home for me." They climbed the front steps slowly and Michael slipped the key into the door, then let it swing wide.

He was the first to speak. "What the ... Holy shit."

Samara's eyes were wide. "How ... When ..."

"I have no idea." They stepped into the foyer and looked around, totally bewildered.

The living room was painted in the slate gray Michael had chosen, with all the woodwork in gleaming white. A nice area rug lay in the middle of the hardwood floor, and a furniture grouping he'd never seen before sat there, matching sofa, loveseat, and chair, with a coffee table and end tables, each holding a lamp. A large TV hung on the wall, complete with a soundbar, the remotes for it and the streaming service on a nice display stand on the coffee table. A few tasteful prints hung here and there, and neutral-colored printed drapes hung at the windows. The bathroom had gotten the same treatment, its walls a pale sage green, and the towels and rugs completed the color scheme. But neither of them could've anticipated the bedroom.

A beautiful bedroom suite greeted them, complete with nightstands, lamps, dresser, chest, and a big four-poster bed. The dusty blue walls held a few nicely framed art pieces, and pale gray curtains cascaded from heavy nickel-plated rods. A pale gray comforter set covered the bed, and the blue and gray rugs on either side of the bed were perfect. Michael was feeling a bit light-headed when he heard a voice call out, "Anybody home?"

Before he could move, Carter appeared in the doorway. "So, I see you're admiring our handiwork."

"What ... Who did this?"

"Me and the guys. Oh, and Cruz came all the way here to help. Can you believe that? Amos and Bud came too."

Michael was stunned. All of those men had given up their free time and worked to finish his house? "When ..."

"Your mother's only job was to keep you away from here, and she did it well. We were afraid we wouldn't get it finished before you decided you just had to come home, but I think we did okay. Oh, and before you ask, most of the furniture is rented. We just wanted you to have something to sit on and sleep on, seeing as how you hadn't had a chance to do any of that kind of shopping. The artwork is rented too, but we paid for it all for three months, so there's no rush. Wait 'til you see the kitchen! And the TV and soundbar aren't rented. They're yours. It's a gift from all of us."

"I really don't know what to say except … Thank you, Carter. For everything. I just …" Words simply wouldn't come. How could you tell someone how important they were in your world, and what a difference they'd made in your life? He heard a sound and turned to find Samara weeping. All he could do was take her in his arms and whisper, "Oh, honey."

"Everybody has been so good to me. I can't believe it. Thank you, Carter. Please tell the rest of the guys I said thanks too. I feel so lucky to be here."

Regardless of how unprofessional some people would've seen it to be, Carter hugged Samara and gave her a kiss on the forehead. "We're the lucky ones. You and Michael both make a difference in our lives and in our community. It just wouldn't be the same without you. Oh! I've got something else to show you!" Carter took off with Samara and Michael on his heels, and in minutes, he'd shown them the new kitchen appliances and washer and dryer, all courtesy of Marjorie.

The three friends laughed and talked for over an hour until the front door opened and Sharla stepped in with four pizzas and a small cooler of drinks. They ate and chatted, and Michael couldn't ever remember a time when he was that happy.

There was no question about it. He was living his best life.

SHE WANDERED INTO THE HOUSE, KICKED OFF HER SHOES, and plopped down on the sofa, completely exhausted. All she'd thought about was getting back to work, and she hadn't given any thought to how hard it was going to be after having been down for so long.

It was almost time to turn on the oven for dinner when the doorbell rang, and she hurried off to see who it was. One glance through the peep hole and she almost didn't answer it. Then she thought better of it and threw the door open. "Can I help you?"

"Could we please come in and talk?"

Samara could feel her cheeks burning as she glared at her father. "I don't know that we have anything to talk about."

"We do. Please? Could we?" her mother asked, but to her credit, she wasn't whining. Samara respected her for that.

"Yeah, sure. Come on in." Samara gestured toward the sofa as she rounded the end to sit on the chair. But she didn't speak. Instead, she just waited for them to sit down and make the next move.

Her mother leaned forward, forearms resting on her thighs and hands clasped. "We'll make it quick because we know you don't want us here."

"Mom, it isn't that I don't want you here. It's that you were very cruel to me when I needed understanding and comfort, and you were very rude to Michael and his mother. I won't stand for that. If that's why you're here, to tell me what I'm going to do or how much of a disappointment I am to both of you, you can leave right now. I'm really not interested."

"No, no." Her father sat back on the sofa and sighed.

"We've come to apologize. We shouldn't have treated you that way, and we're both very sorry."

Her mother nodded. "Yes. We are. We've had some long talks about it, and what we did wasn't very kind. I hope you can forgive us."

"This isn't up to just me. You really hurt Michael, you know. He was worried about me and afraid, and you made that even worse. He didn't deserve any of that, not after what he did. He saved my life."

"You wouldn't have been in that position if it hadn't been for him," Bruce threw out.

It was time. It would be hard, but she had to do it. "Do you know why Alex Stadler came after me?"

"Because you were the detective who knew what he'd done and he wanted to eliminate you?" her mom offered.

"No. Because I was reinvestigating some rapes that had taken place across the county. Then the house burned, and I was there working when he came up. He saw me and realized who I was. That was why he did that to me, Mom. He knew me. He was a state trooper at Post 1 when I was there, and he raped me too." Both of her parents gasped, but she didn't care. "Three years ago. I think the post commander knew. That was when he put me and the other two female troopers in the office as clerical staff, which was very offensive, by the way. He'd figured it out, and I don't know if he was trying to protect Stadler or make sure none of us got hurt. That's why I left KSP, to get away from Stadler and that post. I felt so fortunate to have found the job with Trigg County, and even more so when Carter told me he wanted me to do detective duties. It was all I'd ever wanted, and I finally had my chance. And then Stadler showed up and everything was on the line. If it hadn't been for Carter and Michael, and three other law enforcement agents, I probably wouldn't be here now. I'd be dead."

"Samara, why didn't you tell us?" her father asked quietly. "We could've—"

"What? Told me it never would've happened if I wasn't a trooper? Told me what a mess I'd made of my life? I didn't need any of that shit then, just like I don't need it now. So if that's why you're here, you can leave. My life is different now, so much better, and I have Michael and Carter to thank for that."

Just as she was about to say something else, the front door opened and a voice said, "Hey, babe, who … Oh." Michael pointed back over his shoulder. "I'll just wait out here and—"

"Oh no you won't. This is your home. You'll come right on in here. I think my parents have something to say to you."

Michael shook his head. "Oh, that's okay. You don't have to—"

"No. It's *not* okay. It's not okay at all. Mom, Dad, don't you have something you want to say to Michael?"

Her parents looked back and forth at each other until her mother sighed. Bruce cleared his throat. "Hrrmphhhh, uh, we're really sorry for everything we put you through, Michael. That wasn't right of us, and we apologize."

"Yes. We're very sorry," Debra added.

Michael nodded and patted Samara's shoulder from where he stood behind her chair. "Thank you. I accept your apology. I have to tell you, I don't trust you right now, but that's something we can work on together, all four of us. If that's what you want."

Debra had started to cry. "Yes. Very much."

"Okay. I'm more than willing to try. But if you all will excuse me, I'm going in here to take a shower and put on my comfortable clothes. If we don't soon get to the point where we have time to cook for ourselves, I'm going to have to get new uniforms because of all of my mother's casseroles. She's determined to fatten me up."

Bruce chuckled. "That mother of yours is really something."

Michael grinned. "Yeah, but the question is, what?"

That set all four adults in the room to laughing, and the tension was broken. Samara tipped her head back and smiled at the man standing behind her. He had absolutely no idea what he meant to her.

But she had every intention of showing him.

"OH, GOD. SAMARA, GIRL, PLEASE ... SHIT, SHIT, SHIT. Oh, damn, baby, you ... Sam, please ... Oh, fuuuuuuck," he groaned as his body let go and she lapped up every drop he'd given her.

"Good?" she asked as she wiped a finger across her lips and then stuck it in her mouth.

"Good? That's like asking if coal is black or sugar is sweet. Holy hell, angel, I think you could suck a basketball through a vacuum cleaner hose. Come here." As soon as she was in his arms, he gave her a long, deep kiss. When he ended it and pulled back, he grinned at her. "How long do you think it'll take them to catch on?"

"My parents? Long time. Your mom? She's probably

already guessed. Do you think Carter and Sharla will say anything?"

"No. They won't. But I do know they both said they'd be glad when everybody knew because they want to throw us a little party."

"That's really nice of them. Everybody's been so nice to me. I feel so at home here."

"And you love your job," he said and tweaked her nipple to hear her giggle.

"I do love my job. Might have something to do with my boss. He's a real slave driver, but he's the sexiest slave driver I've ever met."

"Oh yeah?"

"Yeah. Very sexy."

"He's got a very sexy employee too."

She snorted. "I'll be sure to let Justin know you said that."

"Girl!" Michael rolled her to her back and crawled between her legs until his cock was resting on her belly. "You tell Watson that and I'll …" Instead of finishing the sentence, he kissed her again and forced his tongue between her lips. The kiss she returned was ferocious, and everything below his waist tightened. "Damn. You're doing it to me again," he muttered against her lips.

She laughed loudly. "Oh, yeah? Is that right? I'm downright magical, huh?"

"I don't know about the rest of you, but that pussy of yours is positively spellbinding." Braced on his hands above her, he leaned down, sucked a nipple between his lips, and pulled to let it snap back. "Okay, those are pretty magical too, but not as magical as that honey pot. That thing is its own wizarding world."

The smile she gave him was incendiary. "Is that right?"

"Oh, yeah." He gave her another kiss, then rose up again. "I just had a thought."

"Uh-oh. Michael's thinking. We're all in trouble now," she said, laughing.

"Oh, haha. Very funny. I don't think we should say anything. I think we should tell Carter and Sharla to go ahead and plan the party but tell everybody it's for something else entirely. Then we'll surprise them and make the announcement."

"Hmmm. That could be fun. And it would keep my parents from saying anything negative. They wouldn't dare do that in front of all our friends and coworkers."

"That's true. Of course, you know Mom will be very hurt that we didn't tell her."

Samara's smile was wistful. "Maybe we should. Maybe we should ask Sharla to let her help. We can tell her and she'll have fun helping plan the party and keep it secret."

"Oh, wait! Better idea! Let's plan the party here and tell everybody it's for Carter and Sharla. Say they've got an announcement to make. And we let them introduce us."

"I like it. 'Ladies and gentlemen, you think this party is for us, but actually, we'd like to introduce you to Mr. and Mrs. Michael Edwards.' My parents will shit."

He couldn't stop laughing. "Oh, that'll be priceless. Hell, nobody will have to give us any gifts. That'll be the best gift of all—the looks on your parents' faces!"

"Oh, god, I can see it now. That little crease in my mother's forehead will be deep enough to stick a marble into it. And my dad's jaw will drop so far that a blue jay will flap in there and build a nest!" Samara barked with laughter.

"You know what?" Michael looked down into those eyes he hoped were still looking back into his when he was eighty. "I don't really care. I've got you, and nothing else matters."

She traced down his cheek with a soft finger and smiled up at him. "You're right. I've got you … and nothing else matters."

"Did you just say I'm right?"

Samara play-frowned. "Uh, no. I don't think so. I think you're wrong about that."

"Of course I am. So whaddya say we see if we can make a little Michael or Samara?"

"Hey, give me a little while, okay?"

Michael stared at her. "How long do you need?"

In a split second, he felt her hand stroke up his length and his shaft hardened painfully. "Oh, I'm thinking a minute. Maybe two," she whispered.

He drew his hips back and slid into her in one smooth stroke that caused her to let out a gasp. Then he stilled, kissed those soft lips, and smiled. "Nope, baby. Time's up."

Bluegrass Dynasty Series

Books included in Susan Stoker's

Police and Fire: Operation Alpha World,

Badge of Honor

ABOUT THE AUTHOR

Deanndra Hall is a working author living in far western Kentucky with her partner of 30+ years, crazy little dogs, and maybe a snake or two. She's written for business, industry, religious institutions, non-profits, and owned her own graphic design business, as well as working as a fiber and textile artist. When she's not writing all things romance from sweet, simple plots to explicit, erotic suspense, she can be found working out at the local gym, hiking, kayaking, reading (of course), or working on a healthy recipe. And wherever she is, chocolate is sure to be nearby.

On the Web: deanndrahall.com
Email: Deanndra@DeanndraHall.com
Amazon: amazon.com/Deanndra-Hall
Bookbub: bookbub.com/authors/deanndra-hall
Facebook: facebook.com/deanndra.hall
Goodreads: goodreads.com/deanndrahall
Instagram: instagram.com/deanndra_hall/
Newsletter: Subscribe!
Pinterest: pinterest.com/deanndrahall
Mailing address:
P.O. Box 3722
Paducah, KY 42002-3722

There are many more books in this fan fiction world than listed here, for an up-to-date list go to www.AcesPress.com

You can also visit our Amazon page at:
http://www.amazon.com/author/operationalpha

Special Forces: Operation Alpha World
Christie Adams: Charity's Heart
Linzi Baxter: Unlocking Dreams
Misha Blake: Flash
Anna Blakely: Rescuing Gracelynn
Julia Bright: Saving Lorelei
Cara Carnes: Protecting Mari
Kendra Mei Chailyn: Beast
Melissa Kay Clarke: Rescuing Annabeth
Samantha A. Cole: Handling Haven
Lorelei Confer: Protecting Sara
KaLyn Cooper: Spring Unveiled
Janie Crouch: Storm
Jordan Dane: Redemption for Avery
Tarina Deaton: Found in the Lost
Riley Edwards: Protecting Olivia
Dorothy Ewels: Knight's Queen
Lila Ferrari: Protecting Joy
Nicole Flockton: Protecting Maria
Hope Ford: Rescuing Karina
Amy Gamet: Guarded by the SEAL
Michele Gwynn: Rescuing Emma
Desiree Holt: Protecting Maddie
Jesse Jacobson: Protecting Honor
Rayne Lewis: Justice for Mary

Kristin Lynn: Worth the Risk
Callie Love & Ann Omasta: Hawaii Hottie
JM Madden: Rescuing Olivia
A.M. Mahler: Griffin
Ellie Masters: Sybil's Protector
Trish McCallan: Hero Under Fire
Rachel McNeely: The SEAL's Surprise Baby
KD Michaels: Saving Laura
Olivia Michaels: Protecting Harper
Annie Miller: Securing Willow
Keira Montclair: Wolf and the Wild Scots
MJ Nightingale: Protecting Beauty
Melinda Owens: Betraying Katie
Victoria Paige: Reclaiming Izabel
Danielle Pays: Defending Sarina
Lainey Reese: Protecting New York
KeKe Renée: Protecting Bria
TL Reeve and Michele Ryan: Extracting Mateo
Deanna L. Rowley: Saving Veronica
Angela Rush: Charlotte
Rose Smith: Saving Satin
Tyler Anne Snell: Cowboy Heat
Lynne St. James: SEAL's Spitfire
Sarah Stone: Shielding Grace
Jen Talty: Burning Desire
Reina Torres, Rescuing Hi'ilani
LJ Vickery: Circus Comes to Town
R. C. Wynne: Shadows Renewed

Delta Team Three Series
Lori Ryan: Nori's Delta
Becca Jameson: Destiny's Delta

Lynne St James, Gwen's Delta
Elle James: Ivy's Delta
Riley Edwards: Hope's Delta

Police and Fire: Operation Alpha World
Freya Barker: Burning for Autumn
B.P. Beth: Scott
Jane Blythe: Salvaging Marigold
Julia Bright, Justice for Amber
Hadley Finn: Exton
Emily Gray: Shelter for Allegra
Alexa Gregory: Backdraft
Deanndra Hall: Shelter for Sharla
Jenna Harte: Dead But Not Forgotten
India Kells: Shadow Killer
Amber Kuhlman: Protecting Paisley
Reina Torres: Justice for Sloane
Aubree Valentine, Justice for Danielle
Maddie Wade: Finding English
Laine Vess: Justice for Lauren

Tarpley VFD Series
Silver James, Fighting for Elena
Deanndra Hall, Fighting for Carly
Haven Rose, Fighting for Calliope
MJ Nightingale, Fighting for Jemma
TL Reeve, Fighting for Brittney
Nicole Flockton, Fighting for Nadia

As you know, this book included at least one character from Susan Stoker's books. To check out more, see below.

SEAL Team Hawaii Series
Finding Elodie
Finding Lexie
Finding Kenna
Finding Monica
Finding Carly
Finding Ashlyn (Feb 2023)
Finding Jodelle (July 2023)

Eagle Point Search & Rescue
Searching for Lilly
Searching for Elsie
Searching for Bristol
Searching for Caryn (April 2023)
Searching for Finley (Sept 2023)
Searching for Heather (TBA)
Searching for Khloe (TBA)

The Refuge Series
Deserving Alaska
Deserving Henley (Jan 2023)
Deserving Reese (May 2023)
Deserving Cora (TBA)
Deserving Lara (TBA)
Deserving Maisy (TBA)
Deserving Ryleigh (TBA)

Delta Team Two Series

Shielding Gillian
Shielding Kinley
Shielding Aspen
Shielding Jayme (novella)
Shielding Riley
Shielding Devyn
Shielding Ember
Shielding Sierra

SEAL of Protection: Legacy Series

Securing Caite (FREE!)
Securing Brenae (novella)
Securing Sidney
Securing Piper
Securing Zoey
Securing Avery
Securing Kalee
Securing Jane

Delta Force Heroes Series

Rescuing Rayne (FREE!)
Rescuing Aimee (novella)
Rescuing Emily
Rescuing Harley
Marrying Emily (novella)
Rescuing Kassie
Rescuing Bryn
Rescuing Casey
Rescuing Sadie (novella)
Rescuing Wendy
Rescuing Mary

Rescuing Macie (novella)
Rescuing Annie

Badge of Honor: Texas Heroes Series

Justice for Mackenzie (FREE!)
Justice for Mickie
Justice for Corrie
Justice for Laine (novella)
Shelter for Elizabeth
Justice for Boone
Shelter for Adeline
Shelter for Sophie
Justice for Erin
Justice for Milena
Shelter for Blythe
Justice for Hope
Shelter for Quinn
Shelter for Koren
Shelter for Penelope

SEAL of Protection Series

Protecting Caroline (FREE!)
Protecting Alabama
Protecting Fiona
Marrying Caroline (novella)
Protecting Summer
Protecting Cheyenne
Protecting Jessyka
Protecting Julie (novella)
Protecting Melody
Protecting the Future
Protecting Kiera (novella)

Protecting Alabama's Kids (novella)
Protecting Dakota

New York Times, *USA Today* and *Wall Street Journal* Bestselling Author Susan Stoker has a heart as big as the state of Tennessee where she lives, but this all American girl has also spent the last fourteen years living in Missouri, California, Colorado, Indiana, and Texas. She's married to a retired Army man who now gets to follow *her* around the country.

www.stokeraces.com
www.AcesPress.com
susan@stokeraces.com

Made in the USA
Coppell, TX
25 November 2022